PROHIBITION

A Charlie Doherty Thriller, Novel Two

TERRENCE MCCAULEY

WOLFPACK
PUBLISHING
— EST 2013 —

Prohibition
Print Edition
© Copyright 2021 (As Revised) Terrence McCauley

Wolfpack Publishing
5130 S. Fort Apache Rd. 215-380
Las Vegas, NV 89148

wolfpackpublishing.com

eBook ISBN 978-1-63977-050-2
Paperback ISBN 978-1-63977-051-9

PROHIBITION

PROHIBITION

Chapter 1

Manhattan - 1930

QUINN WATCHED his prey from the shadow of a doorway.

He eyeballed the second-floor window of the building across the street, taking in the panic of Vinny Ceretti. He watched Ceretti yank a suitcase from the top shelf of a closet and throw it on the bed. The stupid bastard was in such a hurry to skip town that he'd forgotten to pull down the shade.

But Quinn knew people did stupid things when they ran for their lives. He'd seen men act like this before. Many, many times.

Quinn knew Ceretti was clearing out because a man named Fatty Corcoran had been left bleeding on the floor at Ames' Pool Hall halfway across town. Corcoran was Archie Doyle's right hand man, and Archie Doyle was the biggest crime boss in Manhattan, maybe even the country. They didn't call him The Duke of New York for nothing.

Quinn knew Ceretti had set Corcoran up to take a bullet. And Ceretti knew Archie would send Terry Quinn to ask him why.

Quinn watched Ceretti struggle with stubborn dresser drawers, toss clothes in the suitcase, then slam it shut and pull it off the bed.

The light went off. The bastard was on his way down.

Quinn took a final drag on his cigarette and flicked it into the street. Time to go to work.

Ceretti took his time. Quinn figured he was listening for strange noises and scanning odd shadows in the stairwell. Quinn knew it was a fifty-fifty shot he'd come out the front door. He had a man covering the alley just in case.

He spotted Ceretti's head pop out behind the front door. He looked up one side of the street first, then the other. He even looked right at Quinn, but Quinn had done this before. He was too deep in the shadows to be seen.

Ceretti pulled the brim of his cap low over his eyes and began walking quickly along Thirtieth Street, lugging the big suitcase at his side. When he headed east, Quinn knew he was heading toward Penn Station. Quinn already had men there. He had men at Grand Central and all the bus and ferry terminals, too.

Quinn let Ceretti get a good half a block or so ahead, then began to follow on his side of the street, in the shadows.

At six feet, four inches tall and two hundred and ten pounds, Terry Quinn wasn't supposed to be fast or quiet. Most didn't realize he was both until it was too late.

He had no problem keeping up with the much

smaller man. Even in the darkness, Quinn knew these streets like the back of his hand, sidestepping all the cracks and holes in the sidewalk.

Ceretti stayed in the streetlights along Thirty-First Street, like a rat scurrying along the base of a wall back to its hole.

Quinn heard Ceretti's rapid footsteps echo in the rain-soaked streets. Fatigue and panic would take hold. Soon, every step would sound like a whisper: Dead man. Dead man. Ceretti twitched around every few seconds to see if anyone was following him. He saw no one.

Quinn navigated the darkness with ease.

Ceretti wiped at his nose with the back of his hand. He searched desperately for a cab. But Quinn knew no cab would come. He'd ordered them to stay out of the area until further notice. Working for Archie Doyle had its privileges.

Ceretti kept walking. Faster now, peering into alleys and side streets for signs of danger. The lonely sounds of Gotham drifted out of the darkness to greet him – vermin squealing in garbage cans, a dropped liquor bottle rolling along the pavement, cats screeching, mumbled voices, boozy snickering, a husband and wife yelling.

And in this chorus of the night beat the constant, unnerving rhythm of Ceretti's own steps on pavement.

Dead man. Dead man.

In the shadows, Quinn followed.

Ceretti kept his head down as he ducked into Penn Station. He passed beneath the tall columns and imperious stone eagles that glared down with menace in their carved eyes. Quinn followed him in but hung back even further now. He'd posted ten Doyle men throughout the station. Ceretti wasn't going anywhere.

Quinn watched Ceretti make a bee line for the ticket window and push cash across the marble ticket counter at the clerk.

The drowsy old ticket seller handed him his ticket and his change.

Quinn gave Ceretti a long leash now, letting him head to his train unwatched, his ticket to freedom in hand.

Quinn stopped by the ticket window and leaned on the marble ledge. "What track, Mike?"

The ticket seller's sleepy expression didn't change. "Track 88, pulling out in five minutes or so. Better hope he doesn't get wise and look for it on the big board."

Quinn pulled an envelope from his coat and slid it beneath the ticket window. "Thanks. And Archie said you better not piss it all away on the ponies this time."

Mike snatched the envelope and put it beneath the counter, grumbling to himself as Quinn walked away.

Quinn watched Ceretti walk faster now. The little man's suitcase was almost as big as he was. Ceretti didn't look up at the Departure Board. He didn't look at fellow passengers. He didn't look at anything. He just walked as quickly as he could to Track 88 and boarded the train at the first open car.

Quinn hoped he wouldn't have to search the whole damned train for him when a window shade in the fifth car down got pulled down.

Quinn hopped on board just as the train was pulling out of the station. He took his time, moving through the car to Ceretti's cabin. It was the only one with the door closed and the shade pulled down.

Quinn knew Ceretti was desperate and probably armed, a dangerous combination. He pulled the .45 from his shoulder holster and held it at his side. He rapped a knuckle on the glass and heard Ceretti stifle a scream.

"Tickets," Quinn said. "Tickets, please."

"Hold your horses," Ceretti said on the other side of the door, half laughing, half crying. He was still smiling when he opened the door. "I've got it right..."

The smile dropped faster than the ticket when Terry Quinn stepped forward and filled the doorway.

Quinn shoved him hard back into the cabin, sending him bouncing off the wall onto the bench. "Going somewhere, Vinny?"

Ceretti's breath came in shallow spurts. He started to shake. The dark steel of Quinn's .45 glinted in the dim compartment light. "Yeah. I'm heading to Chicago t-to see my m-m-mother. She's sick."

"Since when did you have a mother," Quinn said. "Word has it you're quite the billiards fan these days."

Ceretti's lower lip quivered. "How'd you find me?"

"You set up one of Archie Doyle's best friends to stop a bullet," Quinn said. "He's not the type to just let that kind of thing go."

Ceretti surprised Quinn by wagging his finger at him. "Now that's a goddamned lie. I didn't set up nobody for no shootin'! All I done was set up a lousy pool game between Fatty Corcoran and Johnny the Kid. That's all I done! If I'da known there was lead involved, I'da steered clear of the whole thing, and you know it."

Quinn kept his gun leveled at him. "Why'd you set up the game in the first place?"

Ceretti swallowed hard. "Because some slick, son

5

of a bitch came lookin' for me a couple of days ago. Bastard had a fancy white suit, white hat. Looked like one of them old plantation owners what runs coons and cotton down south. A real high-roller type. Said he was a gamblin' man lookin' to cash in on some action. When I asked him what kind, he says he'd heard Fatty Corcoran was one hell of a pool shark. He asked if Fatty had ever played a boy named Johnny the Kid."

Quinn didn't buy it. "You didn't think nothing of a stranger asking you to set up a pool game with Archie Doyle's best friend and a two-bit pool punk?"

"Sure, but when I asked him if he knew who Fatty Corcoran was, he said it didn't matter," Ceretti stammered. "Action was action and he heard he could make a lot of money bookin' side bets on a game like that. Said there was some extra coin in it for me if I could pull it off."

"Out of all the skels who could set up a game like that, he came to you?" Quinn asked. He aimed the pistol higher. "You're lying, Vinny."

Ceretti threw up his hands. "He'd heard I knew Ira Shapiro and Ira is The Kid's manager. Said he'd heard I knew Fatty from around and thought maybe I could put the game together if I wanted to. And he offered me five hundred to help me want to, plus a percentage on the action he got, so I put them together."

Quinn let out a low whistle. "Five hundred's a lot of money for setting up a pool game, Vinny. You should've known something was up." He raised the gun an inch or two. "And I think you did."

Ceretti balled up in the corner of the bench. He would've crawled through the wall if he could have. "Wait! He said I only got paid if I got Corcoran to show at Ames' and I had to be at Ames' to collect my money. So, I set up the game, went to Ames' and waited. When Fatty walked in, some guy slipped me my money from behind and told me not to turn around. I got the hell out of there and when I got to the street, I heard the shots. That's all I know, Terry. I swear!"

"Where's the five hundred he gave you?"

Ceretti pulled the wad out of his coat and handed it to Quinn. "There it is, Terry, just like I told you. Take it. It's all yours."

Quinn yanked the money out of his hand and put it in his own overcoat pocket.

"See that?" Ceretti said. "I've been on the level with you, ain't I? Told you everythin' I know and even handed over the money. Didn't even make a play for the heater I got in my belt." He even smiled. "That's gotta count for somethin', don't it?"

It didn't. Quinn fired. One shot to the head. The smell of cordite filled the small compartment as Ceretti's corpse slumped back, that stupid smile still on his face.

A few minutes later, the train rolled to a halt at its destination. The Hudson Rail Yards off Thirtieth Street. Ceretti never had a chance.

Quinn knew the cops wouldn't break their ass investigating the murder of a two-bit hood found shot in the head in a deserted rail car in the train yard. Just like he knew none of the night watchmen patrolling the yard would remember seeing the large man in the black overcoat and fedora hop off the train, or remember what direction he headed in.

Because that's how it was on that dark Manhattan morning, back in 1930.

Back when Archie Doyle ran New York.

Chapter 2

QUINN HEARD Fatty Corcoran's screams half a block away from the safe house on Twenty-third and Ninth. One of the boys guarding the front opened the door as Quinn jogged up the steps.

The stairs and hallways and parlor were jammed with Doyle boys itching for orders to tear the city apart for the bastards who wanted Fatty Corcoran dead. The air was smoky and close and humid. It smelled like a locker room.

All conversations stopped and all the men stood a little straighter when Terry Quinn walked through the door.

And Quinn did not like what he saw.

He spotted Sean Baker making his way to him through the crowd.

Baker was a short, slight boy in his mid-twenties with sandy blond hair and a quiet demeanor. He was tougher than he looked and was good at following orders. Quinn mostly relied on him for detail work, particularly around The Longford Lounge.

"Glad you're here," Baker said. "Fatty's been screaming and carrying on enough to wake the dead and..."

But Quinn had other things on his mind. "Our number two guy just got hit and you've got half our crew bunched up in here like sitting ducks. One firebomb through the front window and we won't have enough guys for a baseball game, much less a mob. Spread them out on the streets where they belong."

Baker started blinking fast like he always did when he got nervous. "I thought we should have them around to protect Archie if..."

"Don't think, Sean. Just do."

Another long Corcoran wail rose from the basement, cutting through the thick air of the house. "Jesus," Quinn cursed. "That's Fatty?"

"That's what I was trying to tell you," Baker said. He led Quinn back through the kitchen where even more of the boys were camped out, busy playing cards or reading newspapers. Quinn got hot all over again. Baker should've known better than to have all these guys holed there. It was a massacre waiting to happen.

"There wasn't much blood when we first got Fatty here," Baker continued, "so we figured it was a flesh wound. But when we cut the shirt off him, we saw another bullet lodged in his lower back."

Quinn knew back shots were tricky. It was better than getting gut shot, but not much. "Who's working on him?"

"Archie had me send some of the boys to fetch Doc Brownell. Found him, too. Drunk off his ass over at The Amber Room."

Baker pointed to two Doyle men tending to Doctor John Brownell. One held his head over the sink. The other stood behind him squeezing his stomach. The doctor moaned, wretched and vomited. Then the exercise was repeated.

"We've been pouring coffee down his throat trying to sober him up, but no luck," Baker explained. "Now we're trying another way."

"That'll just burn his throat and make him too sore to move," Quinn said. He yelled over at the two men. "Dump him in an ice-cold shower upstairs and pour water down his throat until he gags on it, then give him some more. That'll flush the booze out of his system faster and with half the effort."

The two men looked at each other, shrugged, and did as they were told.

Then Quinn realized something. "With the doc out of commission, who's working on Fatty?"

"Who do you think?" Baker shrugged. "Archie's still has a knack for patching up guys."

Quinn stopped cold. "What the hell is Archie still doing here? I told you to get him upstate two hours ago."

Baker blinked. "He wouldn't go until he knew Fatty was getting taken care of. Good thing, too, because when Brownell turned up tight, the boss had to work on Fatty himself."

Quinn pushed open the basement door and headed downstairs. The acrid stench of blood and sweat hit him hard and he fought the urge to gag. Quinn heard Corcoran wail again, then a commotion and muted groans, followed by a familiar bellow.

"Hold him still, ya goddamned ninnies!" Archie Doyle hollered at the five men struggling to hold on to Corcoran's thick arms and legs. "How the hell can I work on him if he's flopping all over the damn table?

Hold him fast! Donohue – keep that chloroform over his nose 'til I say otherwise."

"But any more'll kill him, boss," Donohue said.

"Any less and I'll kill you," Doyle retorted.

Quinn had seen a lot in his thirty years. This was a first. Fatty Corcoran, all three hundred and forty pounds of him, lying on a butcher's block that now served as a make-shift operating table. Corcoran was flat on his side as five of the strongest men in the Doyle mob – other than Quinn, struggled to hold his arms and legs still. A naked, yellow bulb hanging from the low ceiling was the only light in the room, casting a harsh glow on the men wrestling to keep Corcoran alive despite himself.

Quinn saw Doyle was getting the worst of it, struggling to prop up Fatty's bulk with one hand while he fought to get a better look at the bleeding wound with the other. Doyle's arms and undershirt were drenched in sweat and blood. His forehead was streaked red from numerous attempts to wipe the sweat from his brow.

"I can't find the bullet," Doyle grunted as he tried to keep the large man on his side. "I don't know if it hit anything vital."

"Aw, come on, boss," pleaded Jimmy Cain as he helped hold Corcoran down. Cain was Fatty's most loyal boy. Quinn knew if Cain could've changed places with Fatty, he would have. "They say you used to be good at puttin' guys back together in the old days. You've just gotta help him out now."

"What does it look like I'm trying to do?" Doyle said as he strained to shoulder the large man further on his side. He took a thin steel rod from a bottle of whiskey on a shelf near the table. It looked to Quinn like the rods they used to clean the barrel of a Thompson. He saw Doyle's hand shake ever so slightly before he slowly slid the long steel probe into the wound. By then, the chloroform and pain had finally knocked Corcoran out.

Quinn watched Doyle's eyes narrow as they darted back and forth, slipping the probe along the bullet's path. Slowly, so as to not tear anything that wasn't already bleeding and to feel the lead slug when he hit it. Quinn saw a bead of sweat run down Doyle's nose. He inched the rod around gently, ever so gently, until – his eyes froze.

A slow smile spread across his face. "There you are, you little bastard."

"What is it, boss?" Jimmy Cain asked, eagerly. "Did ya find the slug?"

"I believe I did," Doyle said, still probing. "Looks like it missed his kidney and veered off to the side."

"So, he's gonna to be okay?" Jimmy asked with wide, expectant eyes.

Doyle removed the probe from the wound and tossed it on the table. He stuffed the wound with gauze and eased Fatty back down. "The fat bastard won't be turning any cartwheels in the near term, but he'll probably pull through."

All the men in the room gave a nervous laugh, the kind men give when they were looking for a reason to laugh.

Then Doyle spotted Quinn at the stairs. "What's doing with Doc Brownell?"

Quinn said, "A couple of the boys are pouring him into a shower right now. They'll bring him down as soon as he's ready."

"And the hands of him will be tremblin' like a

kitten in a snowstorm," Doyle said. He thumped the sleeping Corcoran on the shoulder. "Do we know of another man of medicine we can tap to take care of this poor creature?"

"There's a doc in The Foundling Hospital up the street," Quinn said. "He's into us for a couple of grand. I'm sure he wouldn't mind working off some of that nut by lending a hand with Fatty."

Doyle reached for a towel and tried wiping the blood off his face and hands. All he did was smear it. He flung the towel into a far corner of the room. "Baker, take a couple of the boys and fetch this doctor Terry's talking about and be quick about it. Fatty's not bleeding now, but that can change."

"Doctor Peter Dempsey," Quinn told Baker. "Tell the nurse at the front desk of the hospital that you're with me. She'll get in touch with him for us."

Baker was already on his way up the stairs when Quinn called up after him. "And don't forget to spread out those boys like I told you. Send some to the Lounge, some to the club house and the rest of them in cars on our side of Fifth Avenue. I want them ready go if we need them."

Doyle turned to the men who'd helped him manage Corcoran. "Donohue, bandage our large friend here the best you can and watch him until the doctor arrives. The rest of you, head upstairs and fetch yourselves a drink or two. Christ knows you've earned it."

The only one who hesitated was Corcoran's loyal Jimmy Cain. "I don't mean no disrespect, boss, but I don't trust no baby doctor to take care of Mr. Corcoran."

"The organs are the same in an adult as in a baby,

except bigger." He added, "And in the case of our Mr. Corcoran here, a lot bigger." Doyle smiled at his own joke. "Go up and get your beer, kid. Fatty'll be fine."

But Cain pulled up a stool and took a seat beside his boss. The others went upstairs.

Doyle motioned for Quinn to follow him out the back door to the small yard behind the brownstone.

Even though Doyle was almost a full foot shorter at five feet six inches tall, Quinn always thought of Aloysius 'Archie' Doyle was an imposing man. His thick shock of unruly gray hair and bushy gray eyebrows framed a deep-set gaze. Years spent working the docks and slaughterhouses of the Manhattan waterfront left him broad shouldered and barrel-chested. His forearms were huge, almost deformed. He was fifty-one years old and was stronger than most kids in their twenties.

Fatty Corcoran and Frank Sanders had both been with him since childhood. Ward bosses paid them to break teamster strikes and scare off organizers. They got paid to get out the vote on election day and made sure people voted early and often. The boys at Tammany Hall liked Doyle's style. His gang got results. Eventually, the bosses depended on him.

Doyle turned dependence into power. With power came money, enough money to expand into the rackets, like booze and gambling and joy houses.

When Prohibition came, the floodgates opened. Speakeasies and gambling dens popped up all over town. Soon, the places Doyle didn't own, he controlled or supplied booze to. Most of them were dives.

The Longford Lounge wasn't. It was Doyle's pride and joy and the best of all worlds, a glamorous nightclub upstairs, a world class casino downstairs. Only high rollers need apply. Celebrities. Politicians. Everyone in between and sideways. The place was jammed every night. Money poured in.

Doyle always made money and wasn't shy about spreading it around. No one complained. The cops got their share. Judges, DAs, mayors, and aldermen too. Everyone bathed in the same dirty water.

With more money came even more power, more influence. Soon, most of the elected officials in the city lined up outside Doyle's door, hat in hand asking for contributions. Asking if his boys could get out the vote.

They promised gratitude. They pledged loyalty. Doyle demanded servitude and got it cheap. The employee had become the boss. Archie's empire grew far and deep and wide. It grew huge.

Quinn had been there for most of it. He knew Doyle hadn't gotten big because he was the toughest or the smartest. He got big because he played the game better than anyone. His speakeasies were safe – even the dives. His booze didn't make you go blind. His gambling joints weren't rigged, and they paid out to winners on time. The few joy houses he ran had clean girls who were well paid.

The cops liked him because he stayed out of narcotics. He kept the gunplay to a minimum. Chicago had Capone and his bombings, drive-by shootings, dead civilians, open warfare. New York had Doyle, who kept things quiet, damned near respectable.

And he paid Quinn to keep it that way.

In over five years, there hadn't been a pint of booze sold or roulette wheel spun, or a politician elected in ten states without Archie Doyle's okay.

One nod from Archie could get a guy killed or send him to the halls of congress.

With success and power came fame. And it was the fame that worried Quinn most. Doyle's sense of humor and easy smile made him a tabloid favorite. Pictures of Doyle with fighters, movie stars and Broadway actresses always made good copy.

But Doyle's Golden Rule still held in newsrooms all over the city: Nothing about Archie in print without his okay. Ever.

Break the Golden Rule and Terry Quinn comes by to ask you why.

But lately, Doyle had been giving his say so more and more. Doyle used to shun the spotlight, but he'd been drawing a lot of ink the past month or so. Quinn didn't know why.

It was a bad time to be famous for being rich. The stock market had tanked a few months back. People were losing their jobs. Money was tight. Bread lines got longer every day. People didn't have money for food, much less for a shot of whiskey or a roll of the dice. After a solid ten-year run, the Doyle operation was starting to slow.

Quinn thought Archie needed to focus on business, not getting his picture in the paper. But he wasn't paid to think.

Doyle went to an old slop sink in the back yard and began washing his hands with brown soap. The irony of the head of the biggest criminal empire in the country scrubbing blood off his hands wasn't wasted on Quinn.

Quinn leaned against the doorway and watched his boss. "It don't come off, you know?"

Doyle winked at him. "It ain't supposed to, kid." He scrubbed at the blood anyway.

Quinn lit a cigarette and drew the smoke deep into

his lungs. "I thought we agreed you'd blow town for a while until I found who hit Fatty and why."

Doyle shrugged. "And we was all set to go, too. Then Jimmy Cain and Baker tell me the doc is too drunk to stand, much less operate on anybody. What was I supposed to do? Leave one of my best friends bleeding to death in a lousy basement? I've known the guy since we was three, for Chrissake."

"You were supposed to leave when we heard Fatty was shot," Quinn pressed. "It's not safe for you to be around while there's trouble like this, especially when we don't know who's behind it."

Doyle waved it off. "There's been trouble sniffin' around me since I was a baby. Besides, the boys woulda thought me yellow if I left one of my own in his time of need. And they'd be right, too."

"They're not paid to think," Quinn argued. "They're paid to do what they're told." Doyle chuckled. "That's what I've always liked about you, kid. You're all heart. Did you get a chance to solve that problem we talked about?" He kept scrubbing.

Quinn nodded, exhaling a long plume of smoke through his nose. "Good," Doyle said. "Whereabouts?"

There was no need to say it when a gesture would do. Quinn tapped his forehead. Doyle spat into the sink. "Too quick for him, the bastard. Get anything out of him before he went across?"

"Something about a high roller from out of town in a white hat," Quinn said, "who hired him to set up a pool game between Fatty and some pool punk. Said they didn't tell him it was a hit."

"What do you think?" Doyle asked.

"Who knows?" Quinn shrugged. "I'll check it

anyway. But here's an interesting tidbit – The Kid is stake-horsed by one of Howard Rothman's boys – Ira Shapiro."

"No kidding?" Doyle said as he turned off the water and dried his hands with a towel hanging on a hook above the sink. "Ceretti ain't creative enough to make all that up on his own. But why would somebody hire a guy to do a half-assed job of hitting poor Fatty?"

Quinn perked up. "What do you mean half-assed?"

"The hole in his back," Doyle elaborated. "It's a .22. Any button man worth shit wouldn't use less than a .45 on a mark Fatty's size."

"I know I wouldn't," Quinn agreed.

Doyle tossed the towel aside and patted Quinn on the face. "You always was a perfectionist, kid, even back when you was in the ring. Maybe our shooter wasn't so picky." Then he pointed at the cigarette. "Got an extra one for me?"

Quinn fished out his cigarette case and let Doyle choose one of his Luckies. "All we got right now is a lot of maybes," Doyle said as Quinn lit it for him. "But we know Ceretti was no mastermind. He didn't have the brains or the balls to set up Fatty unless someone put him up to it. We need to know who that someone is, kid, and we need to know soon."

Quinn heard something new in Doyle's voice. Saw something new in his eyes. Things he'd seen and heard in other men many times. It wasn't fear. Archie wasn't afraid of anyone or anything.

No, he convinced himself. It wasn't fear, but it was close. "Don't worry, boss. I'll handle it."

Doyle didn't seem to hear him. "Christ, this couldn't have come at a worse possible time. Fatty and me got some things on the burner right now that might get queered by all this."

Quinn knew Doyle liked his secrets kept secret. He hated nosy bastards, so Quinn was sure to choose his words carefully. "Boss, it's probably none of my business, but if you need me to..."

But Doyle talked over him. "This thing is big, kid, too big to let you in on it yet on account of so much ain't settled. Maybe in a couple of days, but not now." He took a drag and pointed it at Quinn. "But if this thing I'm hatching takes off, it could change everything. Change it permanent and forever."

Quinn had a million questions, but kept his mouth shut. Doyle would tell him everything in his own way and in his own time. Besides, curious types didn't last long in this business. "What do you want me to do, boss?"

The old Archie returned. "What's the name of the clown Fatty was shooting pool with? Kid Jones or something?"

"Johnny The Kid," Quinn said. "Blew in from Brooklyn about two months ago. Been lighting up pool halls with trick shots ever since."

Doyle brooded. "Fatty's always fashioned himself a pool shark. Stands to reason he'd be suckered into playing him. Setting up that game was probably the easiest dough Ceretti ever made."

"And the last dough he'll ever make."

Doyle smiled. "Fatty usually shoots over at Knickerbocker Billiards on

Amsterdam. Who picked Ames?"

"Beats me, boss. We won't know much until I do some digging."

"So, Ira Shapiro runs Johnny the Kid," Doyle

connected the dots. "And Howard Rothman runs Shapiro. Kind of a coincidence that Shaprio's boy just happened to be playing Fatty when he got shot, ain't it?"

"Coincidences happen, boss."

"Coincidences are bullshit," Doyle snapped. "What do you plan to do about it?"

"Shapiro and his cronies hang their hats in a dive called Pete's on Third Avenue. Figured I'd swing by. See what shakes loose."

"Just tread lightly, kid," Archie Doyle cautioned. "The east side's Rothman Territory and Shapiro is Rothman's best earner. The last thing I need right now is a goddamned street war, especially with this thing Fatty and me got brewing. Got me?"

"Don't worry." Quinn dropped his dead cigarette and crushed it beneath his shoe. "You know I hate violence."

Chapter 3

THREE IN THE MORNING.

Dead time.

Quinn stood in the alley across from Pete's Billiards. Away from the streetlights. He was on the east side now. Rothman Territory. Behind enemy lines. Quinn couldn't afford attention.

A light mist started falling. Everything seemed quieter than it should.

Quiet suited Quinn just fine.

He never rushed jobs like this. Rushing led to mistakes. Mistakes landed you in jail or the morgue. He always looked over a joint first to get the lay of the land. To see who was who and what was what. When he knew as much as he could about the set up, he made his move.

'Pete's Billiards' was still etched in faded gold stenciling on the window, even though "Pete" had been dead for years. It was Ira Shapiro's joint now. A run-down hellhole with a couple of pool tables in the back and a sandwich counter that hadn't sold sandwiches in years. It was a juice joint for hop heads too down on their luck to drink elsewhere, but somehow scraped up enough to buy some of Shapiro's rotgut.

The cops left Shapiro alone because he was Howard Rothman's boy and Howard Rothman was a jack-of-all-crooked-trades. A power broker, more gambler than gangster, more crooked than straight. As an attorney, he'd represented some of the biggest hoods around. When he couldn't get them off or buy the jury, he greased the wheels of justice and bought the judge instead. Howard Rothman was an enterprising man.

Over time, Rothman was able to buy a piece of the action of every major gambling organization in the state. The rules were simple: take Howard Rothman on as a partner or you got raided. Everyone except Archie Doyle's joints, of course. By that time, Archie had already grown as big as he'd wanted in the gambling racket. Rothman took the rest. Rothman and Doyle had an unwritten truce.

It was a cozy set up. When the gambling dens needed money, they borrowed from Rothman. When they needed booze, they went to Archie. When the politicians and judges wanted to lay a bet, they went to Rothman.

When they needed votes and protection, they went to Archie.

Doyle ruled the streets. Rothman ruled the cloak-rooms. Doyle and Rothman were two sides of the same coin. That unwritten truce had held for the last ten years.

Until tonight. Maybe.

From the alley, Quinn watched Shapiro act out a story from behind the counter, waving his long, skinny arms while three goons laughed. Shapiro was about five foot ten and too thin for his height. He had black curly hair and pockmarked skin that made him look tougher than he was.

Quinn could tell the men were big, but soft. Probably bullies used to using their size to scare the hell out of normal people.

Quinn hated bullies. Bullies rarely had the balls to face their own weaknesses. Quinn knew his weaknesses all too well. The ring had taught him that. How far he could run in eight minutes. How many jabs he could throw in a three-minute round. How many shots he could take to the head before he got dizzy.

How to let a bum hang around long enough to make a fight look good. And how hard he had to hit a man to kill him.

But he'd never learned how to take a dive. And that's why he was standing in an alley on a damp November night, watching four assholes laughing it up in Pete's Billiards.

They told him to dive for another contender. Quinn beat him to death in the ring instead. Five years ago, last month. It felt like yesterday.

They took his license and killed his career. Men like Shapiro and his three goons. Men who placed bets on a game they knew nothing about.

They called themselves tough but didn't know true pain. Maybe they'd learn that lesson tonight.

But Doyle's words came back to him.

Tread lightly.

He'd try. He owed Doyle that much. He owed Doyle everything.

Quinn saw one of Shapiro's crew wasn't laughing. A young skinny kid of about twenty or so, sitting alone at the counter. He wore a faded green jacket and held his head in his hands. That must be Johnny the Kid. He looked too scared to enjoy Shapiro's story.

Other than The Kid, Shapiro and his three goons put the count at four. They looked loose. Happy. Maybe a little drunk.

They'd never see him coming. Until it was too late. Quinn crossed the street.

Shapiro and his three goons stopped laughing when the small bell above the door tinkled as Quinn walked inside and closed the door behind him.

Each of them slid off their stools and formed a semi-circle before him. He saw Johnny the Kid eyeing him over his shoulder from the counter. Poor bastard looked trapped. Scared.

Tread lightly.

"Evening, boys," Quinn said, looking each man in the eye. "Hope I'm not interrupting anything private."

"Well, if it ain't Terry Quinn come in outta the rain," Shapiro said from behind the counter. "What brings Archie Doyle's black hand out on a night like this?"

"Just out for a stroll on a soft night in the city," Quinn said. "Saw the lights on, figured I'd come in here where it's warm and dry." He looked at Shapiro. "Hear about Fatty?"

Shapiro put his hand over his heart. "My heart bled when I heard the news. Him and Johnny here were shootin' pool when it happened. Poor kid came back hysterical. Barely able to talk, even. When I finally got the story out of him, I was floored. We was all floored, wasn't we boys?"

The three goons nodded at the same time. Quinn had sized up each of them from across the street. The one to his left was a lightweight – short and stocky. He looked mean but had scared eyes and a weak jaw.

The one on the right was a middleweight. Big hands but his feet were too far apart. He wouldn't move quickly without shifting his weight. The third one had shifted behind him, so Quinn couldn't see him. But he wasn't a threat.

"Bad break for Fatty," Shapiro sucked his teeth. "Sure, I've had my run-ins with the big lug same as everyone else. But the poor bastard didn't deserve to buy it in a lousy, stinkin' pool room like that. And him and Archie bein' boyhood friends and all. Frank Sanders, too." Shapiro set up a bottle of whiskey and two shot glasses from behind the counter. "Hey, you collectin' for Fatty's widow and kids? I'll be glad to pass the hat amongst my boys if you'd like."

"He's not married," Quinn said. He waited for Shapiro to pour the shots before adding, "He's not dead, either."

Quinn watched Shapiro's eyes shimmy. His hand shook as he put the bottle back on the countertop. "No shit?"

"The bullets missed all the vital organs," Quinn said. "Looks like he'll be fine."

Shapiro managed a quick smile. "And thank God for that. Hey, let's have a drink on it, to Fatty's health and all." He grabbed the bottle and topped the shots. "I just figured he bought the farm after hearin' the way The Kid told it." He reached over and gently knocked the Kid in the head. "Must've exaggerated some. Ain't that right, Johnny?"

Johnny flinched and stifled a sob.

Quinn knew he needed to talk to Johnny but getting him out of there would be tricky.

Tread lightly.

"Looks like Johnny's still pretty shook up by the whole thing," Quinn said. "Seeing a guy get gunned down can rattle anyone, especially a young kid like this." Quinn managed a small smile of his own. "Blood's nothing new to a couple of old hands like you and me, eh Ira?"

Shapiro downed his shot.

Quinn left his on the counter. "Maybe I should take him outside for a little walk. Might calm him down some."

"That's awful nice of you," Shapiro said, "but The Kid's doin' just fine. Besides, it's past closin' and we've got to be gettin' home anyways. I wish you'd come by with the good news earlier. Could've had a few snorts to toast Fatty's good health and all." He motioned to the other shot glass.

"How about one for the road?"

Quinn felt the man behind him shift his weight. The other two started breathing faster. Quinn knew he was bigger than any of them. Taking down a man his size wouldn't be easy. They were getting ready to go to work on Shapiro's signal.

Tread lightly.

"While you're closing up," Quinn said, "Johnny and me could step outside to jaw over what happened at Ames' tonight. By the time you're done, so will we. Say, I'll even run him home for you if you want."

Shapiro offered a crooked smile and poured another shot for himself. "Johnny's been through enough. Come back tomorrow."

Quinn wanted to string this out a little longer. See what shook loose. "But everything's still fresh in his mind. He might remember something important about the shooting. Archie would want me to get it from him before it goes stale in his head."

The goon with the scared eyes on the left took a step forward. "Ira told you to come back tomorrow."

Tread lightly.

Quinn ignored him and spoke to Shapiro instead. "I didn't come here to fight, Ira. I just want to talk to The Kid."

Shapiro laughed and smacked the countertop. "That's rich. Archie Doyle sends his chief goon over here in the middle of the night just to ask questions. You bog trotters really make me laugh."

Quinn said nothing.

Shapiro did all the talking. "I don't particularly give a shit about what Archie wants. This is the east side, fucko. Howard Rothman's side. Not yours. I said you can't talk to Johnny, so you don't talk to him."

Quinn kept his hands open at his side. Loose. Ready. "Archie won't like that."

"Fuck him," Shapiro said. "You bastards sit in your goddamned nightclub expectin' everyone to kiss your asses. Well not me, brother." He poured himself another shot of courage and gulped it down. "Help Mr. Quinn find the front door, boys."

Quinn heard the floorboard behind him squeak.

He snatched the thug with the scared eyes by the neck and threw him into the thug on his right. Both fell back, crashing through tables.

The man standing behind Quinn tried to jump on his back. Quinn shifted and stunned him with an elbow to the throat. The man staggered back, gagging. A left hook that sent him back through the front door glass and into the street.

Out of the corner of his eye, Quinn saw Shapiro

bringing up a .38 from beneath the counter. Quinn hit the deck as three bullets smacked into the wooden tabletops above him.

Quinn pulled his .45 as he rolled to his feet, but Shapiro had already hopped the counter. He was fumbling with the lock on the back door.

Shapiro turned as Quinn stood up. Shapiro jerked up his .38 but Quinn fired first. The bullet hit Shapiro in the right shoulder, bouncing him off the door before crumpling to the floor. The .38 dropped as he fell and skidded down the hall.

Quinn wasn't exactly elated. He'd just shot Howard Rothman's best boy. Rothman wouldn't be happy. Neither would Archie.

The two thugs who'd crashed through the tables made it to their feet. The smell of gun smoke in the air made them careful. Quinn held the .45 on them and they slowly put up their hands.

Quinn waggled the .45 toward the door. "Go outside and drag your playmate back in here."

The middleweight dove for Quinn's gun, but Quinn was ready. He swung it out of reach and brought the butt down hard on the base of his neck. He was out cold before he hit the floor.

Quinn pointed the gun back at the last thug. "What about you?"

"Not me, mister," the man said as he stepped through the gaping door.

He tried to get the unconscious man to his feet but couldn't. He opened the broken door and dragged his friend as gently as he could over shards of broken glass.

"Drag him over next to your boss in the hallway," Quinn said moved to pick up Shapiro's .38.

The middleweight was coming to, trying to pull himself up on all fours. Quinn kicked him in the ribs, and he collapsed back to the floor. "Drag this piece of shit back there, too. Keeping my eye on all of you."

He looked over at Johnny, who was cowering at the corner of the counter. "Take it easy, kid. We'll be out of here in no time."

Quinn watched the last man standing drag the middleweight into the narrow hallway and take a seat on the floor next to his boss. It was quite a scene. Two of them unconscious. Shapiro shot, bleeding heavily from the hole in his shoulder.

"Fine group of boys you hired, Ira," Quinn said. "You always did have an eye for talent."

"Donkey bastard," Shapiro slurred. "Whaddya think Rothman's gonna do when he finds out about this? Your life won't be worth shit by tomorrow."

Quinn fished out a Lucky from his overcoat pocket and lit it. He knew Doyle wouldn't be happy, but he'd get over it. If it was worth it. Quinn had to make it worth it.

"Why don't you want me talking to Johnny, Ira?"

Johnny the Kid whimpered like a sick dog. "Please, God. Please. I don't
want to die. Not me. Not now. Not here."

"Shaddap, you goddamned Mary!" Shapiro yelled from the floor. "Keep your mouth shut, you hear?"

Quinn moved to block Shapiro's view of the Kid. "What are you hiding, Ira?"

Shapiro tried to straighten himself against the back door, but there was too much blood on the floor. His blood and more of it every second. "Fuck you," Shapiro slurred. "Fuck Archie Doyle...things...are changin' now..." Shapiro faded, and Quinn fired into the door only inches from Shapiro's head.

The shot boomed loud and woke Ira jumped. "Next one catches you in the belly. What's all this about things changing?"

As hurt as he was, Shapiro still managed to try spitting at Quinn. "You'll find out soon enough, you son of a bitch."

Quinn wanted more, but a loud banging noise from the front of the pool hall cut him off. He turned to see Officer Liam O'Hara rapping on the busted door with his nightstick.

He was red haired and barrel-chested, with a thick, drooping mustache that covered most of his mouth. O'Hara wasn't only one of New York's Finest, but one of Doyle's finest, too. He'd been on Archie's payroll for years and was a frequent guest at the Longford Lounge. O'Hara had a habit of running behind on his tab. Quinn had a habit of forgetting about it.

"Well, if it ain't Terry Quinn himself come downtown to pay us a visit," O'Hara boomed as he strode into Pete's. Shards of broken glass crackled beneath his shoes as he walked inside. "Looks like a helluva party."

"Evening, Liam," Quinn said. O'Hara might've been a crooked cop, but he was still a cop. Quinn stowed his .45 in his pocket to avoid any awkward questions. "Just a minor disagreement is all."

O'Hara kept kicking glass out of his way, then spotted Shapiro and the other two laying in the hallway. "Sweet Jesus, what happened to them?"

"Beats me," Quinn said. "I was just passing by when I heard shots. I think it was an attempted burglary."

O'Hara cocked an eyebrow up at him. "Just

passing by, eh?" He looked down at Shapiro. "That how it happened, Ira?"

Shapiro was bleeding badly from the wound. His head lolled around, and his words were thick through sagging lips. "Donkey bastards," he slurred. "Can't trust them fucks..."

O'Hara peered down at the wound. "It looks like a forty-five slug. That's the same caliber you carry, isn't it, Terry?"

"Small world," Quinn said.

O'Hara cleared his throat. He tapped the only conscious Shapiro thug on the shoulder. "What about you, Smitty? Did you see how it happened? Was it a burglar who done all this?" It was more of a statement than a question.

Smitty looked up at Quinn, then at O'Hara and said, "That's the way it happened, Officer. Lousy burglars jumped us. Neighborhood's been goin' downhill lately. Gettin' so a man can't hardly make an honest livin' around here no more."

O'Hara pulled out his notebook and started writing. "Burglars."

Quinn didn't like his tone. "That's what I told you."

"So you did," O'Hara said. "So you did. Who am I to say otherwise?"

He spotted Johnny the Kid sitting at the counter with his head in his arms, sobbing. "What about him?"

"He's nobody," Quinn said. "Stumbled in here a couple of minutes after me, lit to the gills. I doubt anything he says would make much sense."

"If you say so," O'Hara said. "I'm not looking for any trouble."

"Glad to hear it," Quinn palmed O'Hara a twenty.

"I think I'd better get this boozer a cab and let you boys get to work."

"You're a good man, Terry Quinn," O'Hara said as he made the bill disappear. "If we had more like you, this city would be a beautiful place to live."

Quinn eased Johnny off the stool and edged him toward the door. "Don't forget to call a doctor for old Ira over there. He looks pretty bad."

O'Hara went back to writing in his notebook. "For a pillar of the community such as Ira Shapiro, you can rest assured I'll do my damnedest to make sure he gets the finest medical care possible – right after I finish writing me notes."

Quinn placed a large, heavy hand on the back of Johnny the Kid's neck and steered him out the front door, crunching broken glass on their way as they did so.

Quinn doubted O'Hara would let it go at that and the policeman didn't disappoint. "Try not to stumble upon any more burglars on your way home," he called after them. "One mess like this per night is more than enough. And be sure to give Fatty my regards. We're all praying for him."

Chapter 4

"YOU'RE NOT GONNA KILL me, are you, mister?" Johnny cried.

Quinn steered him west, walking as far away from Pete's as quickly as possible. He glanced back to make sure no one was following them. "Start talking, Johnny."

"I don't know nothin', mister, honest." Johnny said. "Mr. Shapiro can tell you a lot more than I ever could."

"The cops have him, but I've got you," Quinn said. "Tell me what happened back at Ames' tonight and I'll let you skate with a couple of bucks in your pocket. That's a square deal for a pool shark like you."

"I'm not a shark," Johnny sniffled.

"Shut up." Quinn clipped him in the back of the head and shoved him further down the street. "Tell me what happened before Ames' yesterday."

"I was shootin' a couple of games in a joint on Delancey when I saw Mr. Shapiro arguin' with some guy outside on the street."

"Who? What's his name?"

"I don't know, I never saw him before."

"Then what did he look like?"

"A little taller than me. Older, too. Wore a white hat and a white suit, too."

Quinn stopped cold. It was the same guy Ceretti had described. "What'd they talk about?"

"I couldn't hear," Johnny said, "but the guy in white did a lot of pointin' and yellin'. I never saw Mr. Shapiro take guff like from anyone."

"Then what?"

"The man in white took off and Mr. Shapiro came back inside. Told me to get some rest because we had a big money game that night. The kind of game that could put me in the money if I did good." Then Johnny started with the tears. "I swear I didn't know that fat man worked for Archie Doyle, mister. No one told me nothin' about him."

Johnny started to buckle. Quinn grabbed him by the back of the neck and kept him moving. "Did you see this clown in the white suit at Ames'? While you were shooting pool with Fatty?"

"He might've been there. I don't know. When I play, I don't look around, mister. Ask anyone."

Quinn knew the truth when he heard it and he was hearing it then. He was either too scared to lie or the best actor since Lionel Barrymore. Quinn shoved the hustler against a building and pulled out a pad and pen from inside his overcoat pocket. He scribbled a name and number on a sheet of paper, ripped it off and handed it to the hustler.

"That's the name and address of Sander's Billiards up in Inwood. Go there and ask for a Frank Sanders.

Give him that piece of paper and tell him I sent you. He'll take care of you after that."

Johnny didn't even bother to look at the piece of paper. He folded it over and put it in his back pocket. "Why do I have to go all the way up there?"

Johnny flinched when Quinn went to clip him again. "Because I told you too, stupid. And because there's nowhere else for you to go. If you head back to Shapiro, you'll wind up in a body bag. He'll figure you told me something, even though you didn't."

The Kid looked like he was going to cry again. "That's not fair."

"Fair's got nothing to do with it. You're better off without him anyway."

Quinn spotted a cab from the Bradley Cab Company and hailed it. Bradley Cab was one of Doyle's companies, so Quinn knew Johnny would make it up to Frank's joint alright.

Quinn pushed The Kid in the back seat, then threw a couple of twenties at him. "Take that and keep your head down if you know what's good for you. Have Frank call me once you get settled."

The driver recognized Quinn and started with the small talk, but Quinn cut him off. "Take this kid up to Frank's place and step on it. Anyone gets in your way, run them over."

Quinn slammed the door shut and watched the cab take off along Third Street until it disappeared into the early morning fog. No one was tailing it.

Quinn hoped he hadn't made a mistake by letting Johnny live.

He probably should've plugged Johnny just like he'd killed Ceretti. To send the right message for all the wrong people. But Ceretti was different. He was in the

Life. He should've known better than to set up a pool game for Fatty without asking questions. Greed and stupidity got him killed.

Johnny wasn't in the Life yet. He was just a dumb kid who got caught up in the middle of something he didn't understand. And, despite his reputation, Quinn didn't like killing people just for the hell of it. Murder could become an easy solution for most problems. Murder could become a habit and habits made you sloppy. Sloppy got you killed.

Quinn had enough bad habits already.

Johnny the Kid deserved a chance for something more than the Life.

Something better. Quinn had blown his chances for something more. The Life was all he had left.

It was all he'd ever wanted, and he damned himself for it.

QUINN KNEW he had to get to a phone and call Doyle. There was probably a payphone in the drugstore across the street, but it was closed.

There were some speakeasies around, but this was the east side. They were all Rothman's dives. Word about Shapiro would be getting around. He had to get back to the west side and fast.

Quinn decided to drive back home to the Longford Lounge and call Doyle from there. He knew Doyle would be sore at first, but The Kid's information on the man in the white suit made it almost worth it. Find him, find why Fatty took a bullet.

Quinn's pocket watch said it was past three-thirty in the morning, that uneasy, undefined part of the day that was no longer dark enough to be night, but not bright enough to be morning. The back end of twilight. The prelude to dawn. Quinn loved this time of day. It defied exact definition and rules.

Ambiguity had always been a close friend of his.

He stayed alert as he walked back to his car. Rothman might already have some boys on the prowl looking to even the score for Shapiro. But the only thing he heard was the creaky wheels of a horse drawn milk wagon on its way to the warehouse to pick up its first shipment of the day.

When Quinn turned the corner off Third Avenue, he saw two men in long overcoats lingering in the middle of the block near his car. The much bigger one was standing next to the streetlight near his Roadster.

The shorter of the two was leaning against the hood of the car. Hat pushed back high on his head, smoke from his cigarette drifted up, mingling with the light from the streetlamp. Both men looked at him as he got closer. He recognized them by their shapes before he ever saw their faces.

"Evening, Detective Doherty," Quinn said to the man leaning against his car. He looked at the larger man. "How's it going, Halloran? Ready for another day of swiping apples from guinea push carts?"

Detective 'Big Jim' Halloran lived up to his name. He was Quinn's size, but a few years older and a few inches softer around the middle. His long, lantern jaw set on edge and his thin lips grew thinner. "Not yet, wise guy, but I know an old maid who's gonna get her lights put out if she keeps running her mouth like that."

"Don't mind my partner," Doherty said. "He's not used to being up this late. He's kinda cranky."

Charlie Doherty might've had a hangdog look, but his eyes were anything but lazy. His short, cropped hair was graying at the temples. His face bore the lines of a man who'd witnessed a lifetime of human frailty and degradation. He had the air of a man who took everything in stride because there was very little in this world that surprised Doherty any longer. It was tough not to like Charlie Doherty.

He'd also been on Archie's payroll longer than Quinn. Going on ten years or more. But just like O'Hara, Quinn knew Doherty was still a cop. And he still had a job to do.

"You criminal types caused quite a ruckus tonight," Doherty said. "Chief Carmichael's banging the war drum pretty hard."

"How is Andy these days?" Quinn asked. "Haven't seen him around the club house in a while. Tell him Archie misses his company."

"Save the malarkey for your customers," Halloran advised. "What're you doing on this side of town?"

Quinn didn't mind cops, not even crooked cops. But cops like Halloran were thugs who were too dumb to make good criminals. That made giving him a hard time that much more fun. "I'm out for a stroll," Quinn leaned against his car next to Doherty. "What's your excuse?"

"The Doyle mob got it rough tonight," Doherty said. "Word is that Terry Quinn was sent out to set things right."

Quinn pushed his hat back high on his head, just like Doherty's. He lit a cigarette and drew the smoke deep into his lungs. "You've been reading those dime novels again, Charlie. You always get very suspicious when you read those things."

Doherty smiled.

Halloran didn't. "Enough bullshit, Quinn. What are you doing over here?"

Quinn didn't like his attitude. "I went for a walk. Is that against the law or didn't you get that far in detective school?"

Halloran snatched him by the lapels of his overcoat and yanked him off the car. His cigarette fell from his mouth.

"You smug son of a bitch," Halloran said. "You always think you're so goddamned smart, don't you? Above it all. Well, you ain't above it all anymore, stupid. What happened to Fatty tonight proved it."

Quinn didn't like being manhandled. He could've done something about it, but Halloran was still a cop. "Get him off me, Charlie, or I swear..."

"Let him go, Jimmy," Doherty said from his spot against the car. "He baits you whenever he sees you."

Halloran shoved Quinn back against the car. Quinn winked and made a show of straightening his tie for Halloran's benefit.

"I wouldn't be so smug if I were you," Doherty said. "We were on our way to question Shapiro and Johnny the Kid when we saw you working over his boys. So why don't you come clean and tell us what the hell happened in there? We're going to find out eventually."

Since they'd probably seen everything, Quinn no reason to stall. "I swung by Shapiro's place to speak to The Kid about Fatty's shooting. Shapiro put his boys on me instead. Two got hurt and Ira took a couple of shots at me. He caught one in the shoulder, but he'll live."

"Real neat story," Halloran conceded. "All wrapped up in a bow."

"You saw what happened," Quinn added. "You tell me if I'm lying."

"That's pretty much how we saw it play out, too," Doherty admitted.

"We saw you leave with The Kid after O'Hara showed up. What'd he tell you?"

Quinn decided to keep that part to himself. The man in the white hat wasn't much of a lead, but it was the only one he had. Giving it to Doherty and Halloran would be like pissing it away.

"He said Shapiro was edgy all day, then told him he was playing in a big money game up at Ames'. Said he didn't know who Fatty was until the lead started flying. Call me a sucker, but I believed him."

"That's it?" Halloran said. "Nothing else?"

Quinn shrugged again. "Some people just aren't too smart. You know what that's like, don't you, Halloran?"

Doherty got between them before Halloran could grab him again. "Let's you and me go for a walk, Terry."

When they had gotten halfway down the block, Doherty said, "Why do you keep riding him like that?"

Quinn lit another cigarette. "It's fun."

"You ought to lay off him," Doherty said. "He hates your guts. One day, he might do something when I'm not there to keep him calm."

"The day that simp gets the jump on me, I deserve what I get."

Doherty chuckled. "Modesty's not one of your failings, is it?"

Quinn smoked his cigarette.

"You know why we never come down as hard on Archie as we have on the others?" Doherty asked.

"Because Archie owns the mayor, the chief of police and every ward boss in town?" Quinn elbowed Doherty. "Not to mention the interest he's taken in a certain Vice detective's career. No offense, Charlie, but everyone knows you didn't get your shield based on your skills as a policeman."

"That's part of it," Doherty admitted, "but we leave Doyle alone because he's smart. At least, he used to be."

"What the hell are you talking about?"

"Doyle's never adopted the guineas' love for violence, and he runs tight gambling houses. You don't run guns or white powder and your booze is cheap and decent."

"Tell me something I don't already know."

"Your low profile has been your greatest asset," Doherty went on. "But nights like tonight don't help. People are taking notice. People in Albany, like Governor Roosevelt. Now, I know you're not going to like hearing this, but Archie's been letting things get out of hand and it's been going on for a while now."

"Bullshit. Archie's as strong as he ever was."

But Doherty had a point to make. "I know you owe the man a lot and so do I, but he's been in the papers a lot lately. Parties. Show biz people. Sports guys. It doesn't look good. People think he's getting soft and someone taking a shot at Fatty tonight proves it. Maybe someone should remind him about paying more attention to business."

"This is rich," Quinn countered. "Some punk takes a pot shot at Fatty and everyone thinks the sky is falling."

"Would someone have had the balls to even think about shooting Fatty a year ago?" Doherty asked. "Six months ago?"

Quinn wanted to say something but couldn't.

"This wasn't an accident, Quinn. It was a warning that if he's not going to pay attention to the street, someone else will. Like it or not, Archie looks shaky right now. I know it's not easy to hear, but you know I'm right."

"Archie's still in charge and he's going to keep being in charge. If people need to be reminded of that fact, I'll remind them."

"You don't listen so good," Doherty warned. "I just told you we leave you alone because you boys run a tight shop. You start getting sloppy, then we've got to start paying more attention to you." Doherty lightly poked him in the chest. "And that hurts all of us."

Quinn looked down at the finger, then at Doherty. Quinn didn't like lectures. He liked being poked even less.

"More attention could hurt a lot of people," he said. "Wives could find out where their cop husbands really spend their nights. Newspapers might find out just how much Chief Carmichael gets paid off every month."

"You bastard," Doherty said. "Here I am, giving you fair warning and treating you like a friend and..."

"You're talking like a goddamned spectator," Quinn accused. "An innocent bystander watching a parade go by. But you're not. You're in that line of marchers right next to us, Charlie, and you'd better start acting that way."

Doherty tried to say something, but Quinn talked over him. "You were right when you said Doyle's connected to a lot of people in this town. So, if he goes down, a lot of other people go with him. Including Mayor Walker and Chief Carmichael." Quinn poked Doherty in the chest. "Including you."

"Christ," Doherty sighed. "What do you want me to do?"

"I need information. Do you and the boy genius back there have any leads on the shooter?"

"No," Doherty admitted. "No one got a clear look at the bastard. He got away before anyone got a good look at him."

Doherty was tough to read, but Quinn figured he was telling the truth.

With Doherty, you could never be sure. "Let me know if you turn anything up. I'll do the same. The quicker this goes away; the quicker things go back to normal. Now let's get back to Halloran. He's beginning to look lonesome."

Quinn started back toward his car when Doherty grabbed his arm. "We work together, and we work smart, understand. Any more bloodshed and Albany's going to get involved. No one wants that."

"Bloodshed?" Quinn smiled. "Come on, Charlie. You know I hate violence."

Chapter 5

QUINN HIT AN ALL-NIGHT drug store west of Fifth Avenue and called Frank Sanders, letting him know Johnny the Kid was on his way.

Then he made the call he'd been dreading. Archie. There was no way to sugar coat it and there was no way to avoid it. He just picked up the phone and dialed.

He knew Archie was a light sleeper and he picked up on the first ring. Quinn told him what had happened with Shapiro. About the fight. About the shooting. He saved the lead on the man in the white suit for dessert.

Archie seemed distant. He told Quinn not to worry about Shapiro. He told him good work on the man in the white suit. Then he told him 'Good night'. Click.

Quinn sat in the booth for a while after hanging up. He'd expected anger, excitement, something. Deadpan wasn't Doyle's style. Maybe Fatty's shooting took more out of him than Quinn thought? Maybe that other plan he was hatching was bothering him?

Quinn tried to forget what Doherty had said. Maybe Archie didn't care anymore?

It didn't matter. Either way, Quinn still had to find the bastard in the white hat, but it was too early to do anything about it. He decided to kill some time and rest up for a while.

It was almost five o'clock in the morning when Quinn got back to The Longford Lounge. He sipped black coffee at the bar and read about Fatty's shooting in the early edition of The New York Journal. He had an apartment upstairs but was too worked up to sleep just yet.

The raw smells of the nightclub always relaxed him: stale smoke, spilled booze, body washes and colognes that still hung in the air from the night before, all rushed together to form a unique perfume. It was Quinn's idea of heaven. Other than the orphanage, it was the only kind of home he had ever really known.

The Longford Lounge was Doyle's pride and joy; an old warehouse overdone with oak paneling; mirrors, chandeliers, and gold trim wherever they could put it. Quinn thought it was just this side of gaudy, but that's the way Archie wanted it. And since the place was jammed every night, no one seemed to mind.

The bar and kitchen officially closed at three o'clock in the morning, but the party continued until well past sunrise for the high-rollers and professional gamblers in the casino downstairs. The casino easily brought in five times more a night than the restaurant ever could. Considering The Longford Lounge was one of the most popular clubs in the city; that was saying something.

It was one of the few places in town where the

booze flowed freely. The cops knew all about it and were well paid to forget about it.

Quinn sipped his coffee and watched a well-heeled drunk in a dinner jacket stumble on the way out the door. Francois Deveraux, the maitre'd, grabbed the rummy and poured him into a cab. A few hours before, the man had been dressed to the nines for a night of cocktails, dinner, and dancing. Now he looked ridiculous in the coming light of a new day. Quinn took another swig of coffee.

"Would you look at the dumb bastard," said Tommy Delaney, the head bartender, as he washed the last batch of martini glasses. "All that money and no sense."

Quinn might've been in charge of the Lounge on paper, but Delaney and Francois ran the place. Delaney had been with the Lounge longer than Quinn and customers loved him. Ladies loved his dark Irish features and pale blue eyes. Men liked his stories and his dry sense of humor. The brogue made everything funnier.

"How'd we do tonight?" Quinn asked, going back to his paper.

"Grand," Tommy said. "No one's got any money these days, except when they come here."

"Anybody ask about Fatty?"

"Chi Chi and Rascal Parker drifted by," Tommy offered. "They showed appropriate concern. Wendell Bixby was in, too. Sniffing around for items for that damned column of his. All he got was gossip."

"He'd better talk to Archie before he prints anything." Tommy smiled. "I think he remembers what happened the last time." Quinn took another hit of coffee. "Let's hope I don't have to remind him."

Francois Deveraux locked the front door, then took a seat one stool over from Quinn. Deveraux was a wiry man of about fifty, whose hairline had receded to the middle of his forehead long ago. His pencil thin mustache gave him dash. Doyle paid him extra to put on a French accent for the customers, so he did. No one needed to know he was actually Fred Deavers, an old safe cracker and jewel thief out of New Orleans.

"Thank Christ that's over," Fred said, dropping the phony accent. Delaney set him up with his customary Chardonnay. Any man asking for wine would've gotten thrown out on his ear. Fred got whatever he wanted.

"I thought that last group would never leave," Fred said. "That last one dropped five large on the roulette wheel, and that ain't the record, either. People are spending like there's no tomorrow. I don't know where the money's coming from."

"As long as it's coming here," Quinn said, "who cares?"

"True," Fred said as he took a sip of wine. "How's Fatty holding up?"

"He'll live," Quinn went back to scanning the newspaper article on Fatty.

The reporter told the rough details of what had happened. Witnesses had seen two men running from the scene right after it happened, but there was no motive for the shooting. The victim was "Francis Corcoran, an accountant and local businessman from the west side of Manhattan".

Quinn was relieved it didn't mention Archie. The Golden Rule still held.

Tommy said, "Chi-Chi Castanengo called. Asked you to swing by his shine stand first thing this morning. Said he had something to tell you."

Quinn made a mental note to remember that. Chi-Chi always had the best dirt. He might've even heard something about the bastard in the white suit. "Did Walker swing by on his way home last night?"

Fred shook his head. "Nope. Guess Fatty getting shot kept him away."

Quinn wasn't pleased. Last night was Thursday night. Mayor James J. Walker's night to hold court at The Longford Lounge. Walker loved the nightlife and beautiful women and gambling in Doyle's casino downstairs. He enjoyed Doyle's payoffs most of all and Doyle's bully boys getting out the vote for him come Election Day.

Without Doyle's support in public office, Walker would've been just another skinny piano player with an easy smile. He should've at least called to check on Archie. After all, Walker was only the mayor. Mayors got themselves elected and un-elected all the time. There was only one Archie Doyle.

Walker skipping his weekly appearance wasn't a good sign. He remembered Doherty's warning about Archie looking weak. Quinn would have to do something about it.

Tommy brought Quinn out of it by saying, "We did have a bit of variety in our program last evening. 'Herself' dropped by. Made quite the spectacle of herself. Again."

Quinn let the newspaper drop. Alice Mulgrew. Platinum blonde. All curves. All woman. And all hung up on Terry Quinn. He fished out a cigarette from his case on the bar, slid one into the corner of his mouth and lit it.

He held on to the smoke before he let it out slow.

Christ. Alice always had that effect on men. Lately, she'd been having that effect on Quinn, too.

Alice was the kind of woman that could destroy a man just by being around him. Smart when she had to be. Dumb when she wanted to be. She knew exactly how to play him, but Quinn didn't give her much credit for that. He wasn't a complicated man.

She'd been a damned nice distraction to have around, but Quinn didn't need distractions now.

"What shit did she pull this time?"

"She waltzed in here about eleven or so, asking for you," Tommy said. "I told her I didn't know where you were or when you'd be coming back. She called me a fucking no-good liar, same as always when she's tipsy and cantankerous. Then she took a spot at the bar and, as regally as she pleased, ordered a dry gin martini straight up with an olive."

Quinn's anger spiked. Gin sent Alice off her rocker. "And you gave it to her?"

"Calm down," Delaney said. "I slipped her the watered-down stuff, but the mere idea of good gin was enough to set her off on one of her tirades. How you're a no-good louse and how she..."

Quinn waived him down. "I got the idea."

Fred took over. "It got so bad that I had to bring her up to your place upstairs. It was the only way to get her to shut up. She passed out after a while. She's been up there a few hours now."

Quinn knew he'd regret asking the question, but he had to know. "What was she wearing?"

Fred leaned in close. "Your favorite. The black dress with the pearls. She looked downright edible, if you ask me, and you can punch me in the face for saying so."

Quinn didn't want to hit anyone. He wanted to go to sleep. And with a drunken Alice Mulgrew in his bed, the one thing he wouldn't get was sleep. Gin made her angry. It also made her horny as hell. "She still upstairs?"

Tommy nodded. "In your bed. Right now. You lucky bastard."

Quinn dropped his head into his hands. He knew the dress. How it showed off every line of her body. Alice was no beauty, but she was striking. Short, platinum blonde hair. Dark black eyes. Full lips. Smooth alabaster skin. She could trap a man for life if he wasn't careful. And Quinn had always been a careful man.

He wanted to go upstairs, to let her push away what had been a rotten night.

But he'd also lose time in finding the shooter. And that bastard in the white hat, too, if he even existed.

Sure, Alice would've been a good time, but loyalty to Archie came first. Always.

Quinn slid off the stool and pocketed his cigarette case. He had a couple of ideas on where to start looking.

"There's a good man," Tommy said, watching him stand. "Give her a proper easing out of her hangover."

"Not today." Quinn set his hat on his head and started on his way. "Give her a couple of hours to sleep it off, then check on her for me." He patted Deavers on the shoulder as he headed out of the bar. "I'll call later to see if anyone's looking for me."

Tommy put the glass he'd been washing back on the bar and slapped himself in the head. "Ah, Christ, Terry. I'd almost forgotten to tell you about Frank Sanders."

Quinn had forgotten about him, too. About putting Johnny the Kid in the cab up to the Heights to see him. It seemed like a month ago. Even longer. "What about him?"

"He called just before you came in," Tommy said, "but I was so busy with the clean-up that I forgot to give you the message. He said he's still on the look out for that package you sent, but that it hadn't arrived yet. Said you'd know what he meant."

Quinn knew that meant The Kid never made it to Sander's pool hall. It meant that he'd either been stopped before he'd gotten there, or he'd panicked and run away on his own.

Either way, he was probably dead someplace with a hole in his head.

Quinn knew he didn't owe Johnny the Kid anything. But Johnny didn't deserve to die.

Quinn stomped out his cigarette in one of the ashtrays on the bar. A great start to a miserable fucking day.

Quinn knew every gin joint and joy house in New York City worth knowing. Each one drew its own roster of stool pigeons, snitches, degenerates, and gossip mongers who had someone with a theory on who shot Fatty and why. But the La Kaye Club on 45th Street off 6th had something none of the others had: Mary "Texas" Guinan. The woman heard everything. If people were talking, Guinan was listening.

If this bastard in the white suit was a high roller, Guinan would know where to find him.

He could hear her familiar greeting from halfway up the block. "Hello, suckers!" she bellowed to two drunks who'd stumbled into the place in front of Quinn. "We've got plenty of gin, gals and giggles to keep you jumpin' for a while, so come on in and take a load off."

She was a stout five feet tall, but her stark blonde hair and bright red dress made her look like a movie star. The drunks who'd just stumbled out of the Lounge looked ridiculous in evening wear. But on Guinan, it somehow just looked right.

When Quinn ducked through the door, Guinan forgot all about her customers. "Well as I live and breathe, if it ain't my favorite tough guy." She threw open her fleshy arms and pulled Quinn down to plant a big kiss on his cheek. "You big, beautiful hunk'a man, you! Where you been keepin' yourself all this time?"

"I'm around," Quinn said. "Been busy."

"So I've heard," she said. "Your joint's one of the few still makin' money these days. Would you just look at the two shitbirds I coaxed in here? Have you ever seen a sorrier pair? You know times are tough when you can't hardly make a dishonest livin' peddlin' hooch and pretty gals." Her painted face grew a little darker. "Heard about what happened to poor Fatty last night. How's he doin'?"

Quinn kept the details to a minimum. "Pulling through as well as a guy with a bullet in him could."

"Fatty's a pain in the ass and a drunk," Guinan said, "but he's basically good people. Any idea who did it?"

"Maybe," Quinn said. "That's why I'm here."

She waited for him to say more, but he didn't. "Still a conversationalist, aren't you, kid?" She smiled as she linked her arm through his and pulled him inside. "Let's sit for a spell and see what we can do to help you and Archie out. Anything for you two. Anything at all."

It might've been almost six in the morning outside, but it was still happy hour inside the La Kaye Club. There was a dozen or so people in various stages of drunkenness from all walks of life. Some sipped straight shots. Others nursed glasses of Archie Doyle's beer. A couple of showgirls known as Guinan's Graduates were putting on some kind of floorshow.

Calling it a floorshow was a stretch. The stage was only big enough for five girls to wiggle around a bit. The whole place was cramped and hot and close. The Longford Lounge's smell had a hint of opulence and joy amid the corruption of excess. La Kaye had an underlying stench of desperation, like the old gym where he used to train.

Guinan plopped her sizable bottom on a barstool, but Quinn kept standing. He never sat when he drank, and he knew he'd be drinking with Guinan.

She pounded on the bar until she got the bartender's attention. "Lenny, two shots of whiskey a piece," she ordered, then lowered her voice. "The good stuff. Not that piss water we peddle to the rest of the saps."

Lenny didn't look happy. "Mr. Kaye don't like you drinking while you're working."

Guinan took a swing at him, but Lenny ducked. He grabbed the closest bottle of whiskey and slid four shot glasses at them before retreating to the other side of the bar.

"You'd think with all the people outta work these days, I could get some decent help around here," Guinan said as she poured the two shots herself.

"Like the old sayin' goes: If you want something done right..." She toasted Quinn with her glass, and they drank.

The burn hit the back of his throat and went all the way down. It wasn't the worst whiskey he'd ever tasted, but it was close.

Guinan licked her chops and set the glass down with a slap and poured two more. "Mother's milk. So, what do you want to know?"

Quinn began, "When I started shaking the trees about who shot Fatty, I heard about a new guy in town. He's not the shooter, but he went through a lot of trouble to set up that game with Fatty. He may or may not be involved, but he's not on the level either."

"Not on the level?" Guinan laughed. "In this town? Shit, Terry. He'd stick out more if he wasn't crooked. What's his name?"

"I don't know," Quinn said, "but he's probably about five six or so. Stocky. Brown eyes. Beard and mustache. Wears a white suit and hat. Probably a high roller or likes to act..."

When Guinan stiffened, Quinn realized he'd hit something. "You know him."

Guinan futzed with her shot glass and avoided eye contact. "Sounds like a guy I know — at least, know a little."

"Who is he, Mary?" Quinn asked again. "It's important."

"Must be for you to call me by my right name," Guinan said. "He says he's from Savannah, but his accent slips when he's drunk. Sounds more like a Connecticut Yankee then, but I can't be sure. Goes by the name of Simon Wallace, or at least he does whenever he's in here."

Now the bastard in white had a name: Simon Wallace.

Quinn wanted more, but he knew Guinan would

dry up if he pushed her too hard too fast. Tread lightly still applied.

"Tell me about him."

"Not much to tell," Guinan said. She took another shot and refilled her glass. Quinn left his untouched.

"He's been in here a couple of times over the past six months or so whenever he's been in town. Brings a bodyguard who'd just sit there while Wallace drank. Makes a lot of noise about how he was a sportin' man who made his livin' on gamblin'. Judgin' by the way he throws money around, the boy's got to have an income from somewhere."

"Did you believe him?" Quinn asked.

"I don't know. He claimed he also owned a bunch of different businesses down south. He says he keeps an apartment here but doesn't say where. When I asked him specifics, just bein' conversational, he clammed up. I never could tell for sure, but I always got the feelin' he was afraid of sayin' too much."

She grabbed for another shot, but Quinn covered her glass. "What else, Mary? Tell me."

Guinan took his hand in hers. "It's not him lyin' about himself that bothered me. Hell, everyone wants to be someone else, especially in a bar. But I always felt it was more than just play actin' with him. Like he was hidin' somethin' big, or at least somethin' he thought was big, and would do almost anythin' to keep it hidden." She shivered and downed another shot. Quinn let her. "I guess that's why I never asked him too many questions."

Quinn changed the subject. "Ever see his body-guard before?"

"No, but he's a mean lookin' bastard. Not as mean as you, though."

"Wallace ever come in here with anyone other than his bodyguard?"

Guinan offered a weak smile and poured another pair of shots. "I don't know about you, but my buzz is leavin' me but quick. How about another?"

Quinn turned his glass over. "Who else was he here with, Mary?" Guinan closed her eyes and breathed deep. "Before I tell you, you have to promise me you won't do anythin' crazy."

"I don't make promises," Quinn said. "Who was he here with?"

"Howard Rothman," she blurted out.

Quinn felt the blood rise in his neck. Simon Wallace got Ceretti to set up Fatty Corcoran to play Johnny the Kid. Johnny the Kid was managed by Ira Shapiro. Shapiro was Howard Rothman's boy. Howard Rothman had drinks with Simon Wallace. One big goddamned circle. Quinn almost got dizzy.

"Shit, I knew that'd make you mad."

"Skip it," Quinn fought to stay focused. "How often were they here?"

"Two or three times," Guinan said. "It was never just them. There was always a bigger group of people, the typical hangers-on you always see around a big spender like Rothman. Wallace and Rothman seemed friendly enough, but they just didn't act like friends."

But Quinn barely heard her. The old anger began to flood through him once again. The Rothman-Wallace connection meant a move on Doyle's territory and that meant open warfare, something Archie had managed to avoid for a decade.

Quinn almost jumped when Guinan took his hand again. "I know you'd do anythin' to protect Archie, but you've got to make sure you don't do anythin' stupid.

Rothman's not just some two-bit bookie anymore and he hasn't been for a long time. He's got people to back him and pride to boot."

"I don't care..."

"Listen to me," Guinan demanded as she put both hands on each side of his face and said, "I know you love Archie and so do I, but guys like him always land on their feet. It's the people like you and me who end up gettin' killed."

Quinn gently took her hands and lowered them. "We're not going to lie down and take the strap from anyone."

"Who said you should?" Guinan asked. "Just don't do anythin' on your own. You already stirred up a lot of trouble by shootin' Shapiro this mornin'."

"So, you heard about that already?"

"Word is he shot first, but Rothman might see it as payback for Fatty. Either way, you'll need to be careful from here on in. Tell Archie what you find and let him handle it. It's his fight more than it is yours. Now promise me you won't do somethin' stupid."

Quinn managed a smile. Guinan might be a blabbermouth, but she was a caring soul who was far more sensitive than the brash, tough broad she played for the customers. "I told you I don't make promises."

"Well, you're makin' one to me," she said as she slid Quinn's glass to him and refilled her own. "Here and now."

Quinn looked at the glass of bad whiskey and smiled. Rot gut booze for a rot gut promise. He clinked his glass with hers. "I'll drink to that."

Chapter 6

A LACK of sleep and Guinan's bad whiskey made Quinn more sluggish than normal. Luckily, the November wind kicked up cold and helped bring him around.

He didn't have time for sleep. The Rothman and Wallace connection still stung pretty bad. It might be just a coincidence, or it might be a coordinated move against Archie. Other than Rothman and Wallace there was probably only one other man who might know for certain.

The shooter.

Quinn fought off a yawn as he went through the revolving doors of the Algonquin Hotel on West 44th Street. It wasn't hard to spot Hermando "Chi Chi" Castanengo's shoeshine stand at the back of the lobby.

Chi Chi ran half the hotel shine stands in the city, thanks to Archie Doyle. Fatty Corcoran had been a customer of Chi Chi's for years, so when the little Guatemalan told Fatty he wanted to borrow money to expand, he got Archie to put him in charge of all of

Doyle's hotel stands. Shining shoes had always been secondary. The stands were great cover for Doyle's bookmaking business.

The stands were also great places to find dirt. Women talked in beauty parlors. Guys talked when they got their hair cut and their shoes shined. Shine boys passed along things they heard to interested parties for a price. Some of the information was gold. Some of it was worthless.

Chi Chi was a good filter and he only called Quinn when he had something solid. He knew better than to waste Quinn's time.

Quinn found him perched in the shine stall next to the payphone. One of his guys snapped a rag across his spats while Chi Chi read the Racing Form. Rumor had it that the little man had his shoes shined three times a day, and it showed. The black and white spats shined like glass. They clashed hard with his red suit and matching fedora. Quinn thought Chi Chi looked like a pimp in a third-rate whorehouse, but loud was the little man's style.

Quinn caught their reflection as he climbed onto the stall next to the bookie. Chi Chi's small frame and bright red suit made him look like a child next to Quinn in his dark hat and overcoat. The shine boys knew the drill and made themselves scarce.

You didn't eavesdrop on Quinn and Chi Chi.

"Look at what the kitty cat drag in," Chi Chi said. His thick Spanish accent held contempt for the last two letters of most words. "Tommy tell you I call looking for you last night? I hear you have a busy night last night, my friend. Ira Shapiro, bang bang." The bookie sucked his teeth. "All that trouble for nothing. If you just come to Chi Chi first, you would've saved a lot of trouble."

Quinn would have been more surprised if Chi Chi hadn't known about the Shapiro thing by now. "Things don't always play out easy, Cheech. Last night played out harder than I wanted."

"Hard ain't the half of it," the bookie said. "You shoot up one of Rothman's dives – and his best earner. For why? To pump a low life pool hall flake like Johnny the Keed for informations on who shoot Fatty? Informations he don't have, but I do."

"I get preached to on Sundays, amigo. Tell me why I'm here?"

"First things first," the bookie folded his newspaper closed. "How's Fatty doing? I hear many bad things about him. I hear he dying. I hear he can't walk no more. What do you say?"

"He's fine," Quinn lied. "Doc says he'll be back to turning cartwheels across the floor by the end of the week. Who's asking?"

"A lot of peoples owe Fatty money, so if he were to, *se va morir,* God forbid," the bookie crossed himself quickly, "people think maybe their debt die with him." The bookie sucked his teeth again. "Los *animales en esta ciudad.*"

Quinn had been afraid of shit like this starting up. Archie looking shaky. People testing boundaries, second-guessing the way things had been for a decade. Cracks were showing in the Doyle foundation, and it was only 7:00 AM. The more people talked and wondered, the wider the cracks would get. There was only one way to stop it: nail the shooter and remind everyone that Archie Doyle is still in charge.

"A debt owed to Fatty is a debt owed to Archie,"

Quinn explained. "Payment is expected in full and on time. They hold out, I'll come ask them why."

The bookie threw up his arms in surrender. "Of course! I'm just passing on what I hear."

"Then how about passing on what you heard about what happened at Ames' last night?"

"I hear somethings that you might use. But I have to pay for my informations sometimes too. I was wondering if there was some kind of reward for..."

A night's worth of frustration boiled over. Quinn grabbed the bookie's leg and dug his fingers deep into the man's thigh. Slow and hard.

Chi Chi stifled a scream and squirmed in his chair.

Quinn leaned closer. "How's this for a reward? You tell me what you know, and I won't snap your fucking leg."

Chi Chi nodded like his head would fall off. Quinn let go.

"God damn those tempers of yours." Chi Chi rubbed his sore leg. "Why you treat an old friend that way?"

Quinn went to grab his leg again and the bookie couldn't start his story fast enough. "I hear the shooter could be Carmine Zito!"

"Zito?" Quinn knew the name. "The button man for the Harlem dagos?"

Chi Chi shook his head. "Sometimes, but he work for anyone if the money's good. He tough and he don't work cheap, so if he shoot Fatty, someone pay him plenty to keep his mouth shut."

Quinn already figured that. "What else do you know about this guy?"

"No one know what he look like," Chi Chi said. "Tall, short, fat, bald, curly hair, ugly, handsome." A smug grin spread across his small face. "But I know what he look like."

Quinn hated dragging out information like this, but he played along. "How?"

No one was within ear shot, but Chi Chi beckoned him closer anyway. "I know this girl who is what you might call 'a woman of easy virtue'. She says she and this Zito sometimes, you know..." the bookie made a fist and jiggled it as though milking a cow, "...for money. He never say what he do for a living and get angry when she ask him. She get curious one day and went sniffing in his closet while he sleeping. She find many guns in a bag in his closet. She also know he disappear for days and bring this bag with him. He never tell her where he goes, but she see train tickets in his house sometimes."

Quinn knew a whore's word was damned thin. Lots of people kept guns around. But it was the solid lead he had. "And she's sure she saw this same guy shoot Fatty last night?"

Chi Chi nodded. "She see his face clearly as he pull the trigger. She say he was wearing a hat, but he has a scar on his face she know from anywheres. She is certain. *Absolutemente.*"

The bookie slowly leaned back in his chair. A proud man. "How's that for informations, eh?"

Quinn wasn't entirely sold, but he was interested. "She mention this to anyone else?"

The bookie tucked his fingers into his red vest and grinned. "Just to her Uncle Chi Chi. She call last night after Fatty was shot, very hysterical. She afraid maybe Zito saw her and might shoot her too to keep her quiet. So, I invite her over to my place – just to calm her down and, maybe, you know..."

"You're a real gentleman, Cheech. What time did she get to your place?"

"A little before midnight, I think, but it's hard to say because when she got there, we..."

Quinn drove his fingers back into the bookie's leg, "You were too busy laying pipe to this bar frau instead of letting me know? The bastard's probably three states away by now!"

"He no skip town!" Chi Chi squealed as he tried to pry Quinn's fingers from his leg. "No one know who he is or what he look like! Why run?"

Quinn released the leg with a shove and tried to calm down. All that bullshit with Shapiro wouldn't have happened if Chi Chi had told him this hours ago. But then he realized he probably wouldn't have talked to Johnny the Kid and heard more about Simon Wallace. Maybe there was no harm after all. If Zito was still in town.

He tried soothing the bookie's busted ego. "You're a good boy, Chi Chi. Sorry I got rough, but this thing with Fatty's been tough."

The bookie kept massaging his wounded leg. "You really gotta do something about those damned tempers of yours. Find Jesus in your heart, maybe."

Quinn laughed, really laughed, for the first time all day. "Let's worry about finding one mystery man at a time." He dug a wad of twenties out of his pocket, peeled off five of them and slapped them in the bookie's hand. "Now, let's get this twist of yours on the phone and see if she remembers where Zito hangs his hat."

Chapter 7

IT TOOK Chi-Chi a good dose of begging and threatening before the girl gave up the address.

Zito lived on Ninth Street and First Avenue, a tenement neighborhood teeming with immigrants. Italians, Germans, Jews, Greeks, and a few Micks right off the boat sprinkled in for good measure. It was the kind of neighborhood where a four-story dump could house over a hundred people – and often did. The street was teeming with life, lined with push-cart vendors and customers haggling for apples, clothing, rugs, fish, fresh killed chickens, and hand rolled cigars.

They made it a point not to look at the large man in the black overcoat as he moved through the crowded street. They didn't see him walk up the stoop and enter the building, either. This was the kind of neighborhood where curiosity got you killed, and everyone had plenty of troubles of their own.

It was Quinn's kind of neighborhood.

The rats in the stairwell didn't give an inch as he

walked up the four flights to Zito's place. Top floor. Tenement Penthouse suite.

The lock on Zito's door was the typical flimsy hunk of metal found on most tenement doors. Quinn figured a pro would've put a better piece of hardware on his door. Maybe Zito thought a better lock would draw attention. Or maybe the whore was lying about this guy.

Quinn didn't have the luxury of maybes. There was only one way to find out.

He put his ear against the door and listened. All he heard was some faint snoring.

Good. Sleepers were easier to sneak up on.

He checked the hall for any bystanders, then pulled his .45. He put his shoulder against the door and pushed. Slow. Steady pressure.

The wood creaked, then the lock snapped. He tensed for the sound of metal hitting the floor. Nothing. He listened for the snoring to stop. It didn't.

Quinn opened the door and slid inside the apartment. A floorboard creaked, but Zito kept snoring away. Quinn closed the door with a quiet click and took a moment to get his bearings.

A torn, yellowed shade tried in vain to block out the morning sun. An old painting of a three-mast ship hung crooked on the wall by the window, faded and blackened. The wallpaper was yellowed like the window shade and peeling. One leg of the bureau was crooked and the whole piece was warped.

Quinn could tell Zito wasn't much of a decorator, but he was a music fan. A brand-new RCA radio and Victrola cabinet stood prominently in the corner of the room. The shiny, new cherry wood finish was in stark contrast to its surroundings. Zito must've had a big payday to drop coin on a new music box. Maybe Chi-Chi's whore had been right about this guy after all.

The snoring grew loud again as Quinn's eyes adjusted to the weak light. The rest of the room looked like the apartment of a man who'd just come home from a hard day's work – if that work involved gunplay.

Dark clothes and a cap were tossed over the back of the chair near the door. That matched the description of what people saw the shooter wearing as he ran out of Ames'. Quinn spotted a gun cleaning kit on a table with grease covered cleaning rags balled up next to it.

Quinn saw a naked man asleep on a Murphy bed near the window. He figured this must be Carmine Zito. He watched the gunman sleep for a while. If this really was Zito, all the descriptions he'd heard about him were wrong.

He was about thirty-five or forty. Average height and build. Black curly hair and a good head start on a two-day growth. A long scar ran down the left side of his face from his jaw to his hairline. Just the way Chi Chi's whore said.

To Quinn, Zito looked like any of the millions of other men who went to work in the slaughterhouses, grocery stores and fish markets in New York City every morning. He didn't look like the kind of man who killed for money. But the best ones never did. The ability to blend in was probably Zito's greatest weapon.

Blending in had never been an option for Quinn.

Quinn saw Zito was sleeping flat on his back, naked, slack-jawed and snoring deeply. Normally Quinn would've just wasted the guy and toss the room for clues. Keeping him alive could complicate things. Fatty's shooting was already complicated enough.

But Quinn needed answers, not corpses. He should at least question the bastard, find out who hired him and why. He could always kill him later.

Quinn saw Zito's left hand was tucked beneath the pillow, probably wrapped around a gun, or at least right next to one. Quinn slept the same way.

He couldn't grab the gun without reaching over Zito. That would put him in a vulnerable spot if the man woke up.

Quinn had to make the gun come to him. He holstered his .45 again. Time to wake up Sleeping Beauty.

Quinn drove a fist down hard into Zito's stomach. The sleeping man jackknifed up in bed, bellowing, hugging his aching belly with both arms. Quinn grabbed him by the back of the neck with his right hand and jerked him forward as he stabbed beneath the pillow with his left.

He pulled out a .22 revolver – the same kind of slug Archie had pulled out of Fatty the night before. Quinn flipped the gun butt-side-out and brained Zito on the back of the head with it. The gunman's list of ailments was growing fast.

Quinn toed one of the kitchen chairs to the side of the bed and sat down. Zito cradled his head and gut and whimpered. The poor bastard had just gotten himself yanked out of dreamland by a gut punch and a pistol whipping. It wasn't exactly breakfast in bed, but it was all Quinn had on the menu that morning.

Zito rubbed his head and gut at the same time. "Who the hell are you?"

"The last guy on earth you'll ever see unless you're smart enough to tell me what I want to know."

Zito squinted at him. "Wait a minute...I know you." His eyes opened wider. "Christ, you're Terry Quinn, ain't you?"

Quinn kept Zito's .22 leveled at him while he fished out his cigarette case, selected a Lucky and lit it with one hand. "You know me?"

"I know what you done to Charlie Murphy," Zito said. "And what you done John Calabrese up in the Bronx."

Quinn let out a long stream of smoke through his nose. "Some of my best work."

Zito's eyes stayed wide. "What the hell do you want with me, mister?"

"You shot Fatty Corcoran, dimwit," Quinn accused. "What did you expect? A dozen roses?"

Quinn watched Zito forget all about his sore head and gut. His eyes went vacant, then darted around the room. His mouth started quivering and his hands started to shake.

Zito stammered. "That fat man in Ames' was Fatty Corcoran?"

"As if you didn't know."

"Jesus," Zito whispered. He inched to the far side of the bed, away from Quinn. The trembling got worse. "Jesus Christ. Jesus Christ. Listen, mister, you gotta believe me. I didn't mean to..."

"You didn't mean to what? You didn't mean to shoot him, or you didn't mean to leave him alive? Which is it?"

Zito popped sweat. "I didn't mean to shoot Fatty Corcoran." He fidgeted with the sheet like a little kid who'd just pissed the bed. Quinn wondered if he had.

"I mean I shot him, yeah, but I didn't mean to shoot him." He ran his hand nervously over his unruly hair. "Fatty Corcoran? Oh, sweet Jesus, what did I do?"

Zito's whimpering surprised Quinn. He held back giving Zito another slap to steady him down. He'd seen a lot of liars act this way before he'd killed them, but something about Zito's act rang genuine. He decided to switch tactics. Keep the guinea off balance.

"Take it easy," Quinn said. "If I'd wanted you dead, you would've woken up that way." He tossed his cigarette case on the bed. His lighter followed.

The .22 stayed level.

Zito looked at the case, then at Quinn. He slowly reached for the cigarettes with an unsteady hand.

"That's better," Quinn approved. "No sense in getting too nervous, Carmine. You and me are just a couple of guys chewing the fat is all. So just lay back, relax, and tell me everything from the beginning. Who hired you to kill Fatty?"

Zito was shaking bad now, worse than before. Quinn wondered if he was going into shock. Zito barely got the cigarette in his mouth. He fumbled with the lighter. But Quinn wasn't dumb enough to fall for that old trick. He saw how it could play out: reach over to give him a light and Zito makes a play for the gun. Fuck him if he can't light it himself.

Zito gave up trying to light it and tossed cigarette and lighter aside. "What's the use? You ain't gonna believe me anyhow. You'll just plug me anyway. Christ!"

"Maybe, maybe not. Who hired you to shoot Fatty?"

"Nobody," Zito quickly waved his hands. "I mean I used to pull jobs for the O'Bannion boys in Chicago,

69

the Kansas City combine and so on. I get on a train, do the job, get paid and come back. But that kinda work's been slow lately, and I ate into most of what I had squirreled away for a rainy day. I was getting pretty desperate..."

"My heart bleeds. Get to the fucking point."

Zito took a deep breath and began again. "A couple of days ago, I woke up and found a paper bag on the floor at the foot of my bed. Somebody must've climbed down the fire escape and tossed it in the window while I was sleeping. I opened it up and found a thousand bucks in tens and twenties in there with a note card inside."

Quinn hadn't been buying the story until then. "A note? What kind of note?"

"See for yourself," Zito said, pointing quickly over to the RCA cabinet.

"I put it in there with the record player after I read it."

Quinn looked over at the cabinet. It still looked too formal for a dump like this. Just as Quinn knew there was a gun under that pillow, he figured Zito probably had one or two firearms stashed in other places in the apartment as well. "Anything in there I should know about?"

"I got a .45 stashed next to the player. Just in case."

Quinn slowly got out of his chair. He kept the .22 trained on Zito's chest. He peeked behind the cabinet. No extra wires coming out of it. It didn't look rigged, or booby trapped.

Quinn opened the lid slowly. He found the .45 nestled against the turntable, just like Zito said. He also saw a small white envelope about the size of a calling card next to it. He pocketed Zito's .45 and took the note back to his chair. He pulled the card out of the envelope with one hand.

The other still held the .22 on Zito.

The handwriting on the card was impressively neat. It read:

I have it on good authority that you are a man who knows how to solve problems. I have a problem that requires solving of a permanent nature. Please accept this one thousand dollars as a retainer for your services. Do a good job, and you shall receive twice this amount afterward.

Regrettably, it will be impossible to give you much advanced notice of when I may need you, and for what purpose. I shall give you all the notice I can. Please remain in your apartment each evening for the next three days so I will know how to find you.

You have a reputation for discretion, Mr. Zito. Please, keep it that way.

Talk soon,
  Me.

Quinn re-read the note. The tone was fancy and stiff. He couldn't understand why anyone would write down anything like this in the first place. "Any idea on who sent this?"

Zito shook his head. "Half the people who hire me can't hardly read, much less write. I don't exactly advertise, either so I don't know how they found me. Normally, I'd be steamed about someone sneaking into my place while I slept, but a thousand bucks does a lot to water down my temper, especially these days."

Quinn pocketed the note. "So, you get the note and the money. Then what?"

"I waited, just like he told me to," Zito said. "A grand is more money than I've seen in one place in a long time. But I wanted to be ready so that when the guy came back, I could grab him and find out how he found me.

"Then yesterday, around five or so, someone bangs on my door. By the time I get over there, there was nobody in the hallway. Just a sack laying against my door. When I open it up, it has another grand in it and another note." Zito took another note card from the table next to his Murphy bed and handed it to Quinn. "Here. Read it for yourself."

The handwriting was completely different: bold, blocky letters. It read:

ames pool hall, tonight, 11:00 PM. get there early. give $500 to vinny ceretti at the bar. we know you know who he is. make sure he gets all the money, or you don't get the rest of yours. when vinnie leaves, kill the fat man playing pool. we'll be watching.

Quinn re read the note. Two notes, two different people. No way of telling why or who wrote them. No sense in wasting time trying to figure it out yet.

"You knew Ceretti?" Quinn asked. "How'd they know that?"

Zito shrugged. "I don't know. We wasn't pals or nothing. I just knew

him from around. You know how it is."

It made sense to Quinn. Ceretti was always sniffing around, looking to scrounge up a buck. He scurried a broad path. "What did you do next?"

"I showed up early," Zito continued. "I waited until Johnny the Kid started playing pool. I spotted Ceretti, stood behind him so he couldn't see me. Ceretti's a rat and he woulda given me up in five seconds flat after the shooting if he saw me. I gave him the money, told him to scram. I shot the fat guy playing pool, just like the note told me to do. It was too crowded for a head shot, so I got in close and shot him as best I could. If I knew the guy was that fat, I woulda brought the .45 instead to do the job right. But I'd been paid to do a job and I went to work with what I had." Zito caught himself and added: "Shit, I mean, in this case, I'm glad I didn't have the .45 because..."

"Skip it. You mean to tell me you didn't recognize Fatty when you saw him?"

"Sure, I know who he is, but I never saw him before. If I'd known who it was, I never would've done the job. And I sure as hell wouldn't still be here if I did."

Quinn sat quiet for a while. He watched Zito fidget as he ran through the gunman's story in his mind.

The whole damned thing was so ridiculous, it just might be true. The note. The small caliber weapon he brought to do the job. Things weren't adding up to a hoax. If Zito knew who he'd hit, he would've run. Why take the chance writing the notes himself? Quinn could've just as easily killed him and found them when he tossed the room after.

Things were looking up for Mr. Zito. "So, you shoot Fatty with the pop gun, get downstairs and take off. Then what?"

Zito shrugged. "I came back here, and someone had thrown another bag of money through my window. Two g's this time, just like they promised. No note. A lot of it was in singles. I didn't get the chance to count it, but I'm sure it's close to two grand. I put the money under the bed with the first thousand they gave me and went to sleep. Next thing I know, you're giving me the wake-up call."

Quinn still had one question. "What did you do with Johnny the Kid?"

"Nothing. What would I bother with him for?"

Quinn saw Zito was telling the truth. Again. "You said the money they gave you is under the bed?"

"Almost three grand, except for the five hundred I gave Ceretti."

"Show me." Quinn cocked back the hammer on the .22. "And do it real slow."

"With the beating you gave me, slow's the only speed I got."

He creaked off the bed, cradling his gut. The naked man kept his other arm away from his body and in full view. "I'll lift the bed up with my leg, nice and easy. When the bed comes up, you'll see a shotgun on top of the bag. I'm not going anywhere near it, so don't get nervous."

Zito slipped his foot under the bed and eased it up. The springs caught and pulled it back into the wall with a loud snap. A large duffel bag and a .12 gauge lay on the floor, just as Zito had said. The Italian backed up against his RCA cabinet, as far away from the shotgun as he could possibly go in the tiny room.

Quinn got up, eased the shotgun off the bag with his foot and moved it over to the side. Zito was still close enough to kick him in the face if he tried to pick it up and he didn't want to give him the chance.

"You are a careful boy, aren't you, Carmine? Smart, too. I'll bet you're just smart enough to let me walk out of here with all your money and not make a stink about it."

"Why are you doing this for me...?"

"I won't be happy, but there ain't a whole hell of a lot I can do about it right now."

Quinn liked Zito's style. His gut told him Zito would make a better ally than a corpse. He might prove useful before all of this was over. "You're smart, Carmine. Smart all the way around the track. I like that."

Quinn lifted the sack on to the table where Zito had his gun cleaning set and opened it. Some of the money was bundled, but most of it was just as the gunman had said, lose tens, twenties, and lots of singles. Like someone scrambled to get the money together at the last minute.

Quinn pulled out a two-hundred-dollar stack and tossed it to Zito. "That'll keep you afloat for a while. But you won't need much where you're going."

Zito let the stack hit him in the chest and fall to the floor. He looked at the gun. "You're still gonna kill me? After all that?"

"Don't be a dope." Quinn opened the cylinder of the .22. and dumped the shells on the floor. "You're the only link I've got to whoever wanted Fatty dead. Besides, I've got big plans for you." He tossed the empty gun to Zito, then looked at the clock on the wall. 8:20 AM. "Do you know where the Chauncey Arms is?"

Zito began pulling on some clothes. "Thirty-ninth and ninth?"

"Twenty-ninth and ninth," Quinn repeated. "It ain't The Algonquin, but your employers will never find you there if they come looking. Ask for Joey, the manager. Tell him I sent you and he'll set you up fine. Stay there until I call for you. And don't get any ideas about rabbiting on me." Quinn held up the sack. "You'll get this back when all this is over."

He took Zito's .45 from his pocket, ejected the magazine left it on the table. "You're going to need this, the shotgun, too. I'll call you personally when I need you. If someone else calls saying I told them to call you, hang up and get the hell out of there. If they come knocking at the door..." He looked at the shotgun, then at Zito. "You'll know what to do."

Quinn picked up the duffel bag and headed for the door.

"Why are you doing this for me," Zito asked, "after what I did to Mr. Corcoran?"

Quinn paused halfway out the door. "Someone's running a game on you, just like they're running a game on Archie. And when I find out who they are, I'm going to make them pay."

"I don't like people using me, mister. When you need me, I'll be ready."

Quinn closed the door behind him and bounded down the stairs, past the rats and the street vendors. And none of them bothered to look his way.

Chapter 8

IT WAS close to noon by the time Quinn got back to his apartment above the Longford Lounge. He was dizzy from the lack of sleep.

The apartment was empty, but he could tell Alice had been there. The rumpled bed sheets outlined where she'd slept. The air still smelled of her: cheap gin and that tonic she used to keep her hair flat. She always said it smelled like honey. He thought it smelled like hair tonic and it gave him a headache. Images came to him – her long white neck, the way her...

Quinn shook it off. She wasn't his girl. She wasn't his friend. She was a distraction, and he had no time for distractions.

He pulled up the corner of the red rug in the middle of the room. He removed a cut out panel from the floor and opened the combination lock of the floor safe beneath it. He put in Zito's money for safe keeping. If Zito played along, he'd get his money back. The trouble was Quinn didn't know what game they were playing yet. But he had a feeling he'd figure it out soon enough.

He'd been wearing the same clothes for the past two days. He tossed his shoulder holster on the bed, peeled off his clothes and stepped into the shower. The hot water beat down on his neck and shoulders. The water felt good on his sore hands. Ira's punks might've been soft, but they had hard heads.

He shut off the water and toweled off. He caught a glimpse of himself in the mirror on the back of the bathroom door. Alice had once told him he was so ugly, he was handsome. She liked to trace his scars and ask about them.

A knife fight with Richie Dago had left him with a purple six-inch scar that stretched from his stomach to his ribs. His right shoulder was still a bit out of joint from the wicked left hook he'd caught from Big John Genet in The Garden back in '25. The left shoulder had been separated when he burst through a door looking for Brody and the money he owed Archie. Quinn's nose had been busted more times than he could count. His jaw too.

He smiled at his reflection. Alice was right. If ugly was handsome, Terry Quinn was beautiful.

Quinn stretched out naked on his king-sized bed. Some of Alice's body heat was still in the sheets and it relaxed him.

He wanted to sleep, but his mind was too crowded. Too busy. He started piecing together everything he'd learned instead.

Wallace paid Ceretti to set up the game with Fatty Corcoran. Wallace knew Rothman and Shapiro, who backed Johnny the Kid. It stands to reason that Wallace had also hired Zito to shoot Fatty. He could've just been what he claimed to be: a sporting man who wanted to bet on a pool game. But it was an awfully big coincidence that Fatty happened to get shot during that game. And like Doyle had taught him, coincidences were bullshit.

Zito said he didn't know who hired him. Quinn knew he shouldn't believe him, but he did. Finding Wallace was the key. At the least, he was mixed up in this somehow. At the most, he'd planned it. Quinn would worry about why later. For now, one thing mattered: finding Simon Wallace.

Behind all this loomed Doyle's mystery project. It was important enough to worry Doyle and that worried Quinn. Archie never got rattled and he didn't exaggerate. Whatever it was must be big. The faster Quinn found out who shot Fatty and why, the better Archie would sleep at night. He wished Guinan had known where the bastard lived; life would've been much easier.

Quinn knew Doyle's organization had over a hundred guns on the street and a small army of snitches who'd sell out their mother for a cigarette. One word to them, they'd tear the city apart looking for Wallace. But the cops would kick up a storm and Archie couldn't afford that kind of trouble.

Quinn could look for Wallace himself, but ten different people would give him ten different answers. No one would admit they didn't know where Wallace lived. He'd waste the whole day.

So Quinn made a phone call instead. Time for Detective Doherty to start earning his keep.

When Doherty came to the phone, Quinn said, "I need you to start asking around about a guy named Simon Wallace."

He heard Doherty write the name down. "He the shooter?"

"No, but he might be involved," Quinn explained. "I don't know exactly how, but his name keeps popping up. I could have my boys look for him, but I know that wouldn't end well."

"You're a lot of things, Terry, but dumb isn't one of them," Doherty admitted. "I'll get the word out and swing by the Lounge tonight. Let you know what I find."

Quinn hung up the phone and went back in bed. Let Doherty's people look for Wallace. He'd pay them a nice finder's fee and get the chance to question them himself. His mind raced, thinking of all the angles. Who was Wallace? Was he even involved? What was his beef with Fatty?

His mind sought answers. His body craved sleep more. The darkness of his mind rose up and enveloped him.

AFTER A GOOD SLEEP, Quinn got dressed for work. He wore a midnight blue tuxedo, silk bow tie, matching cummerbund. And the .45, of course, but the jacket had been tailored to conceal his holster.

Alice always told him the tuxedo made him look more intimidating than usual. She liked the way the tuxedo jacket showed the lines of his shoulders and how the starched collar made his neck look even thicker than it already was. She liked his hair when it was slicked straight back and how it showed off his dark eyes.

Quinn knew she was sneaking into his thoughts

again. He reminded himself she's just a distraction. He pushed her memory away. Tonight wasn't the time for romance.

It was closer to six o'clock by the time Quinn got to his perch atop the elevated dining area of The Longford Lounge. Normally this was the best part of his day, watching the swaying crowd of revelers drinking and dancing the night away. A couple of fat cats at the bar were treating a client to steaks and martinis. A couple of loud rich boys made passes at a cigarette girl.

Wendell Bixby nursed a Manhattan at the far end of the bar. The New York American's star gossip columnist was listening to a pretty, young blonde whispering in his ear. Quinn figured Bixby was pumping her for dirt for the next day's column. The scribbler was always looking for the skinny. He paid well for it, too. Times were tough and there was no shortage of people lining up to give it to him.

Prohibition had turned the place into a gold mine and the Crash only seemed to help business. Bread lines grew longer by the day. Dozens of speakeasies and nightclubs had closed all over the city since the stock market tanked a few months before. The Lounge was one of the few truly swanky places south of Harlem still open. On any given night, customers might see William Powell, Fay Wray, Jean Arthur, Gary Cooper, Babe Ruth sipping Side Cars, martinis, or Old Fashions.

The nightly receipts proved the casino in the basement was the real draw. As poor as people were, they always found enough money for another spin of the wheel or the roll of the dice. Lady Luck was always just one card away. Blackjack, poker, craps, and roulette. The Four Horsemen of the Apocalypse.

The band finished their number, and the band-leader introduced a new performer to the stage: Miss Alice Mulgrew.

Quinn didn't know she was part of the show. He tried to get Fred Deavers' eye to find out what the hell was going on, but he was busy handling the crowd at the front door.

The Lounge patrons applauded as the spotlight hit her and she smiled her crooked smile. The sequins of her nude-colored cocktail dress caught the smoky light. She almost glowed. Her hair was no longer platinum blonde, but black. Short, silky, and smooth. Her lips were as red as her skin was white and the dress showed off every curve of her body.

The crowd hushed and every eye in the place was on her.

Her eyes skipped over the crowd as the band warmed up. When they settled on Quinn, all thoughts of Wallace and Shapiro and Fatty Corcoran went right out the window. He took another drag and told himself it was just the dress and the lighting. But when she went into her song, he couldn't help but smile. 'Someone to Watch Over Me'.

He'd told her it was his favorite song the last time they'd gone to bed together.

Alice wasn't a great singer, but she could sell a song better than most. Her throaty voice gave the lyrics that extra melancholy that always got to Quinn.

And Alice knew it.

He had to remind himself again that she was just a distraction.

Quinn was surprised to see Frank Sanders limping his way up the stairs toward him. Even though Archie had given him control over Washington Heights and

Inwood, Sanders looked more like a dock worker than a crime boss. He was a fifty-year-old flat-faced, chinless Irishman with sad eyes and a sour expression. He always wore a rumpled brown suit, brown tie and a beat-up brown fedora plopped on his head.

Quinn had heard all the war stories of when Fatty, Sanders and Doyle were breaking legs for the Dead Rabbits years before. Doyle always said it just as easily could've been Sanders' mob if Frank had wanted it bad enough. But Frank seemed content with running his pool halls and speakeasies, taxi concessions and numbers games up in northern Manhattan.

"Archie sent for me," Sanders said, skipping the pleasantries. "Some kind of pow-wow he wants with me and Walker tonight."

Archie hadn't told Quinn about any meeting with Sanders and Mayor Walker. Then again, it was his place. He didn't have to tell Quinn anything.

"Any word on the bastard what shot the fat man?" Sanders asked. Quinn already had Zito under wraps and that's where he was going to stay. If people knew he had him, they'd want to know where he was. Best to keep that to himself, even from Archie.

"I hear it's some clown named Carmine Zito," Quinn offered. "But keep that to yourself. The cops are afraid of a war breaking out and I don't blame them. I've got some people running him down now."

"Keep looking," Sanders said. "We need to hang that bastard by his balls. You got my message about Johnny? He never showed. Neither did the cab."

That struck Quinn as strange. "The cab too?" Now Quinn knew Johnny must be dead. "Anyone find them yet?"

"No, but we're looking. I bet Rothman grabbed

him out of revenge for what you done to Shapiro. They oughta give you a medal for that, by the way. Someone should've put a bullet in that little bastard a long time ago. He's still in the hospital, but he's supposed to pull through."

Quinn didn't care about Shapiro. He wouldn't die from a shoulder wound. It was Johnny going missing that was bothering him. "I should've dropped Johnny off at your place myself, but I had troubles of my own with the cops."

"Which ones?"

"Ours, Halloran and Doherty. They're worried about what Rothman hitting back over me shooting Ira."

Sanders waved it down. "Archie'll square that with Howard. That's probably part of why he wanted to meet tonight." Sanders pulled his pants up over his gut. "Circle the wagons. Whip everyone into shape. Who else is coming?"

Quinn figured he'd find out soon enough, so he told him. "I didn't know anything about it until you got here."

Out of the corner of his eye, Quinn saw Frank Deavers waving his red handkerchief at him. The standard sign that Mayor Walker had arrived. "Looks like Little Jimsy's on his way in. You'd better head back and jaw with Archie before I bring him in. It'll take him a couple of minutes to work the room before we make it back there."

Sanders went back to see Archie while Quinn went to the front to escort Walker through the crowd. Alice had finished her song and moved off the stage to a long chorus of applause. The band stuck up something lively. Quinn made his way to the door through the dancing patrons at the bar. A few of the regulars tried to talk to Quinn as he moved through. He cut through them without stopping until he reached the front door.

"Our man on his way in?" Quinn asked Deveraux.

Deveraux leaned in close to Quinn and dropped the French accent. "Walker's glad handing some civilians on the sidewalk. He's wearing a white tie and tails, for Christ sake. He don't know how to play it small, does he?"

As if on cue, Mayor James J. Walker strode into the Lounge with a beautiful brunette on his arm and a big grin on his thin face. "Whaddya know and whaddya say, boys?" He whisked off his top hat and tossed it to the hat check girl. "Where's the party?"

Quinn gave the bandleader the signal and the band struck up "Will You Love Me in December, As You Do in May", the song the mayor had written as a young man in 1905. A cheer went up from the customers and everyone strained their necks to see the man the papers had dubbed "The Night Mayor of New York City".

Walker slid the black mink stole from the brunette's shoulders, revealing a tall, thin girl in a sleeveless black evening gown and pearls. Walker was in white tie and tails with a white scarf around his neck. He pumped Deveraux's hand and the brunette swooned as the maître 'd laid on the French. Then the mayor shook Quinn's hand.

"Hello, kid. How's the crowd tonight? Nice and mellow or drunk and rowdy?"

"A little bit of both, your honor," Quinn replied.

"Fine, fine. That's just the way I like it," Walker then turned his attention to the young woman on his arm. "Darling, I forgot to introduce you. Terry, this is my good friend Betty Compton, the brightest star of the New York stage."

Quinn had met her several times before, but Walker never remembered. Quinn made a show of bowing at the waist. "Always a pleasure to see you, Miss Compton."

"That's what I always tell her every morning, ain't that right, baby," Walker laughed, playfully elbowing Quinn in the stomach. "Well, no sense in putting off temptation any longer. Why don't you lead the way, my good man, so we can get down to the serious business of drinking." He turned back to the small group that had followed him in. "Once more into the breach and all that, eh, boys?"

Quinn led the mayor, Miss Compton, and the entourage of Walker's sycophants through the crowd. The mayor had a meeting with Doyle but was in no hurry at all. Once "Will You Love Me" played out, they broke into a rendition of "Sidewalks of New York", the song from his mentor, Governor Al Smith's presidential campaign of 1928.

Walker shook every hand and slapped every back he could reach. Quinn was amazed how he remembered all the regulars' names and even some of the strangers too, as though he'd remembered them from that time he saw them. Everyone wanted to like him and to think of him as one of their own. Walker was happy to oblige.

Everyone knew Jimmy Walker was owned lock, stock, and barrel by the Tammany Hall machine in general and to Archie Doyle in particular. He was as crooked as they came, but no one seemed to mind. If anything, they seemed to respect him for his honesty about his dishonesty.

When Quinn finally got Walker to his table, Walker pulled Quinn aside. "Does Archie need to see me right this second or is he busy with other things because I sure could use a couple of drinks first?"

Quinn knew Walker's version of "getting settled in" involved two or three glasses of champagne. He didn't know why Doyle wanted to see him, but he was sure he'd want Walker sober. "I think Mr. Doyle was hoping to see you as soon as you arrived."

Quinn saw Walker's frown, then added, "I'm sure we can have champagne brought to the back room."

Walker's frown disappeared. He made a flimsy excuse to his table about needing to meet with some pesky constituents. He kissed Betty's hand before he followed Quinn to the back room.

The little man trotted alongside Quinn and tugged on his arm. "Listen, kid, between you, me and the lamp post – what the hell is going on? Someone goes after Fatty last night; you almost kill Shapiro right after. Word has it he might lose an eye."

Quinn loved rumors. "I winged him in the shoulder, sir."

"Whatever," Walker said. He'd never been big on letting facts change his mind. "My phone's been ringing off the hook all day long with people wondering if hell's about to break loose. You know I love Archie like a brother, but he should've played it smart and headed to that horse farm of his until all this blows over."

Quinn led the mayor to the meeting room at the back of the club. "Mr. Doyle figures it's safe to act like its business as usual, and from what I've seen, he's pretty good at figuring things."

"I sure hope so," Walker cautioned, "because I'd

hate like hell to hear his name read at mass in the morning."

Quinn doubted the little shit had been inside a church since the day he was married, but he let it slide.

Quinn lightly rapped his knuckle on the French doors of the back room. He heard what sounded like Doyle and Sanders arguing. He'd never heard the two men argue about anything in all the years he'd been working for Doyle.

After a moment or two, Doyle yelled, "Come in!"

Chapter 9

THE BACK ROOM of The Longford Lounge was nick-named 'Doyle's Court'. It was where Archie Doyle talked business over cocktails and cigars without fear of anyone listening in.

Hunter green wallpaper, dim lighting, and faded paintings of some of Doyle's prize racehorses hung on the walls. Doyle and Sanders had been drinking brandy and smoking thick Cubans. A thin cloud of blue cigar smoke hovered over the table like a dirty halo.

The flushed look on the two crime bosses' faces told Quinn that they'd been arguing. They barely acknowledged the mayor as Walker slid behind them into the room.

To the rest of the world, he was a celebrity. Mayor Jimmy Walker. Tabloid darling. Hero to the common man. In Doyle's Court, he was still Lil' Jimsy from the old neighborhood. A likable kid who'd made good because men like Doyle and Sanders let him make good.

"Take a load off, Jimsy," Doyle waved his black cigar at one of the vacant chairs at the table. "We got champagne already chilled and all the trimmings."

Quinn saw that Walker felt the tension in the room, too. He might've been crooked, but he wasn't stupid. He smiled his thanks anyway. "That's swell of you guys. Just swell. Thanks for thinking about me."

"No thanks needed, Jimsy," Doyle said as he pulled a bottle of champagne from the chill stand and poured a tall glass for the mayor. "What we've got here is a real occasion. A night for the books you'll be able to tell your grandchildren about someday."

Sanders pulled the cigar from him mouth and said, "Goddamn it, Archie, I'm begging you to think about this some more before..."

Doyle shut him up with a glare.

Sanders flicked an ash from his cigar into an ashtray. Quinn knew no one ever held Doyle's stare for long.

"What's the rumpus, Jimsy?" Sanders asked the mayor. "I ain't seen you since The Flood."

"It's been a long time, Frank," Walker forced a laugh. "I don't get up to the Heights as much as I'd like to these days. But at least I get to stop in on Archie at least a couple of times a week and help him get rid of some of that champagne he stocks." He toasted all of them with his champagne flute and drank.

"Oh, you're a big help in that department," Doyle sneered. "You blow in here, buy a round for the house and run outta here without putting your hand in your pocket once. You're a real class act, Jimsy."

"Ah," Walker grinned, "but The Longford Lounge benefits tenfold by being known as the place where

Mayor Walker hangs his hat whilst out for a night on the town, doesn't it, Archie?"

But Doyle wasn't grinning. "The mayor forgets that he's only mayor because I let him to be mayor."

Quinn could tell Doyle was not in a good mood. Time to make himself scarce. "I'll be out on the floor if anyone needs me."

"I need you here," Doyle told him. "Take a seat next to the good mayor over there."

Quinn froze. He thought he was hearing things. This was the first time Doyle had asked him to join a meeting. Why would he? Quinn was just the hired help.

"I ain't asking you to quote scripture, goddamn it," Doyle boomed. "Sit your ass in the goddamned chair."

Quinn closed the door behind him and did as he was told.

Walker didn't seem to like the idea. "Everyone here knows how fond I am of Terry here, but I need to talk about some things he probably shouldn't hear." He touched Quinn's arm. "Again, no offense."

"What about?" Doyle asked. "That Shapiro nonsense? Don't worry about that. I'll iron that out with Rothman on my own."

"I'm talking about the whole damned thing," Walker elaborated. "Fatty getting shot's got a lot of people scared shitless. And Terry shooting Shapiro's joint looks like you blame Rothman for Fatty, which is a little presumptive on your part, I might add. No one wants New York to turn into another Chicago."

"I'm not Capone," Doyle declared. "I got more sense in my little finger than that fatty little guinea had in his whole head. Terry shooting Shapiro wasn't planned, but it wasn't his fault either."

"That's debatable," Walker retorted. "Rothman says..."

Doyle didn't care what Rothman said. "Shapiro's goons jumped him, and Shapiro shot at him. What was the kid supposed to do?"

"And I don't care who did what to whom. I care about what happens next. Governor Roosevelt's people have been looking for a reason to go after me since the gimp got elected. Any more bloodshed, and I mean any and I'll get the blame from Albany, not you."

"Fuck Albany," Sanders said. "Nothing but a bunch of goddamned farmers up there anyways. What do they know?"

Doyle ignored Sanders. "There's not going to be anymore bloodshed, believe me. We'll find the bastard who shot Fatty and that'll be that."

Walker surprised Quinn by showing this much backbone. "That's not enough anymore, Archie. I need you to sit down with Rothman soon so I can tell those bastards up in Albany that this thing won't boil over. You've got the city, but Rothman's bought a lot of favors in the legislature. There's a whole big state outside of the city, my friend and he's bought up a lot of assemblymen and senators."

Doyle grew very still. He slowly took the cigar out of his mouth. "You talking down to me, you son of a bitch?"

"No, I'm telling you the way things are and how to protect your investment. And that investment is me. Please, please have a sit down with Rothman. Smooth this shit over and end this thing once and for all. Roosevelt's made no secret about having his eyes on the White House in two years and he's planning on using my neck as a steppingstone. The bastard's got his

Good Government brigades crawling over every agency in the city. The boys at Tammany don't sleep nights."

Doyle motioned for him to calm down. "And I'm telling you that, soon, Roosevelt and his Goo Goos will be a distant, bad memory. For you, for me and for all of us."

Walker first looked at Quinn, then at Sanders. "What the hell are you talking about?" Then his eyes popped wide. "Christ, you're not going to kill him, are you?"

Doyle smiled. "I'm going to do better than that. I'm going to beat the gimp at his own game."

Walker hesitated. "What game?"

"Politics. Just look at what's going on in today's world. Money's drying up. People are losing their jobs, their homes. Hell, even the gin mills and gambling parlors are going belly up. That means there's a lot of crooks out of work getting that lean hungry look while they all chase the same buck. Eventually they all start looking at the guy on top of the mountain and that guy is me. That's why we've gotta start looking to the future. And the best place for the future is politics."

Sanders spoke up. "Archie, for Christ sake. I really want to talk about this another..."

But Doyle talked over him. "There'd be anarchy if we just pulled outta the street all at once. That's why I want to start backing away slowly. Let the other gangs get pieces at a time. Sally Lucania has been pushing me for more territory for a while. Maybe I'll give him some. We've already got the permanent stuff – the docks, cab stands, restaurants, warehouses, but our main source of income is from gambling and booze. We're gonna be screwed out of that once the feds repeal Prohibition in a few years or so. The quicker we get legit, the better. And we get legit by getting Al Smith elected the next president of the United States."

Quinn sat very still. He couldn't believe this was Archie's big plan. Owning a mayor in the city you ran was one thing. Owning a president was different.

Walker stopped rubbing his temples. "That's it? Electing Al Smith as President of the United States will solve all our problems in one big swoop."

Doyle plucked his cigar from the ashtray and leaned slowly back in his chair. "That's my big plan."

"He tried running two years ago and lost remember?" Walker reminded. "Hoover mopped the floor with him back in '28 because the people of this fine country will never vote for a Catholic to be president, plain and simple. And even if they did and even if they elected Al president, he'd have a whole country to worry about, not just us."

Doyle puffed long and slow on his Havana. He held the rich smoke in his mouth for a while before he slowly let it escape from his mouth in broad circles. "A lot's changed in two years, Jimsy. People had money to burn back then. Now, they're scrimping and saving just to get by. Come 1932, they're gonna want a man who knows what it's like to grow up poor, who knows what they're going through. They'll want a man who knows what it's like to go to bed hungry and cold. A man like Al Smith – Man of the People. The time is right for a move like this, Jimmy. Think about it and you'll realize how right I really am."

Quinn saw Walker's lips move, but no words came out. Walker's eyes softened and he sank back in his chair. Quinn could see the idea was beginning to take root in his mind.

A broad smile spread across Doyle's face. "I ain't saying it's gonna be easy. I'm just saying it's possible. Instead of just running New York, we'll run the whole damned country. And we'll run it legal."

Quinn watched Walker sit back in his chair and sip his champagne. "I'm not completely sold, but I'm man enough to admit that you could be on to something here – if Al goes for it."

Doyle laughed to himself and popped the cigar back in his mouth.

"That's why I want you to swing by his place tomorrow and find out if he's interested in throwing his hat in the ring one more time. We need to get him on board and fast."

"My powers of persuasion will be much stronger once I have a chance to test Lady Luck's kindness on your roulette wheel downstairs," Walker said, with another toast of his champagne glass. "Terry, do you think I could sneak down there without Ms. Compton or my other friends seeing me? I'd like a couple of minutes alone to work the room, and I can't do that with a bunch of spectators following me around."

Quinn looked to Doyle for permission. Archie nodded and got up and walked to the door. "I'll bring you down the back way, your honor. I'll have Ms. Compton and your friends brought down whenever you're ready."

Walker drained his glass and laid it back on the table. "Frank, it's always a pleasure. And as for you, Archie, you've given me quite a bit to think about. I'll be in touch in a couple of days." He came around the table and slapped both of them on the back on his way toward the door.

Doyle focused on his cigar instead. "You be in

touch tomorrow afternoon like I told you. I'll be very disappointed if I don't hear from you by three o'clock." The ash fell into the ashtray. "Very disappointed."

Quinn saw the mayor stand a little straighter. He wasn't used to being spoken to this way.

"I'll have something for you by tomorrow afternoon. I promise. I'd like to leave now."

Doyle nodded at Quinn and Quinn opened the door.

"Good luck on the tables, Jimsy," Doyle called after him. "I'll be down there myself after Frankie and me finish up here."

Quinn escorted Walker through the small dining room to the hallway behind one of the curtains.

When they were out of earshot, Walker queried, "What the hell was that all about?"

Quinn said nothing.

"His world's falling apart and he's playing king maker?" Walker went on. Then, as was Walker's custom, he switched gears. "But, if we could get Al to run and if we could do it the right way this time, that half-baked scheme of his might work."

"That would make Archie very happy," Quinn conceded.

They walked through the back of the kitchen, past the two men guarding the rear stairwell. Quinn escorted him down to the casino, two flights below.

When they got to the lower landing, they were greeted by an orchestra of gambling sounds. A marble ball rolling along the track of a roulette wheel, the muffled scramble of dice rolling along the felt of the craps table, the gentle clink of chips, and the cheers and moans of hitting a winning number.

"Good luck on the roulette wheel, Your Honor, and let us know if you need anything."

For the first time in all the years Quinn had known him, Walker didn't rush into the casino.

"I got a real bad feeling off Archie tonight, Quinn. And I don't mean because he got sore at me at the end there. It's almost like he was...afraid...or desperate. I've never heard him sound like that before."

Quinn lied. "I'm sorry you feel that way, sir. I'm sure he's just tired."

But Walker didn't look so sure. "Maybe you're right. Maybe the whole thing with Fatty's been harder on him than I thought."

Walker offered him a weak smile and a pat on the arm. Then he slipped into the casino.

The mayor's words haunted Quinn as he walked up the back stairs. Running Al Smith again for president might be a tough sell, but Archie wasn't desperate. Impossible.

But it was. Quinn had seen fear in enough men to know he'd seen it in Archie that evening. Did he really think Al Smith being president was his shot at respectability? Quinn was glad he didn't have to answer. He just did what he was told. Let the bigger brains worry about politics, Prohibition, and the future. He had a saloon to run, money to earn, and a man in a white suit to find.

Chapter 10

QUINN GOT BACK UPSTAIRS and walked through the main dining room of the Lounge. He waved to some of the better patrons who called out to him. Being social was good for business. Everyone wanted to know the guy who ran the joint. Everyone wanted to look like a big shot to their friends and mistresses. As long as they kept shelling out the dough, Quinn let them think whatever the hell they wanted.

Wendell Bixby, the gossip monger for the Journal-American, kept trying to catch his eye. Quinn let them all wait. Quinn took a cigarette from his case and lit it. "What's the disposition?" he asked Tommy.

"The usual assortment of fine ladies and gentlemen and everything in between," Tommy said. "We've a booming business at the bar, the tables are full, and your colored band is keeping them hopping, which should make them all good and thirsty." He poured enough gin and vermouth for three martinis into the tumbler and gave it a couple of good shakes.

"Even New York's Finest seem to be having a ball over there."

Quinn found the cops' reflections in the large mirror behind the bar. Doherty and Halloran had parked themselves at the bar near the door. Their cheap suits, bad ties, and hang dog expressions screamed out 'copper' to anyone who saw them. They casually eyeballed the crowd while they downed highballs. Older and thinner, Doherty did a better job of blending in than Halloran, but not by much.

Doherty caught Quinn's stare in the mirror and toasted him with the highball glass. Quinn offered a salute with his cigarette.

"They give you any trouble?" Quinn asked Tommy.

"That big bastard Halloran had the gall to demand the best rum in the house, but I've been giving them that watered down paint we got from The Peacock after it closed down last week."

"Just make sure they don't go blind."

"Never fear," Tommy said. "Besides, you've got bigger worries before you." He poked his thumb over his left shoulder and said, "Her Grace has been acting up again."

Quinn saw Alice laughing it up at a table with a couple of banker types. Quinn didn't like her flirting with guys twice her age. He didn't like her hitting the sauce so hard after getting plastered the night before. He didn't like the way she leaned forward to show her cleavage when she laughed.

He didn't like hearing her sloppy cackle that caused people to look at her. He didn't like that he was starting to give a damn about her.

"What's she drinking?" he asked Tommy.

"Her hosts are paying for Dewar's, but I know how wild she gets on the good stuff," Tommy said, placing lemon rinds in the glasses of the newly poured martinis. "I'm serving her the same watered-down stuff your boys in blue are having. I won't let her get too loaded; I promise."

That was one of the reasons why Quinn liked Tommy. He knew how to save his customers from themselves. "You'd better deliver those martinis before they get warm."

Quinn felt something strike him on the shoulder. He turned to see Alice swaying in front of him, ready to hit him again with her purse.

"You dirty, cold hearted son of a bitch," she slurred. Her left eyebrow was cocked. A thick strand of black hair had fallen over one eye. Her nude-colored evening gown was hanging a little lower in the front than it should've been. The brown beauty mark on her left breast showed. He remembered another mark on her stomach. There was a third matching mark on her inner thigh. Kissing them in the right sequence drove her wild. As drunk as she was, she looked beautiful.

Quinn laid his cigarette in the ashtray. "Didn't leave anything out, did you, sister?"

"You left me alone last night," she slurred. "How dare you treat me like shit when there's guys all over this city that'd give anything to turn out the light with me lying next to them?"

She was beginning to draw the attention and catcalls from the bar. Quinn knew he'd have to calm her down before she made a scene. "Sorry, angel, but something came up." He tried to gently take her arm. "Why don't we go upstairs right now where we can talk?"

Alice wrenched her arm free. "You mean somewhere so I'll be nice and quiet, you goddamn bastard. How can you look at me like I'm nothing to you in front of all these people? Like I'm some cheap whore you paid off after you had your fun. All Doyle and those sons-a-bitches want to do is use you. I love you."

Quinn pulled her closer to him. "If you'd been sober long enough, you'd see things have been a little busy around here the last couple of days. Now, let me take you upstairs."

Tommy placed a steaming cup of black coffee on the bar in front of her. "Drink up, darlin'. A little cup o' joe right now will do you a world of good."

"Sure, sure," Alice slurred again. She looked at the coffee like it was poison. "Drink coffee. Get her upstairs. Let her sleep it off. Anything to shut the drunken bitch up so your customers can go on having fun." The crowd cheered and toasted the sentiment.

Alice's eyes flickered. Quinn moved to catch her. She rebounded and backed away from him. "It's always Archie Doyle, isn't it? You and that cheap hood sitting on top of all your money looking down at the rest of us like we was shit."

She hauled off and swung her bag with all her might. She missed wildly and spun completely around. The entire bar cheered and called out for more. Quinn grabbed her before she fell and gently wrapped his arms around her shoulders to hold her up. She reeked like one of Doyle's breweries.

She broke down into sobs and buried her face in his chest. Her head hung to one side, revealing the length of her white neck. He fought the longing stirring inside him. There'd be plenty of time to get laid later.

Alice was right. Time to shut the drunken bitch up and get her upstairs. Quinn beckoned Sean Baker over and handed Alice off to him. He made sure his hand wasn't high enough to touch her breast or too far behind to touch her ass. He handed Baker the key to his apartment upstairs. "Bring her up to my place and lock her in. Let her sleep it off for a while."

"Okay, boss," Baker said, struggling against Alice's dead weight "but there's a man at the door who..."

"Whoever it is can wait. She's more important."

The patrons at the bar cheered and raised glasses at the weeping Alice as Baker led her from the room. For the reputation of the Lounge, and for other reasons he dare not admit to himself, Quinn wanted to get their focus off her. He knew alcohol was the best way to do that. "Tommy, give the bar a round on the house."

Another loud cheer went up. Tommy got busy filling glasses. Quinn made the rounds to all the regular patrons at the bar. He winked away the trouble with Alice. Wendell Bixby tried to get his eye again, but Quinn ignored him. The scribbler was only looking for an item for his damned column.

Quinn went over to Doherty and Halloran to see if they had anything on Simon Wallace.

Halloran toasted him before he drained his glass. "You're a regular Rudolph Valentino, my friend. For a common hooch punk, you've sure got a way with the ladies. And what a set she has on her."

Quinn's temper spiked. "What would you know about a set, Jim? You haven't been anywhere near a teat since you were in diapers."

Halloran spat out his rum and threw his glass to the floor. He wiped his mouth with the back of his hand. He reared up to his full six feet three inches. He almost matched Quinn eye to eye. "That mouth of yours is gonna get you killed one day, hooch punk."

Quinn glared back and grinned hard. "But not tonight and not by you."

"That's enough, Jim," Doherty scolded him from his barstool. "Go outside and cool off for a while."

But Halloran held his ground. "You and I are going to dance real soon, Quinn. You hear me? Real soon."

Quinn gave Halloran the smirk he saved just for him as the cop turned and stormed out of the place.

Doherty watched him leave, then turned back to his rum. "Jim's had a rough night. We just pulled Johnny the Kid off a meat hook over on the East side about an hour ago. Cab driver, too."

Quinn bit into his cigarette. He'd figured The Kid and the cabbie were dead. Knowing for sure didn't make him feel any better about it.

Doherty continued. "Looks like whoever it was took their time, too. They hacked out his tongue and put it in his back pocket for good measure. Guess someone thought he talked. No twenty-year-old deserves to end up like that. Poor kid wasn't old enough to deserve the end of a meat hook." He drank and put his glass down. "You know, if I hadn't seen you send the Kid off in a cab with my own two eyes, I would've figured you for the job."

"Meat hooks and hack jobs aren't my style. You know that."

Doherty seemed to buy that. "Where'd you say you sent him off to again?"

"I didn't say." Quinn wasn't about to tell Doherty now, especially after

Johnny the Kid wound up dead. The less the police knew, the better. "What about Simon Wallace?"

"Nothing yet," Doherty said, "but we're looking around. Oh, I forgot to tell you: Vinny Ceretti turned up. Some railroad detectives found him in a train car with a .45 slug through his belly this morning."

Quinn knew he'd shot Ceretti in the head but wasn't dumb enough to correct him. "Another pillar of society crumbles. I'm all broken up."

"You should be. Things are getting out of hand; first Corcoran, then Ceretti, Shapiro, Johnny the Kid, and the cabbie. That's four separate examples of violence involving the Doyle and Rothman mobs in less than twenty-four hours. Two dead bodies that I know about. More to come, I'm sure. I saw Walker in here tonight and I'm sure he told you if you can't keep a lid on things, we'll have to do it for you."

Quinn wondered what Doherty would've thought if he knew Doyle was planning on owning the White House, too. He probably wouldn't believe him. Quinn wished he'd be lying. "Just make sure your boys in blue remember who's buttering your bread. The good wind still blows from Archie Doyle's direction, and until that wind changes, he's still the boss."

Doherty nodded slow. "For your sake, I hope that wind doesn't blow into a storm."

Before Quinn could answer him, Baker was at his side and handed him back his keys. "I put Miss Mulgrew on the bed and came right back. She was wailing pretty loud when I left."

"Let her. No one'll hear her from up there."

Baker whispered up to him. "I tried telling you before that there's a man outside who's asking for you personally, boss. He wouldn't give his name but said you might know him. I figured he was a friend of yours."

"Wonderful." Quinn stabbed out his cigarette in Doherty's ashtray. "When it rains, it pours, don't it, Charlie?"

The detective smiled a boozy smile. "Every cloud's got a silver lining, or so they tell me."

Quinn followed Baker to the entrance where Deavers was waiting for them. "Sorry about this, monsieur," Francois Deveraux said in character, "but a gentleman insists on bringing an associate inside with him who is not properly dressed."

Quinn stepped through the curtain. He stopped dead when he saw who it was.

Chapter 11

THE MAN WAS JUST how Quinn had pictured he would be. About five feet six inches tall. Around fifty years old. A light brown beard trimmed to give his fleshy face the illusion of a jaw line.

A white, broad brimmed fedora tilted to the left. He held himself with a forced elegance, with one hand dipped in the pocket of his white cashmere overcoat. The other hand held a black walking stick that supported his weight. He had a strangely passive expression, like he was trying to look bored.

Quinn knew this was the man he'd been looking for. Simon Wallace. This was the man in white.

The ex-boxer in Quinn wanted to drag the bastard downstairs to beat a confession out of him. His pride was wounded because this man had the balls to walk into his place not twenty-four hours after Fatty got shot.

But Quinn knew Wallace must've come there for a reason. He'd let the man make whatever play he'd come there to make.

He could always beat the hell out of Wallace later.

"I'm Terry Quinn," he extended his hand to Wallace. "What seems to be the problem?"

The man in white regarded the large hand for a moment before shaking it lightly. It was the limp kind of handshake that pissed Quinn off. "This French poodle you have guarding the door barks at me every time I attempt to bring my associate inside with me."

Quinn sized up the associate. He looked like the muscle that Guinan had described that morning. A little taller than his employer but much broader and thicker. He wore a dark cap, a gray turtleneck and a blue pea coat that had seen better days. Quinn bet he was a bully boy from one of the slaughterhouses along the east river.

Quinn remembered what Doherty had said about finding The Kid on a meat hook. He bet there was a connection.

"Francois is only enforcing a standard policy we have here at The Longford Lounge about proper attire," Quinn explained. "Your associate isn't wearing a coat and tie, so he can't be allowed into the club. You, however, meet our dress code and are more than welcome to join us inside, Mister...?"

The man in the white hat ignored the question. "Then you must have some kind of shirt, tie and jacket on reserve that he could borrow?"

"No."

Baker tried to pull Quinn to the side. "Terry, I think this guy could be a real high roller. Can't we..."

Quinn ignored him and spoke to the man in the white hat. "Your associate also violates our policy against having firearms in the club."

The man's left eyebrow rose. "What makes you think he's armed?"

"The bulge on the left side of his coat. If I'm wrong, dinner's on me, but if I'm right, he'll have to wait outside for you until you're ready to leave, if you decide to come inside. I can assure you our staff is more than capable of providing you with a safe, enjoyable evening."

The man tapped his walking stick against his leg for a moment, then looked up at Quinn. "I suppose these terms are nonnegotiable?" He tilted a billfold out of his inside jacket pocket.

"Your money's good at the bar. Not with me."

The man turned to his hired muscle and sighed. "I'm dreadfully sorry about this, Carl, but you'll have to go for a walk. Meet me in front in about two hours."

Carl did as he was told without saying a word. The man in the white hat faced Quinn and held his hands out from his sides. "Now that I'm completely at your mercy, Mr. Quinn, may I please finally go inside and have a drink?"

Quinn motioned to the cloak room. "By all means. Would you like to check your hat and coat first, Mister...?"

The man in the white pulled off the glove of his right hand one finger at a time. "Wallace, Simon Wallace, an entrepreneur late of Savannah and many parts west. I understand you've been looking for me."

Quinn worked to keep his expression from changing. The link to Fatty's shooting was standing right in front of him. "Pleasure to meet you, Mr. Wallace."

He watched Wallace hand over his walking stick and hat to the coat check girl first, then pulled off the other glove one finger at a time with great ceremony.

He slipped out of his overcoat and laid it on the half door. He smiled and gave her a little bow when the girl handed him his ticket.

Quinn saw that Wallace had had a lot of practice at acting like he had money. He'd seen plenty of to-the-manor-born types and this wasn't it. There was something different behind the man's small brown eyes, something hard and permanent that couldn't be hidden by phony accent and fancy clothes. It was something that came from going to bed hungry more than once. From scraping and fighting to stay alive. Quinn knew the look well. He saw it every time he looked in a mirror.

There was a reason why Wallace wanted to be seen as a lightweight. There was a reason why he'd come to the Lounge. Quinn had to know why. For Fatty Corcoran's sake. And Archie Doyle's sake, too.

"I believe this is your first visit to the Lounge before, Mr. Wallace." Quinn escorted him inside.

"Yes. But the Lounge's reputation for quality of service and gaming has reached the shores of San Francisco and the parlors of Savannah and Louisiana."

"You said you're from Savannah. Where you are from originally?"

Wallace smiled. "I said I was a man of many parts, Mr. Quinn."

Quinn let it go. "You also mentioned you're an entrepreneur. What kind?"

"A very successful one, I assure you. In many industries far too numerous to mention. Lately, I've prided myself on being a man of action, one who takes time to enjoy the more exciting aspects of life."

"Is that what brings you to New York?" Quinn

asked as they moved toward the bar. "Action and adventure?"

"If that's what one seeks, what better place in the world than here?" Wallace found a spot at the bar and caught Tommy's attention. "A Manhattan, straight up and sweet." He didn't look to Quinn to pay for it. Quinn didn't offer. "I'm particularly looking forward to availing myself of the many places of entertainment in this town."

Quinn saw this guy liked to talk. Quinn loved talkers. They told you everything if you let them run their mouths enough.

"One place you might like," Quinn suggested, "is Texas Guinan's Le Kaye Club on Broadway. Ever been there?"

Tommy served Wallace his Manhattan, before he could answer. He picked up the rock glass and sipped. Pinky extended.

Hand shaking just a little.

Wallace regarded the tan liquor as he swallowed, then smiled warmly. It was a smile more of relief than pleasure. The first real expression the little bastard showed yet. Wallace didn't just enjoy that drink. He needed it. That information could be useful somewhere down the line. Just like Zito.

Wallace licked his lips. "Your man makes a damned fine drink, sir. The only thing I prefer to good liquor is a good game of chance. And to answer your question, not only have I heard of Tex's club, I've been there several times. A charming little place, but a bit too loud for what I'm looking for this evening."

"And what might that be?"

"Risk, Mr. Quinn," Wallace's eyes flashed big. "Action gets my blood rushing and quickens my senses.

And as I was saying before we were so pleasantly inter-rupted," he said, hoisting his Manhattan, "I under-stand your Lounge has one of the finest gaming floors this side of the Mississippi."

Quinn wouldn't admit to having a casino down-stairs to a stranger. Especially not to a stranger who probably had a hand in shooting Fatty. He decided to prod him a little. "What's your game, Mr. Wallace?" He let the question hang for a moment. "Poker? Roulette? Blackjack? Craps?"

The man sipped his Manhattan again. "I've always had a particular fondness of cards with a terrible weakness for blackjack."

Quinn saw his shot and took it. "I would've marked you for a pool player."

A twinkle appeared in Wallace's eyes. "I'm afraid I've always seen billiards, or pool as you put it, as a sport for the rougher set. But I find all games of chance invigorating. Don't you?"

Quinn shook his head. "Never liked chance. I like taking matters into my own hands."

Wallace bit his lower lip. "There's something to be said for a man brave enough and bold enough to try to control his own destiny, I suppose. But I've always found that attempting to control destiny – fate, if you will – is often dangerous and, if I may say so, foolish. Wouldn't you agree?"

"Not me." Quinn bent a fraction of an inch closer to Wallace. "I've never been smart enough to know when to quit."

Wallace didn't back away from the larger man. His eyes moved over Quinn's face. "Most boxers don't," Wallace toasted him.

Quinn stood upright and smiled. The little bastard

couldn't resist showing what he knew. "You saw me fight?"

"I have fond memories of reading about your ring career and was sad to see it end much too soon and on such a tragic note." Wallace quickly waved off the moment with a toast. "Ah, to the bravery of youth, sir. And now that I think you're quite sure that I'm not a Treasury Agent sent to raid this establishment, I understand you have a gambling establishment on the premises. I wish to play."

The little bastard has balls, Quinn thought. "It's only open to members of The Longford Lounge and its guests but can be used by non-members for a small service fee."

"Ah, yes," Wallace said. "The ever present 'fees' of such places. How much?"

"One thousand dollars. Cash on the barrelhead. No personal checks or IOUs accepted."

Wallace raised his eyebrows. "You call that a small fee?"

"Whatever it is, it's non-negotiable. We allow only the most serious clientele in our game room. The fee splits the pretenders from the real thing. Something you'll appreciate if you decide to play downstairs."

Wallace sighed. "A wise policy. Are there any other accoutrements I might expect with said fee?" He gave a rakish grin. "Particularly those of the female persuasion?"

"I run a square joint, Mr. Wallace. Booze, broads, and blackjack are a dangerous mix. Besides, the cops in this precinct don't like call girls or cat houses, so we keep out of that business. If you want company for later, the floor manager downstairs might be able to have something sent over to your hotel. But while you're in here, your wick stays dry."

Wallace laughed. "Well put, sir. I wish they were that frank in Monte Carlo." Quinn watched his hand move toward the billfold in his suit jacket again. "Shall I pay you or the floor manager downstairs?"

Quinn doubted he'd ever been to Monte Carlo. But he'd have the boys downstairs watch how Wallace played. You could tell a lot about a man by what he played and how he gambled. Just because Wallace liked to take chances didn't mean he knew how to handle the odds.

Quinn whipped out a slip from the inside pocket of his dinner jacket, signed it, and handed it to Wallace. "Give this to the man at the elevator down the hallway to my right. He'll escort you downstairs. The cashier will take the fee and give you however many chips you want. Any problems, have them call me."

Wallace regarded the slip for a moment, then folded it and put it in his pocket. "Thank you so much for your hospitality, Mr. Quinn. Everyone's been so kind to me since I arrived in New York and, except for that unpleasantness with my bodyguard, tonight has been no exception."

"New York's a real friendly town with plenty of action, Mr. Wallace, so long as you're careful about where you look for it."

Wallace's smile dimmed. "Indeed. I'm fortunate to have a great many friends in town to call upon should I need them." He held Quinn's gaze as he extended his hand. "Good evening, young man. I'm sure we'll run into each other again sometime soon."

The moment Wallace got on the elevator; Quinn got

on the house phone and called the floor boss down at the casino. "Hanz," he said when the man picked up, "there's a little guy in white on his way down right now. Warn the table boys to watch him closely, but to not screw with his play. Tell them to watch what he plays and how he bets. If you catch him cheating, let it drift so long as none of the other players raises a stink. Just tell me how he does it."

"Got it, boss," Hanz responded. "Here he comes now."

Quinn's hand shook a little as he put the receiver back on the hook. The bastard was wrapped up in Fatty's shooting somehow. His gut told him to beat the information out of him.

But Quinn figured Wallace was a tougher customer than he let on.

He probably wouldn't crack, or worse, he'd feed them a phony story he'd already cooked up.

No, the smartest play was to keep an eye on him. See what happens. Quinn knew Wallace was mixed up in all of this somehow. Time to find out just how much, starting tonight.

Sean Baker came over and gave him a gentle punch in the arm. He was in a good mood. "Glad you reeled in a live one with that Wallace fella, eh boss? Bet he's gonna drop a lot of coin downstairs..."

Quinn was in no mood for jokes. "Don't you ever, and I mean ever, question me in front of a customer again."

Baker's eyes stammered again. "But I thought..."

"That's the problem, you're not thinking too good lately. Last night, you kept our boys bottled up in the safehouse instead of being on the street where they could do some good. Tonight, you almost let in a guy who everyone, but you could see was packing a gun. What the hell is the matter with you lately?"

Baker didn't look at him. "I'm sorry, Terry. I just thought he looked like a high roller, and you'd want his money is all."

"Let me do the thinking and you do the doing." He saw Baker beginning to shake a little and it stopped his anger cold. This wasn't some punk giving him lip. This was Sean, a reliable kid who'd just made some mistakes lately.

Quinn couldn't blame him. With Fatty getting shot and everything else that had happened, it was tough for anyone to know what to do. Even Quinn. The words came tough, but they were necessary. "Look, I'm sorry I got mad, but we can't afford mistakes right now. Understand?"

Baker nodded. Quinn thumped him on the back and said, "Good. Now get back to the front door and try not to let anyone in here with a fucking howitzer."

Baker straightened himself out and went back to work. Quinn rolled his neck. Muscles popped and relaxed a little.

Quinn took a cigarette from his case and lit it. He held on to the smoke for a long time before letting it go.

He felt like his entire world was falling apart before his very eyes. Fatty getting shot. Doyle's crazy play for Al Smith in the White House in '33. Albany putting a bullseye on Walker's back. Alice pulling shit in front of everyone. Johnny the Kid hanging on a meat hook. Simon Wallace walking in the place. Baker turning flaky. And Zito, the gunman, quietly holed up in the Chauncey Arms downtown.

Of all the threads in this mess, Wallace worried

him most. Sure, he had Hanz and his boys keeping an eye on him downstairs. Then what? He had to know where Wallace was going. But if he had one of Doyle's men trail him, word might get back to Archie, and Quinn couldn't afford that. Doyle had the White House on the brain. Nothing else seemed to matter.

Quinn got a sharp twist in his gut. He'd never held anything back from Archie before.

Quinn was now on his own.

If he couldn't use one of his own people to trail Wallace, then who could he trust?

Then the tobacco kicked in. He knew the right man for the job. He headed back out to the bar.

CHARLIE DOHERTY WAS on his fourth rum on the rocks. He was woozy, but sober enough. "What's the place turning into anyhow?" Doherty asked him. "Hell, I can remember a time when you wouldn't have let a swish like him stand in front of the joint, much less go downstairs." Doherty flicked his cigarette at the ashtray but missed wide. "Shit, you won't even let me go downstairs."

"You and your men have the run of the pool room during the day and after hours," Quinn reminded, "but at night it's paying customers only. Besides, I've got something better for you to do."

"Oh yeah?" Doherty showed in drunken interest. "Like what?"

"Like following up on a lead on who might've hung The Kid on a meat hook tonight?"

Doherty's buzz evaporated. "Tell me."

"Your boyfriend in the white suit, that's Simon

Wallace."

"The guy we've been looking for all day?" Doherty
slid off the barstool and buttoned his jacket with boozy
resolve. "Let's go grab him."

Quinn put his hand on the detective's shoulder and
guided him back to the stool. "He's not going
anywhere for a while. Besides, Wallace is a crafty son
of a bitch who'll just give you the run around if you
corner him like a criminal."

"Not if I drag his ass down to the station and have
Halloran work on him for a few hours," Doherty said.

Quinn shook his head. "I'd have my own boys
doing that right now if it would do any good."

Doherty smiled. "I thought you hated violence."
Quinn smiled too. "All right, smart guy," Doherty said.
"What do you want me to do about it?"

"Have Halloran follow the little bastard to see
where he flops next. Halloran's not good for much, but
he's pretty good at tailing people. Normally I'd send
one of my boys to do it, but I don't want word to get
out that we might be interested in him."

Doherty thought about it a moment. "Holding out
on Archie, eh?"

Quinn already had an answer for that. "I'm just
not wasting his time by getting his hopes up." He
almost believed it himself. "When I find out more
about who Wallace is and what he's up to, I'll let
Archie know."

Doherty seemed to buy it. "We've got a better
chance of figuring Wallace's game if we watch him
from afar anyway. I'll go find Halloran. He's probably
still walking around the block after that steaming you
gave him."

Doherty stopped and stumbled a bit on his way to

the door. "That was some good thinking, Quinn. You would've made a pretty good cop."

"I'm not that much of a businessman. I'll leave police work to you more enterprising types."

Doherty went to find Halloran, and Quinn took his spot at the bar.

Tommy cleared Doherty's glass and wiped the spot clean. "It's a night of characters, eh, Terry?"

"You don't know the half of it." Quinn crunched out his half-smoked cigarette in the ashtray. "Set me up with a Cutty, neat."

Tommy froze in mid-wipe. He looked carefully at Quinn. "Terry, are you sure you'll be wanting to start in with the spirits so early in the evening? Why not leave them alone until after closing?"

Quinn glared at the bartender.

Tommy cleared his throat. "You know how it makes you sometimes."

Quinn's glare held. Tommy reluctantly retreated to fetch the drink. "And don't water it down like you usually do. I just need a little to take the edge off is all."

Quinn lit another cigarette and breathed the smoke deep into his lungs.

He wondered if Tommy was right, then decided he was dead wrong. After the night he'd had? One drink wouldn't hurt.

Tommy placed the glass of Cutty in front of him and moved away.

Quinn let the drink sit while he took in the Lounge. His lounge. Heads were bobbing to the smooth beat of the band. Dancers swung around the dance floor. Quinn found his own head bouncing to the rhythm of the drums. For a minute or two, Quinn didn't think about presidents, mayors, gunmen or bosses. Right now, there was just rhythm.

The rhythm of the music. The rhythm of his club. The rhythm of his casino downstairs.

That was all Quinn really had. And for now, that was all he really wanted.

Chapter 12

THE WORLD slowly came back to Terry Quinn.

He wasn't asleep. He wasn't awake, either. He was too much of one and not enough of the other. He wasn't sure how long he'd been like this. A few seconds? Minutes? What little feeling he had in his head felt like it was laying on something soft. A pillow? Probably.

Feeling gradually returned to his neck. Then his arms. Then his chest.

They were on something soft too. His arms were stretched out from his sides. On a bed? Definitely. He made fists with his hands. They didn't hurt. Good. He probably hadn't hurt anyone last night.

But felt drafty and cold. Almost naked. He didn't have the energy to open his eyes.

But he heard someone groaning in the distance.

Maybe he had hit someone after all? He couldn't remember who it was. He didn't try. He had a soft, quiet place all to himself and his head didn't hurt yet. He knew he should enjoy this peace while it lasted.

The headache was going to be a doozie.

His eyelids parted. A wood paneled ceiling came into focus, just like the one in his bedroom. He realized that this was his bedroom and his own bed.

But where the hell was that groaning coming from?

His head felt like it was made of glass. It would break if he moved it. He moved his eyes instead. He followed the ceiling down until it fell away from view. He looked down further and saw a woman on top of him.

Her head arched back. Her arms on the bed behind her, grinding herself around his erection. Her neck had one small brown beauty mark on it. There was another one on the inside of her left breast. His eyes trailed down her body, where he found another beauty mark on her thigh. He recognized her right away.

Alice.

She moaned again. She grinded harder and faster. She threw her head forward. She brought her arms around to his shoulders to support her weight. Her eyes were closed. Her mouth was drawn into a sneer. She ground him harder now. She made a sound halfway between a squeak and a moan. He felt her nails dig into his shoulder.

All feeling rushed back to the rest of his body. Her stomach felt smooth against his. Her breasts felt warm and soft as they swayed back and forth against his chest. They matched the rhythm of her hips. Something hot spilled over him and he felt himself losing control.

Alice scooped her hands behind his head and slipped her tongue in his mouth. His pelvis matched the rhythm of hers. She bounced harder. She moaned louder. Her tongue moved faster and faster until...

Splendid release.

Shiver after shiver went through her body into his. Quinn kept moving his pelvis, bringing it up to meet hers. Her hands slipped off his shoulders, onto the bed and his hands moved up to the back of her head, pulling her mouth closer to his. The rhythm continued. They drank each other's kiss. Her breath tasted like stale cigarettes and cheap gin. So did his. Neither one cared.

She shuddered deeply and broke off the kiss. Another spasm racked her body. She giggled. She lowered herself on him. Another spasm. Another giggle. He let his hands slide down her back, now wet with perspiration. She shot upright with another shake. She put her hands on his ribs to balance herself. He watched her loll her head around. She bit her lower lip and brushed a wisp of black hair from her eye and tucked it behind her ear.

Her makeup from the previous night had faded. What was left was smeared all over her face. Her pale body glistened. She made no move to get off him. She sat back on his thighs. He was still inside her.

She smiled. "God, it took me a long time to get you going," Alice whispered breathlessly, "but when you did..." She raked his chest lightly with her nails. Quinn was sure he was still drunk and couldn't remember much. His first Cutty had been followed by six or seven others. Lots of cigarettes. No food. Same old story.

"How did I get here?" His own voice sounded strange to him.

Alice slowly rubbed her hands up his flat stomach. She grazed it with her nails on their way down. "I don't know how you got here, but I'm glad you came," she giggled.

Alice still sat on top of him with her head lolling around in a slow circle. Normally, she could've stayed there all day if she'd wanted to for all he cared, but his hangover was starting to kick in. He felt nauseous.

"You getting off me anytime soon?" he asked her, still groggy.

Alice shook her head, her eyes still closed, and began to slowly rock back and forth on him. "Not a chance. I'm having way too much fun and you know this is the best way for me to fight a hangover. Besides," she said with a throaty laugh as she whispered in his ear, "I think somebody's ready for number two."

She slowly French kissed the side of his neck and proved herself right. Nausea would just have to wait.

AFTER NUMBER TWO, Alice slid off him and curled up next to him like a well-fed house cat. She hadn't pulled a sheet over herself and the thought of doing it for her never crossed Quinn's mind.

His bare feet on the freezing floor brought him closer to sobriety as he trudged to the bathroom to take a shower. He let the warm water beat down on his head, neck, and shoulders for a while. It didn't kill his headache, but it kept it from getting worse.

Quinn remembered Wallace being there and he wasn't happy with himself. Getting drunk with a prime suspect in the house wasn't the brightest thing he'd ever done. He hoped there wasn't anything else worth remembering.

He quickly toweled himself off and dressed in his

usual white shirt and black suit. He started heading downstairs when he heard Alice say:

"Going somewhere, lover?"

"Gotta go to work."

She laughed and rolled onto her back, still naked among the white sheets. "What work? You smack people around all day and clean up Doyle's messes." Her long hand patted the pillow next to her. Her lips slid into a sly grin. "Come back to bed and I'll put you to work. Work that'll do us both some good."

As tempting as it was, Quinn kept his hand on the doorknob. "Archie needs me."

"Bullshit." Her grin turned into a sneer. "Why do you keep sticking your neck out for that bum anyhow? All he does is use you."

Quinn didn't like anyone running Archie down. Not even Alice. "It's got nothing to do with you."

"It has everything to do with me. With us, if there's ever going to an us."

"There is no 'us'," Quinn countered before he could stop himself.

"That so?" Alice slowly stretched out her white body on the bed. "Then what do you call what happened here last night?"

Quinn was hungover and didn't like being questioned. "This was a nice drunken evening with..."

Alice's cackle cut him off. "For a brave guy, you sure are scared of the truth. This is me you're talking to here and I know you a hell of a lot better than that. I saw you go through women pretty quick – two, maybe three weeks before you move on." That damned cocky smile of hers returned.

"You and me have been doing this little dance at

least four nights a week for three months, Terry. And we weren't drunk every time."

Three months. Quinn hadn't thought about how long they'd been doing whatever it was they'd been doing. Too long for a fling. But he didn't have time for this now. He had to know how Doyle was doing. He needed to know about Wallace and if Halloran was tailing him.

Mostly he just wanted to get out of the room.

"I've got to go to work, okay? Fatty's been shot and Archie..."

"...will get along just fine. There's always going to be something he needs you to handle. If it isn't Fatty getting shot, it's the ward bosses not doing what they're told, or the unions trying to organize one of his warehouses or some cops who forgot they're on the take or some other goddamned thing that ends up with you getting hurt and Archie getting rich."

She stopped yelling and tried a smile. "But it doesn't have to be that way forever, baby."

Quinn wanted to remind her he was making good money, too. Better than other guys in his position. Better than he would've if he'd stayed in boxing, even if he'd won the belt.

But he knew Alice wouldn't understand any of that and he didn't feel like trying to explain it. "He saved my life, Alice. I owe him."

"You've worked for the man for over five years. Any debt you think you owe him was paid a while ago. It's time to think about what you want now. For you. For us."

Quinn didn't want to argue. He grabbed the doorknob again. "I've got to go to work."

He opened the door.

"I love you." She looked up at him from the bed. Tears flowing from her eyes. Not the same kind of tears the rum brought. Real tears. "I love you and I know I shouldn't, but I do. I love you and I don't want to see you killed because of your loyalty to some two-bit party boss who did you a favor once. I know you love him like a father, but you love me, too. I'm not asking you to say it. I can tell you do. And that's supposed to mean something, too."

The word rang in Quinn's ears. Love. He couldn't remember the last time someone had used that word on him, at least someone that mattered.

Most of the women he'd known had used it to keep him from slipping away. None of them had said it the way Alice had. She'd touched him in a strange place. A place he'd always known was there, but never paid attention to before because he'd never had a reason. But he had a reason now.

And she was lying naked on the bed before him.

His loyalty to Doyle stood between them. "It means something, Alice," Quinn continued out the door. "It just can't mean something today."

He closed the door quietly behind him. He told himself he didn't hear Alice's gentle sobbing through the door.

━━━

HE FOUND them sitting around one of the large dining room tables playing cards. Archie Doyle, Frank Sanders, Tommy Delaney, Fred Deavers and Hanz the Pit Boss. All in the same clothes from the night before. Each outfit was in a various state of disrepair.

Tommy's tie was gone, his collar unbuttoned.

Deavers' dinner jacket was off. His sleeves rolled up to his elbows.

Sanders was the only one who looked exactly as he had the night before. Rumpled brown fedora pushed back on his head. Tie pulled down. Collar opened. Cigarette dangling from his mouth. Doyle's dinner coat was on the back of his chair. His bow tie lay on top of his chips. Quinn wondered if he'd bet it.

Doyle puffed on one of his black Cubans and smiled wide at Quinn over his cards. "There he is, boys. Terry Quinn, ex-heavyweight contender, and current world champion mattress polo player. A Dutch master of bed artistry if I've ever heard one."

They all cheered and pounded the table. Quinn gave the finger all around.

He was still smarting from his sparring session with Alice. He grabbed a cup and poured himself some coffee from the side table.

Tommy said to Archie: "Look at the poor lad, boss. We're making him blush."

Doyle shifted one of the cards in his hand. "Considering most of the blood in his body has been residing further south for the last several hours, that's quite an accomplishment."

More table pounding and catcalls. Doyle's tall stack of chips spilled over. He cursed them as riotous bastards.

Quinn took refuge in a booth with his mug of coffee. His mouth was too dry to taste anything, but at least the caffeine would help his headache. He watched Tommy grimace at his lousy hand. He folded, grabbed a bottle of scotch, and slid into the booth opposite Quinn. Tommy was a veteran of Quinn's hangovers.

"Give it to me straight," Quinn asked. "What did I do?"

"Talked with a couple of the customers," the bartender told him. "Drank and made your way upstairs a little before closing time. Unless anyone had seen how much you were drinking, they would've thought you were just tired. No harm done at all, except to yourself."

He poured some of the scotch into Quinn's coffee. "Here. A little hair of the dog that bit you will do you good."

Quinn swallowed the spiked coffee and felt a little better. At least he hadn't made a complete ass of himself. He called over to Hanz, who'd just called Doyle's bet. "What about the guy in the white suit?" He made sure he didn't mention Wallace's name.

Hanz said, "Played roulette and a little blackjack the whole night. That's all. Played it careful, betting odds or evens on roulette and occasionally betting on the groups, but never too much. On blackjack, he always hit on twelve, but never on fifteen and when he got two face cards, never split, or doubled down. A very careful boy."

Quinn wasn't surprised. A guy like Wallace wouldn't blow a wad in a strange house until he got the feel of the joint first. "How much did he walk out of here with?"

"He lost maybe about one hundred total by the end of the night," Hanz said. "But on his way out, he did ask me something strange before he left."

"What?"

"He asked about the billiards room downstairs," Hanz said. "He wanted to get on the list because he heard New York poolrooms were dangerous places."

Doyle looked at Quinn from across the card table. "Sarcastic son of a bitch, ain't he, kid? Who is he?"

"Nobody," Quinn said. He hoped Archie couldn't hear the lie in his voice. "Just some punk who sassed me on his way in. Tried to bring his bodyguard inside and kicked when I told him no. Frankie can tell you all about it."

"Maybe later," Doyle said as he went back to his cards. "By the way, looks like we're famous again. Show him the paper, Tommy."

"Take a look at page seven," Sanders said. "Bixby creep's getting ballsy in his old age."

Tommy handed Quinn the morning addition of The New York Journal. Growing bread lines at soup kitchens had once again replaced Fatty Corcoran's shooting as front-page news. Quinn flipped the broad sheet over to page seven to "Bixby's Box". An outdated picture accompanied Bixby's by-line for the past decade, showing a man with a rakish smile and a thin mustache.

Quinn's red eyes narrowed when he saw the headline of "Bixby's Box".

CRIME KING HOLDS COURT

Doyle Defiant Despite Shooting Spree

Hold the phone, Mr. and Mrs. John Q. New Yorker. The Bixby Box bestows its best to bad boy Archie Doyle for standing firm in the face of danger. Not even a bullet in a comrade's keyster could keep the Big Mick from his daily duties as Grand Poohbah of Patronage and Payola in this City of Towers. Word has it that the Arch-bishop himself held court last night at the lovely Longford Lounge with a powerful and elegant elected official who's known for his nocturnal needs and diminutive stature. So be-ware, street scoundrels and be-have. The ol' grapevine is humming with juice and all of it comes up champagne on ice for the Big Mick and his cronies.

Quinn's eyes narrowed more when he found a second item just below it:

JUICE BELLY JAB-OREE

Movers and shakers weren't the only show at the Double L last night. Fight fans saw an eyeful at the grand bar when the lush-ious songbird Alice Mulgrew went one round with ex-heavy-weight pretender Terry Quinn. The ol' juice belly professed love between lefts but Quinn's fancy footwork kept him out of harms' way. Maybe Sweet Alice should take boxing lessons because to this reporter's ear, her singing lessons ain't cutting it.

Quinn forgot all about his hangover as he crum-pled the paper. Bixby knew the Golden Rule. Doyle doesn't get mentioned in the papers. Bixby had just broken that rule. This was an act of defiance of Archie at the worst possible time. This was the kind of bullshit Quinn had worried about.

"Fine bit of reporting, ain't it," Doyle said. He slipped a card out of one part of his hand and moved it to the end. "Maybe you oughta pay the scribbler a visit? Remind him what happens to people who forget the Golden Rule."

Quinn slipped out of the booth and grabbed his hat and coat. "Don't worry, boss. I'll remind him."

"Good," Doyle said. "I also firmed up a meeting with you, me and Howard Rothman down at the club-house this afternoon to smooth over the Shapiro thing.

Four o'clock sharp. Try not to be late. And try not to shoot any more Rothman people in the meantime."

But Quinn was already out the door when he'd said it.

———

ASIDE FROM BEING the city's leading gossip columnist, Wendell Bixby had been a professional boozehound and degenerate gambler for the better part of the 1920s. His wife and daughter had left him years before, leaving him to the ravages of the nightlife, racing ponies and other vices. He was only forty-five or so, but his love of all things illicit made him look ten years older. Ten hard years older. He was an open grave who filled the emptiness of his life with dirt shoveled from the lives of others.

Next to booze and horses, Bixby lived for his column. He was a schmoozer extraordinaire. He paid for his information and paid well. Free dinners, free rum or with a good word whispered in the right ear to get someone off the proverbial hook. Always chasing a good item.

Bixby was the scourge of socialites, but they always invited him to their cocktail parties. They were too afraid not to. Politicians hated him but always returned his calls. Everyone was afraid of what he'd do to them in his column if they didn't pay him respect. Wendell Bixby swam the murky waters of New York society like a shark. His mouth wide open; scooping up anything – or anyone – in the water in front of him. He magnified people's shortcomings while ignoring his own.

Quinn knew Bixby was a creature of habit. He trolled the same dives day in and day out. It was easier for his snitches to find him that way. Since it was only two o'clock, Quinn figured he'd be at The Stage Left, a speakeasy in an alley on 46th Street off Broadway. Bixby liked to perch there early afternoons.

Quinn's anger had kept his hangover at bay. He walked down the alley as two large rats scurried out of an overturned trash can and ran away from him.

He pounded on the steel door of The Stage Left three times and waited. The eye slot slid open. A pair of mean brown eyes peered out at him.

"Whaddya want?" came a voice from inside.

Quinn pounded the door again. "Open the goddamned door, Tiny." The locks were undone, and the door opened wide. Tiny the doorman was an ex-boxer, too. Much fatter and taller than Quinn, but punch drunk from too many shots to the head. He stood beside the open door, his eyes cast down and his mouth in a pout.

"Sorry, Terry," the oversized man-child whispered. "I was just makin' sure there wasn't no bulls out there pretendin' to be you, is all. I'm sorry."

Quinn walked inside. "No bulls, Tiny. Any assholes in here today?"

Tiny shut the door and bolted it. "Sure. Got 'em by the dozen. Take your pick."

"Wendell Bixby?"

Tiny was only too happy to tell him. "Sittin' by the phone booth in the back all by himself. Think he's waitin' for a call or somethin'."

Quinn walked deeper into the bar. The Stage Left was a dank little joint with low ceilings and sticky floors. Humid, dark, and narrow. He heard a rummy cough from a booth in the shadows. A couple of two-by-fours had been nailed together for posts and some planks of wood formed a bar. It was the kind of place that gave dives a bad name. It was also one of the most successful speakeasies in Doyle's organization.

Quinn ignored the regulars who eyeballed him. They all knew who he was and what he was. The bartender started in on him the moment he saw him. "I don't want no trouble here, Terry. I paid off on Wednesday like I was supposed to and I ain't due for another shipment for four days."

Quinn ignored him, too. He spotted Bixby huddled in a phone booth with his back to the bar. He was booze gaunt and pasty. His hair was thinning fast. A pencil was tucked behind his right ear. He was careful to keep his rum steady on the shelf while rifling his pockets for more change to feed the phone.

Quinn snatched the gossip monger by the back of the neck and yanked him out of the booth. Bixby protested his innocence. Quinn shoved him through the swinging bathroom door.

Bixby bounced off the wall and fell to the floor. He rolled over on his back and looked surprised to see Quinn standing over him. "Jesus Christ, Terry. What's the...?"

Quinn picked him up by the lapels of his sport coat and slammed Bixby hard into the wall. His feet were a good six inches off the ground. "Don't insult me, Wendell. Don't insult me by asking me why I'm here."

Bixby fanned his hands quickly at Quinn. His waxed mustache looked silly above his opened mouth. "Whoa, you got it, big fella. Let's just take it easy."

"I'd like to be taking it easy, Wendell. I wish I was in bed right now, nursing my hangover and making time with my lady, but I can't." Quinn pulled him off the wall. His feet dangled free. "You know why?"

Bixby shook his head fast.

"Because you broke the Golden Rule, dimwit." He slammed the reporter back against the wall. "You got cute and mentioned Archie Doyle in your fucking column today."

"You got it all wrong, tiger," Bixby laid on the charm as much as a guy with his legs dangling six inches off the ground could. "That was just my way of helping the Big Mick out, see? I threw that in there so people would see Archie was still around, same as always. Know what I mean? I was lending a hand. Showing him my loyalty."

Quinn let him slide down the wall and backed off. "Lend a hand, eh?"

"Sure," Bixby said. He fingered his glasses back higher on his nose. "It's the least I could do for him after all the kindness he's shown me. I'd do anything for the big lug if it would help. Power of the press and all that." Quinn hooked a quick right to Bixby's gut. The reporter doubled over, but Quinn slowly eased him back upright. Quinn knew that made the new pain in his belly even worse. "You're insulting me again, Wendell. Don't make me ask you again."

Bixby gasped his answer when he got his wind back. "I put him in my column because it's been a flat week for dirt, and I needed something juicy. How many times can I write about Walker balling some broad, or soused socialites in Central Park? Even that stuff gets stale, and I needed something sweet. I figured the Archie angle was as sweet as I could get. I even watered it down by throwing in that item about that tomato you've been tasting, didn't I? What's the harm?"

"Bullshit." Quinn backhanded Bixby, sending the

scribbler's glasses into the toilet. "Mentioning Archie without permission is against the rules. So, I'm going to ask you one more time. Why would a lowlife gambler like you try to...?"

The answer hit Quinn just as he was asking the question.

What would make a gossip peddler grow enough balls to defy Archie? Something made Bixby do it.

Then he remembered: Bixby was a degenerate gambler. It wasn't a far leap to truth from there.

"Howard Rothman! He made you put Doyle in your column today, didn't he?"

Bixby shook his head. Quinn pushed the reporter's head down toward the toilet. "Your head's going in after your glasses if you don't start singing. How much are you into Rothman for?"

"About four g's," Bixby screamed. "I hit a bad streak at the track and Rothman's been carrying me for the last couple of months. He didn't bug me about my monthly payments until a month ago. He started calling in markers by looking for dope on people."

That was a typical Rothman move. Quinn lowered Bixby so his feet hit the floor. He kept him pinned to the wall. "Go on."

"He's been making me drop subtle hints in my column about dirt I've got on politicians who haven't paid off the markers they owe him," Bixby said. "I usually show what I've got to a mark first so we can figure out appropriate compensation to keep my mouth shut. But Rothman's been pushing me to throw in items that might be kosher and might not. He won't give me enough time to check them."

Quinn knew Rothman was a bookie and bookies liked to get paid – one way or the other. If Bixby couldn't pay him in cash, he'd pay with favors. "Rothman told you to put Archie in your column?"

"He's sore about you drilling Shapiro. He knows Archie doesn't like being in the papers, so he made me put him in my column today to see if Archie would kick." The reporter grunted and rubbed his aching belly.

"He sure kicked all right. The bastard was supposed to have someone here to protect me."

"And he's doing a hell of a job, isn't he?" Quinn let Bixby double over to ease the pulling in his stomach. Since Quinn already had Bixby talking, he might as well press him for some information. "What do you know about a guy named Simon Wallace?"

Bixby shook his head. "Zilch. But I'll do a little digging around for you if you want?"

Quinn didn't know if Halloran and Doherty had gotten anything by following Wallace. He didn't know if Halloran would tell him the truth even if he had. Wallace already knew Quinn was eyeballing him. It didn't matter if Bixby put the word out Quinn was asking about him. It just might stir something up.

Quinn described Wallace to Bixby. "Find out everything there is to know about him. And don't be shy about who you ask."

"Anything for you and Archie, just like always."

Quinn reached into his pocket, peeled three twenties off his wad and stuffed them into Bixby's jacket pocket. "Here's a little throwing around money plus a little more for inspiration. Do a good job and there'll be more where that came from."

Bixby sank to the floor, breathing deep as he clutched his belly, his face looking even more drawn than before. "I'll call you at the Lounge tonight with what I got; I promise."

Quinn pointed down at the glasses floating in the toilet bowl. "And make sure you get yourself some new specs, Bixby. A high roller like you needs flashy cheaters to keep up appearances."

Chapter 13

CONTRARY TO POPULAR BELIEF, Archie Doyle didn't run his empire from the oak paneled world of The Longford Lounge. He ran it from a third-floor office in a rat trap tenement across the street from a row of warehouses off west Twelfth Street. Doyle had decided long ago that a low profile in a poorer part of the city was best for the image of the Party. Better for him to be in the heart of his territory to keep an eye on things.

The Sons of Erin Democratic Party clubhouse had been Doyle's front organization for twenty years and the true center of his power in the city. It was from there that Doyle organized charity drives and gave away free turkeys to the poor. It was where people from the neighborhood came to ask for money to pay the rent or to keep the heat on or get their mother that operation they needed. It was where he met with the boys down at Tammany Hall to get out the vote come Election Day.

It was where careers were begun and ended, where the status quo was defined and defended.

An empire had been born in that old building. And that day, it was a well-protected old building. In light of the Rothman meeting, Quinn had ten men guarding the place: eight downstairs and two on the roof. Doyle thought having men on the roof was a waste. Quinn felt better having two guns with a bird's eye view of the street.

Quinn lounged on the worn leather couch in Doyle's office. Doyle was wearing his Sunday best: grey pinstripe three-piece suit, starched shirt, and red tie. He could've passed for a banker. Doyle always dressed well but took extra effort when meeting with Rothman. The gambler always looked like a million bucks.

This was the first chance Doyle had given Quinn to tell him about everything he'd learned since Fatty's shooting.

Quinn ran through all of it. Johnny the Kid. Zito. The man in white. Wallace. Rothman leaning on Bixby.

He skipped the part about having Zito holed up in a hotel across town and about Wallace being the man in white. He had no choice. Archie might order him to shoot Zito or grab Wallace.

Quinn knew Zito could be useful later. And the more Wallace ran free, the more they'd find out about him. He only hoped Halloran or Doherty had tailed him last night. Neither had returned his calls.

Doyle chewed his cigar while he listened, slowly swiveled back and forth in his squeaky office chair. "Guinea hit men, shot up fat men, sheeneies with big mouths and the bosses what wants them protected. Dirt mongers paying off debt by dishing dirt." Doyle shook his head. "We live charmed lives, don't we, kid?"

"Nature of the business," Quinn agreed. "What do you want me to do about this Bixby situation?"

"I know what you're thinking, but Rothman planting that story with Bixby don't mean he's behind Fatty getting shot. You see, I've known Howard Rothman for almost thirty years. He's not a direct man and shooting Fatty is as direct as it gets."

He pulled his cigar from the corner of his mouth and pointed the wet end at Quinn. "Now, making Bixby put my name in his column? That's more Rothman's style." Doyle smiled. "Who knows? Maybe this Wallace fella's our boy. Your man in white."

Quinn shut his eyes. The jig was up. "How did you find out?"

"I pieced together some things I overheard and whatnot. You never could lie worth a shit, kid. That's why I trust you."

Quinn saw no reason to hold back. "Guinan told me Rothman and Wallace were in her club together a bunch of times. I wanted to know more about Wallace before I told you about him. I still think he's working with Rothman against you somehow."

Doyle didn't seem to think so. "Whaddya got on Wallace so far?"

"Nothing, except he's not what he appears to be, but he's got a lot of money to throw around. I had Halloran and Doherty tail him when he left the Lounge last night. Still haven't heard back."

Doyle popped the cigar back into the corner of his mouth. "Bastards are probably hungover from drinking free booze at our place. Goddamned moochers. I'm gonna have to remind Doherty of his place."

The candlestick phone on his desk rang and Doyle

picked up the earpiece and mouthpiece with one hand. "Yeah?" He smiled at Quinn.

"That so? Well, send him up in a minute or two." He replaced the earpiece in the cradle and sat back.

"The Hebrew's downstairs already," Doyle pulled a gold pocket watch from his vest. "Tried getting the jump on me by showing up early. Let 'im wait." He dropped the watch back in his vest pocket. He smoothed down his gray hair even though it didn't need smoothing.

Doyle cleared his throat. "You know I might have to rap your knuckles in front of him. Make it look like I'm bending his way a little so as he don't cry about me being unfair. Walker's right: half of City Hall and the state legislature makes book with the bastard, so I gotta show him a little bit of courtesy, especially with Jimsy talking to Al for me and all." He cleared his throat again. "You know how it is."

Quinn shrugged. "Don't worry about me, boss. I can take a beating."

Doyle laughed. "You're damned good at dishing 'em out, too, which is what got us into this mess in the first place." He pulled himself out of his chair and shrugged into his suit coat. "I was right about you from the first day I saw you down in Gleason's sparring with Lepaski. Right from the start I could tell you was a kid what saw the whole picture. Wish I had more of it around me. Especially now. It'd add class to this organization, and I like class. I always say it's the one thing you can't have too much of."

Doyle belched as he undid his pants, flattened his shirttails, and zipped them up again. He bellowed for Baker, who was sitting right outside the office.

Baker scrambled in, avoiding eye contact with Quinn.

Quinn figured he was still sore about the dressing down he'd given him last night. Quinn would make it up to him somehow.

"Yeah, boss?"

"Fetch the Jew in here, will ya?" Doyle pulled down his vest and swung on his suit coat.

"No need for fetching for he is already here," Rothman announced as he strode past Baker into the office.

Quinn noticed the differences between the two men.

Doyle the political boss was short and powerful with a thick shock of gray hair.

Rothman the lawyer-gambler was tall and slender and moved like a dancer. He wore a pearl gray over-coat with a matching bowler and suit of the same color. He wore a pale blue tie and silver tiepin. He had a pale complexion, beady eyes and a long, pointed nose that reminded Quinn of a beak.

Rothman tossed his ebony handled walking stick into his left hand as he extended his gloved right hand to Doyle. "How's every little thing, Arch?"

Doyle flicked on the charm as they shook hands. "How've you been, Howard? Grab a seat. Take a load off." Doyle motioned to one of the chairs facing his desk.

Rothman lowered himself into one. He moved it so his back was to Quinn.

Quinn smiled.

"I wish we were meeting under better circumstances," Rothman said. He stretched his long legs along the floor and crossed them at the ankles. Quinn saw his fresh-shined patent leather spats. "That thug of yours caused a hell of a lot of problems for me and my associate."

"Which associate would that be?" Doyle asked as he sat down. "Simon Wallace?"

Quinn was surprised Doyle mentioned Wallace at all.

Rothman didn't flinch. "I spoke to Simon this morning. He raved about the hospitality he received in your joint last night. He particularly raved about Quinn." His smile disappeared. "Too bad the gorilla didn't show the same decorum to poor Ira in Pete's the other night."

Doyle looked surprised. "Shapiro's first name is Ira? You don't say. Ira is a good strong name. You know, it's funny the things you learn about a guy when he catches lead, ain't it? Fatty Corcoran's first name is Aloysius."

"Ira had nothing to do with that," Rothman said.

"Who said he did? But like it or not, one of Shapiro's boys was playing pool with Fatty when he got shot. Don't it stand to reason that we'd like to talk to him about what happened?"

"Talking is one thing," Rothman flicked a thumb over his shoulder toward Quinn. "But that ape went in there with lead on his mind. He sent Shapiro to the hospital with a bullet in his shoulder and two of his boys wound up with busted heads." He slapped the arm rest of his chair. "Do you have any idea how much money Ira brings in for me every week?"

"I ordered Terry to question The Kid – and only The Kid. I even told him to play nice. Shapiro and his boys started up the rough stuff and things got out of hand. Don't make it more than what it was."

Rothman snickered. "My best earner got a bullet in the shoulder and his place busted up. I think things got more than just out of hand."

"Do I look happy about it?" Doyle asked. "But if Terry says he had to get rough, then I have no choice but to believe him."

Quinn didn't know why Archie was coming on this strong, but he was glad. It was the first glimpse of the old Doyle he'd seen in weeks.

"I'm not a heartless man," Rothman said. "I know you're fond of Terry and he's been a good man for you. But Ira's been good for me, too. I can't have Quinn putting my help in the hospital and getting away with it. How the hell would I get anyone to work for me if word gets out that I can't protect my own guys?"

Archie shrugged. "Seems to me like you've still got plenty of people who want to work for you. People like Wendell Bixby."

Rothman laughed. "What makes you think Bixby's working for me?"

"Bixby said so."

Rothman shook his head slowly. "So, you had your gorilla brace Bixby about the item in his column, eh?" The gambler turned back to face Quinn for the first time. "You must be proud of yourself, champ. First you smack around a pool hustler half your size then you brace some red-nosed scribbler with a weakness for the ponies. What's next? Squeezing blind newsies for pocket change?"

Doyle didn't let Quinn answer. "You know I don't like ink, Howard. Ink draws attention and attention draws Feds. Bixby broke the Golden Rule and suffered the consequences just like everyone else. You having him run that item on me right after Fatty's shooting was a shitty thing to do."

"You talk about living by rules? Your boy shoots up one of my joints and you say he's right."

"I didn't say he was right. I said they was both wrong for what they done. I'm trying to get you to say that, too."

Quinn watched the bookie uncross his legs and lean forward in his chair. The Lower East Side returned to his voice. "Let me lay it all out for you so we're both playing off the same sheet music. I got a pool hall property busted up to the tune of a thousand dollars, my best earner laid up with a bullet in his arm and one of the best pool hustlers in the city hung up on a meat hook. Now, I don't know if it was Quinn who hung The Kid up or..."

Quinn's temper spiked as Doyle cut Rothman off. "Be very careful about slinging allegations, Howard. I could start slinging some of my own."

Rothman sat back in his chair, took a deep breath, and folded his hands on his lap. "It's just a little odd that your boy's the last one to see The Kid alive."

"Terry put him in a cab and sent him up to Frank Sanders' joint in the Heights for his own protection. If you don't believe me, ask Doherty and Halloran. They seen him do it."

Rothman laughed. "Doherty and Halloran, eh? You've got every bog-trotter with a badge in your pocket, and I'm supposed to believe what two more Mick cops have to say?" Rothman sucked his teeth. "I didn't get this far by being that stupid."

Doyle's chair squeaked loud as he settled back. He put the Cuban back in his mouth and drew the smoke in slow. "You and me have been running the same streets a lot of years now, ain't we? Probably since we've been able to walk. Going on damned near fifty years for me. About the same amount of time for you, ain't it?"

Rothman slouched in his chair. "I'm not dressed for a stroll down memory lane, Archie. What're you driving at?"

"Sometimes you and me have been on the same side and other times not. But we always respected each other in the end. Respect is the most important thing in our line of work, ain't it? Even more important than friendship."

Doyle continued. "I say things got out of hand that night in Pete's. You disagree. But we both know he didn't go in there to kill nobody because if he did, the meat wagon would've hauled five bodies out of Pete's instead of just one smarmy punk with a hole in his shoulder."

Doyle moved the cigar to the corner of his mouth. "We can go back and forth about this all day long 'til we're blue in the face, but I don't think either of us'll change his mind. So, out of respect to you and our long association, I'll cut you a check right now for five hundred dollars from my own personal account to help cover some of the damage caused by the scuffle. I'll kick in another five hundred to help the sheenie with his shoulder."

Quinn didn't know what the hell was going on. Doyle had just given Rothman every reason in the world to get his connections in the legislature to kick hell out of Walker. Why was he doing this?

Rothman didn't move. "Five. Hundred. Dollars. To cover what Quinn did? That's an insult, Archie. It doesn't even cover the cost of the damage to the tables and chairs."

"Bullshit. Roaches crawl out of the joint to die in the gutter because even they wouldn't be caught dead in the place and you're telling me you need a grand to fix it up? If it went up in a fire, you'd be lucky to get a grand from the insurance company for the whole building. Quinn's good, Howie, but he ain't that good."

Quinn watched Rothman get red. "I wouldn't believe you could be this cold and heartless unless I was hearing it with my own two ears. A man's time and suffering are worth something. The embarrassment of..."

"Stow the sob story, will ya?" Doyle waved him down. "Next, you'll be blaming the poor bastard for your mother's rheumatism and your sister's crabs. I'll tack on another five hundred on account of your overwhelming grief and suffering and wounded pride and anything else that'll make you feel better. How's that?"

But Rothman didn't seem to go for it at first. "Money can only repair so much." Rothman thrust his gloved thumb back toward Quinn. Quinn was beginning to hate that thumb. "I want to know what you intend to do about this?"

Doyle looked over to Quinn. "Terry, you and Shapiro are to play nice from now on, understand?"

"Sure thing, boss," Quinn smiled. "Maybe him and me'll play catch in Central Park, once his shoulder heals up."

Doyle took the cigar from the corner of his mouth and put it in the ashtray. He grinned at Rothman. "See? Now everyone's friends again."

Rothman sat still for a long while. "I'm not happy, Archie."

"And I don't give a shit, Howard." Doyle's grin held. "What's more, I don't have to. I still run this town. Don't forget it."

Rothman bolted up out of his chair. Quinn slid his right hand beneath his suit coat, closer to the .45 hanging beneath his arm. Archie didn't budge.

Rothman glared down at Doyle, eyes narrow and face red. Then he threw back his head and laughed. He stomped his foot, flashing a line of teeth too perfect to be real. He was laughing, but his eyes weren't.

Quinn's hand stayed close to the .45.

"Maybe you're right, Archie," Rothman dabbed at laugh tears that weren't there. "You and me have known each other too long to let a little poolhall scrape get the best of us. Just look at us now, two men at the top looking down at the rest of the whelps scrambling for our crumbs. What we do just happens to be illegal, otherwise we'd be admired like Carnegie or Morgan or Rockefeller. I love Rocky. He's a sucker for taking U Penn and the points."

"Can't say I blame the man," Archie said, "seeing as how I'm guilty of having a few sentimental weaknesses myself."

"Yeah, especially for dried up old boxers," Rothman nodded back toward Quinn. "And since we'll never receive the accolades we deserve, we only rely on our own honor system, an honor among thieves, if you will."

Rothman made a show of pulling his gloves a bit tighter.

Quinn's hand stayed near the .45.

"You and I may have started different," the bookie went on, "but things have evened up now. They've evened up closer than you might think. I'm not that scrawny kid chasing ambulances anymore. So, the next time you have a beef with one of my people, contact me directly instead of sending one of your donkey goons over to shake things up. I expect that kind of courtesy, Archie, because I've earned it. And if I don't get that kind of courtesy – that respect – I'm going to have to take it."

Quinn sprang off the couch to teach Rothman some manners.

Doyle's glare froze him in place.

Doyle slowly started swiveling his chair to and fro again. The piercing squeak cut the air. "You were a two-bit order-taker then, Howard, and you're a two-bit order-taker now. You just have a better wardrobe is all. The tiepin's a nice touch, but it don't change the man who's wearing it. You've got a lot of powerful people making book with you and borrowing your money. Good for you."

Then Doyle stopped swiveling in his chair. "But them same powerful people don't rely on you to get them elected every couple of years. They don't call you when they knock up their mistresses or their kids get arrested or to get them off the hook on the q.t. I'm the one who gets those phone calls in the middle of the night, not you."

Quinn watched Doyle rise out of his chair and come around the desk slowly. He stopped square in front of the bookmaker. He was several inches shorter than Rothman, but he was almost twice as broad. "We didn't choose an easy life, Howard. The best guys like us can hope for is to die in bed." Doyle's eyes narrowed. "Threatening me ain't the best way to realize that hope. It never has been. Get me?"

Quinn watched Rothman trace the inside of his

cheek with his tongue, probably because his mouth had gone dry. The bookie broke off the glare and took a small step back. "Well, I guess that's that, then," his voice cracked. "Fifteen hundred it is. I'll expect one of your boys to drop off the dough by the end of the week." He squared his derby and gave Doyle a two-fingered salute from the brim as he headed for the door.

Rothman didn't look at Quinn as he strode out of the office and went down the stairs.

Doyle took his dead cigar from the ashtray and relit it. He walked to the window, puffing on his cigar. Quinn walked over and joined him.

Together, they watched Rothman and his bodyguards get into his roadster and drive up the street.

"I don't know about you, kid, but I'd say that went pretty much as expected."

Quinn's head was still buzzing. "I was expecting you to rap me on the knuckles, not kick him in the balls."

"Yeah, I know, but the smug way he pranced in here got under my skin. I could tell he wasn't in the mood to talk, so I rode him hard. Besides, I got what I wanted, and, in the end, I learned something in the bargain."

"Which was?" Quinn asked.

"That he didn't have Fatty shot." Doyle slipped out of his jacket and tossed it over the back of his chair. "I hit him with that Wallace remark first thing, and it bounced right off. Didn't even blink. He didn't over-explain how he knew Wallace. He didn't deny it, either. I know he's a gambler and he didn't get rich by blinking while holding a lousy hand. But it was just a feeling I got off him. A look in his eye. He was angry, not vengeful. He even took the fifteen hundred with barely a squawk."

Quinn wasn't so sure. "He's smart enough to work that into his act, boss. Maybe he didn't kick up a fuss about the dough because he's already moving against us?"

But Doyle shook his head. "That's why I pushed him hard at the end when he made that threat. I called his bluff and he just backed down. That ain't the way a man ready to start a war acts, kid. I oughtta know. I've been in enough of them."

Doyle sighed and thrust his hands deep into his pockets. He went back to looking out at the bleak, colorless warehouse across the street. Quinn saw the fading afternoon sunlight showed deep lines on Doyle's face. He saw bags under Doyle's eyes. The boss had been up all night drinking and playing cards. Quinn remembered a time when Doyle could go days without sleep and still look fresh without so much as a ten-minute nap.

But Quinn knew Archie Doyle wasn't a kid anymore. He was no longer a man without limits. Things were changing. The Old Man was growing into his name.

"Rothman didn't set up Fatty," Doyle continued. "That leaves this Wallace punk. Let's put some of our own men on it this time. To hell with Doherty and Halloran. Put a couple of good boys on it who know how to trail a guy, not just blast him. Killing Wallace won't help us figure out why he shot Fatty. Not yet anyway."

Quinn saw the same look in Doyle's eyes that he'd seen while he was talking to Walker. It wasn't fear, but it was close. "And do it fast, kid. Because the quicker this goes away, the more likely Al Smith'll throw his hat in the ring. And now's the time, Terry. I can feel it in my bones." He went back to looking out the window. "Now's the time."

"Sure, boss. But I need to know where Wallace is before I can put some boys on him. Doherty never called me back, remember?"

"Well, the bastard'll call me back." Doyle bellowed out at Sean Baker again. "Get Detective Doherty on the phone, will ya?" No response.

"Baker?"

That's when Quinn heard the tinkling of breaking glass, followed by distant screaming. They were common sounds in that neighborhood, except they sounded close.

Quinn looked out the window and saw a blur of fire pass from the roof of the warehouse across the street onto the clubhouse roof. More breaking glass and more screaming. It took Quinn a second to realize what they were.

Fire-bombs.

Then Quinn saw the heads and shoulders of two men at the roof ledge of the warehouse. They brought around Thompsons and aimed down at Archie's office.

Quinn tackled Doyle to the floor as the machine guns opened up.

Bullets shattered the windows and raked the desk where Doyle had just been standing. Quinn and Doyle were covered in wood splinters and glass. Above the roar of gunfire, Quinn heard the screaming of the men he'd posted on the rooftop. The poor bastards were being burned alive.

Quinn crawled on top of Doyle, staying below the

window line while trying to shield his boss with his own body.

Large bits of wood and dust from the desk and floor were kicked up as the Thompsons spat lead into Doyle's office. The leather couch was ripped open by gunfire. Chunks of stuffing and wood were thrown into the air. Old pictures jumped off the walls as bullets punched them until they shattered and fell.

Quinn figured being close to the window kept them safe from the Tommy guns. The shooters were firing from too high an angle to be able to hit them. He knew it was only a matter of time before they lobbed a fire-bomb through the shattered windows of the office. He and Doyle wouldn't be able to escape the fiery liquid that burned everything it touched.

Quinn thought one of the guns stop firing. The other kept up the assault. Quinn knew a cocktail was coming. He wiggled out of his overcoat and threw it over Doyle's head.

"I think they're getting ready to throw a cocktail at us," Quinn yelled over the gunfire. "My coat'll cover you in case you get splashed. Just throw it off and keep going if it gets you."

But Doyle fought the overcoat. "What about you?"

"I'm right behind you," Quinn screamed into Doyle's ear. "Head for the door."

A fire-bomb sailed through the gaping window and exploded in the middle of the office. Liquid flame shot all over the room. The splintered desk had shielded Quinn and Doyle from the liquid but was now in flames. Both had seen this ploy enough times to know better than to run right away. The cocktail was meant to make them run for the door so they could be picked off by the gunmen.

The room quickly filled with black smoke and the gunfire stopped. The bastards were either reloading or waiting for their shot. Quinn took advantage of the break and the thickening smoke. He popped his head above the windowsill and saw the two men on the roof of the warehouse across the street, about two stories above him. They were slapping fresh ammo drums into their rifles.

Quinn pushed Doyle toward the door. "Crawl toward the hallway. I'll keep 'em busy for a while. Move!"

Doyle took his cue as Quinn rose on one knee and fired four times up at the ledge. One of the shots ricocheted off the ledge and sent chips of cement flying into one gunman's face. Quinn saw him fall back from the ledge. Quinn ducked just as the other one raked the room again with machine gun fire.

All the old targets got hit again. None of the bullets reached Quinn. The smoke was getting thicker by the second. His eyes burned. His lungs ached.

The machine gun roared.

Bullets slapped plaster and wood. Quinn buried his face in the sleeve of his jacket and moved toward where he thought the door was. He'd make a run for it once the last gunman stopped to reload again.

When the gunfire finally stopped, Quinn started crawling. The smoke was billowing now, darker, and thicker even along the floor. But the doorway wasn't where it was supposed to be. He tried not to panic. He knew people got disoriented in fires.

But things got strange fast. He knew the door couldn't be far, but his body was getting heavier. Then the floor felt like it was where the wall was supposed to be. Everything began to spin, and Quinn's legs gave way. He collapsed onto the shards of glass and laid still. He'd take a quick rest and try again in just a second. It was a little cooler on the floor anyway. Calm and quiet, almost peaceful.

He saw a hand with stubby fingers reach through the smoke, grab him by the collar and drag him into the hallway.

No sooner had he hit the hallway floor when another cocktail flashed and exploded in the office. A red ball of flame and heat exploded. The stench of burning plaster and wood snapped Quinn out of it and made him gag dry.

Quinn looked up and saw Archie dragging him into an open closet in the hallway. The door partially blocked the thick smoke from reaching them.

"Laying down on the job ain't your style, kid," Doyle coughed over the gunfire and flame, his face blackened by smoke. "I thought you was giving up on me."

Quinn hacked a couple of dry coughs and pointed down the stairs. They helped each other off the floor and scrambled down to the lobby, crouching low as they moved.

The smoke wasn't as bad on the ground floor, but five of Doyle's men were crouched in the hallway, trading gunfire with shooters on the first floor of the warehouse across the street.

Doyle found Jimmy Cain ordering men to different parts of the first floor. "What's the situation?" Doyle screamed to him over gunfire.

Cain's face had also been blackened from the smoke. He also had a nasty cut on the side of his face. "Looks like they took out our guys on the roof with fire-bombs, then opened fire on your office from the roof top of the warehouse. We tried gettin' over there, but three more guys opened up on us from the ground floor of the warehouse. They clipped three of our boys out front. They've got us pinned down pretty good, too, but we ain't givin' up yet."

Quinn knew a couple of fire-bombs of his own would clear them out of the first floor. But this was Doyle's political headquarters. He never kept booze around in case the feds raided it. The bastards across the street probably knew that, too.

Another long volley of gunfire from the warehouse made them duck. Bullets raked the plaster walls and tore through the air above their heads.

"Is the back way clear?" Quinn shouted.

"I don't know," Cain said. "But we ain't been hit from that direction yet, so it might be."

Doyle bolted down the hallway toward the back door before Quinn could stop him. Quinn, Cain and two extra men ran after him.

Quinn got between Doyle and the back door. "I can't let you go out there, boss."

Doyle tried squeezing past him. His face shined with the glow of combat. "Get outta my way, Goddamn it! I didn't get this far being a pussy, and I ain't gonna start now. Now move!"

Quinn grabbed Doyle's arm, but Doyle cried out and his knees buckled.

That's when Quinn felt a sticky dampness near the shoulder where he grabbed him. The red splotch quickly spread along Doyle's shirt.

Doyle had been shot.

Quinn eased Doyle down the wall to the floor and holstered his automatic under his left arm. He pulled off his own suit jacket, balled it up and put it behind Doyle's head.

"It's just a scratch, goddamn it," Doyle said, biting off the pain. "Get me up."

Quinn ripped open the sleeve of Doyle's shirt at the shoulder. The bullet had entered just above the front of the socket and went straight out the back. The amount of blood told Quinn it might have cut an artery. Doyle would die if they didn't stop the bleeding.

Quinn pulled off his tie and tied it as tight as he could around the wound. He yelled instructions to Cain over the gunfire. "Tear the rest of his shirt into strips and wrap it around the wound as tight as you can. Then take his belt and pull that even tighter. He'll scream like hell, but it's the only thing that'll stop that bleeding until I come back."

Cain grabbed Quinn's arm as he moved to leave. "Where the hell are you going?"

Quinn pulled away and moved down the hall. "Just have your men concentrate their fire on the first floor of the warehouse. Tell them to keep an eye out for me. I'll try to give them signals as I go." He looked down at Doyle. "Just keep him alive until I get back."

Quinn pulled the .45 from his holster and opened the back door. He brought up his automatic and crouched low in the doorway.

The back alley was empty.

He ran through the alley behind the building next door and took a quick left up the side alley toward the warehouse. The alley was long and narrow and couldn't be seen from the warehouse. Perfect cover.

Quinn stopped just short of the mouth of the alley, inching up the rest of the way until he saw the hail of bullets flying back and forth between the Doyle headquarters and the first-floor windows of the warehouse. He couldn't see the last gunman on the roof of the warehouse but was sure they were still there. Quinn knew he had to move and move now.

Quinn darted out in the street, bracing for the impact of a bullet. These were the moments Quinn lived for.

The volley between the warehouse and the club didn't let up. He got to the other side and threw himself flat against the building next to the warehouse. No one had fired at him. From there, he saw how bad the headquarters had been hit. Every window in the two-story building had been shot out. Black smoke billowed out from the second floor and roof.

Three of Doyle's men lay dead in the street, twisted in various death poses. Blood stains spread long and wide beneath their bodies on the sidewalk. The cold air was filled with the acrid stench of gun smoke, death, and blood.

Quinn's skin burned as the salt from his sweat mixed with the black soot from the fire. He wiped his brow on his sleeve and kept moving, inching along the front of the building until he came close to the alley between it and the warehouse.

He looked over at his men in the headquarters, motioning for them to move their fire over further to his right. He didn't want any stray bullets hitting him.

They shifted their fire, just like Quinn wanted. He bobbed his head twice around the corner to check the alley. Nobody there. He sprinted alongside the warehouse looking for a way inside. He found an old wooden door that looked as though it had been kicked in.

He peeked in fast. Nothing there. He moved inside.

Fast and quiet. His .45 swept the area in front of him. It was a cavernous building filled with wooden crates and barrels of all shapes and sizes. Sawdust littered the floor and muffled his footsteps as he crept toward the front of the warehouse. Gunfire erupted at the front of the warehouse again. The sound echoed throughout the building. Quinn jogged down the aisle of crates in a crouched position. His gun led the way. He stopped when he got to the front loading bay, close enough to hear the three gunmen talking.

"How much ammo do these mugs got?" one of them asked. "They gotta be running dry by now."

"Just keep firin' 'til Eddie comes down and tells us to beat it," said another.

Quinn crept up closer. He saw three men firing Thompsons through boarded windows. The floor was littered with spent shells. The gunman on the far left ran out of ammunition and dropped to one knee to reload. Two to one.

Quinn's kind of odds.

Quinn opened fire on the middle gunman first, hitting him twice in the back. His fedora flew. The gunman at the far right spun around, but his rifle stuck in the boarded window as Quinn shot him twice in the chest. He tumbled back into a row of stacked crates.

The last gunman fumbled with his rifle to eject the spent ammo drum. His eyes went wide as he looked up at the approaching Quinn. He dropped the rifle and kicked it away as he fell back, slipping on the piles of spent shells. He raised his shaking hands in front of him. His mouth trembled. His eyes watered.

Quinn approached the man slow. "How many more of you are in here?"

The gunman held his hands far in front of himself

now, cringing with each step Quinn took toward him. "Please, God, please."

"Concentrate." Quinn stopped a few paces in front him and leveled his .45 at him. "How many more of you are in here?"

Then Quinn saw the man's eyes flicker over to something above Quinn's left shoulder. Quinn spun to his right and dropped to a crouch as a gunman on the catwalk opened up on him with a Thompson. Quinn fired back. Sparks flew from the railing. A red mist appeared behind the shooter's head.

Gunman and rifle fell on opposite sides of the catwalk. The sound of wooden crates collapsing beneath the body echoed in the warehouse.

Quinn swept his pistol back around to cover the first gunman. No need. He'd been practically cut in half by his partner's blast.

There were still the bastards on the roof to take care of. Quinn wasn't sure how many rounds he had left in the magazine. He reloaded with a fresh clip anyway. He took the stairs of the metal staircase up to the catwalk two at a time. Fast. Quiet.

The steel door to the roof was open. Gravel crunched softly beneath his feet. He held his gun out in front of him. From there, he saw and smelled the black smoke billowing up from the rooftop of Doyle's head-quarters. He saw the smoldering bodies of Evans and McCluskey, the two men he'd stationed there a few hours ago. The poor bastards died terrible deaths.

Quinn saw the last gunman slumped with his back to the ledge wall. He thought he'd gotten him with a ricochet, and he was right. The cement from the balustrade had racked his face. Blood streamed from cuts on his eyelids and the sides of his face.

The gunman had heard someone coming toward him. He blindly pawed at the gravel around him. "Gussie? That you, Gussie? Did you get the bastard?"

Quinn waved down at Cain's men and beckoned them over. They spilled into the street and into the warehouse. "Sorry, pal. The bastard got Gussie."

The blind man tried kicking himself away from the voice, but he was already as far back against the wall as he could go. Quinn saw a broken Thompson on the ground next to him. A surge of pride filled him. Hell of a shot.

Quinn kicked the rifle away. The blind man stopped groping for it. He laid his hands flat on the gravel beside him. His breathing came quick, uneven but he held his water. He was waiting for the bullet.

Quinn figured him for a pro.

He crouched beside the blinded man, the .45 hung loose in his hand. "Who sent you?"

The blind man banged the back of his head against the ledge in frustration. He wiped at the blood from his eyes, but it kept flowing. "Just kill me and get it over with."

Quinn liked his style. "I killed your entire crew, ace. It's just you and me now. Who sent you to kill Archie Doyle?"

The blind man froze. "Archie Doyle?" He swallowed hard. He looked like he would say something else but didn't. He swallowed hard again and began breathing faster.

Quinn had seen that look before. On Zito's face when he told him he'd shot Fatty Corcoran.

"Archie Doyle," the blind man said, "the New York boss?"

"That's right," Quinn repeated. "Who sent you?"

The man gritted his teeth but kept his mouth shut. Quinn put the barrel of the gun to the man's knee cap. "Start talking or you'll be blind and a cripple." He thumbed back the hammer for effect. "Last time, ace. Who sent you?"

The man's breathing grew shallower as the truth broke free. "I ain't even from here and I sure as shit didn't know we was sent to whack Archie Doyle."

Quinn knew a .45 to the kneecap was a wonderful thing. "Where are you from?"

The blind man couldn't get the words out fast enough. "We're with Lenny Boo's mob out of Kansas City."

Quinn forced the gun barrel hard into the blind man's knee. "Bullshit. Lenny Boo does business with us. Why would he want to take him out like this?"

"I don't know," the blinded man stammered. "He usually tells us who the mark is, but this time he only gave us an address. Said it was a contract job for this new partner of his."

Now they were getting somewhere. "What new partner?" Quinn pressed the barrel harder into his knee. "What's his name?"

"I don't know!" the blind man screamed. "But Lenny said this building was owned by a guy who owed his new partner a lot of money. Told us to shoot it up to teach the owner a lesson. Said we were only supposed to open fire when the guy in the pearl suit left the building, and the place was empty."

Quinn took a step back. They were told to wait until Rothman left the building. Rothman had set up Doyle after all. Jesus. "How many of you did Lenny send?"

"Ten of us out here to hit two places. That's all I know," the blind man said.

Quinn felt himself get dizzy. "What two places? Where are the other five guys?"

"This one and another joint up in midtown, The Longbow or something like that," he screamed. "I don't know for sure. I wasn't in on that one."

Quinn grabbed him by collar and yanked him up. "The Longford Lounge? Is that it, you son of a bitch? The Longford Lounge?" The man quickly nodded, and Quinn squeezed harder. "When goddamn it? When?"

"Now, I think, before the joint opened," the blind man stammered. "They wanted to hit the place while some of the employees were there. Maybe they were going to do it before this job, maybe after it. They didn't tell me what they were going to do, I swear!"

Quinn heard Jimmy Cain and three other men from the headquarters spill out on to the roof. "You all right, Terry?"

Quinn let the blind man drop and holstered his pistol. "I thought I told you to stay with Archie."

"Baker's with him now," Cain said. "I stopped the bleeding and I've got some of the boys putting him in the car to drive him over to Doc Brownell right now."

"I'll drive him over myself," Quinn pushed past him toward the stairway. "Get some boys over to the Lounge right now. They're sending another crew to hit us there, too." He pointed back to the blind man. "Take that piece of shit to the safe house where we got Fatty stashed. Sit on him until I get back. And don't hurt him. Understand?"

Quinn and Cain rumbled down the metal staircase and bolted across the street to the headquarters. What was left of Doyle's gunmen were guarding the front of the club and looked up when they saw Quinn running toward them.

"Get over to the Lounge. They're going to hit us there any second," Quinn bellowed. "Move!"

They all broke toward their sedans and started their engines. Those who couldn't fit in the cars stood on the running boards, Thompsons beneath their overcoats.

Quinn ran into the club house and spotted Baker heading down the hall. "Call the Lounge and tell them to clear out of there, now!"

He found Doyle in one of the inner offices. His shirt had been cut away and used as a tourniquet for the gunshot wound in his left shoulder. Cain had done a good job with the dressing, but there was still a good amount of blood on his T-shirt and pants.

Doyle grabbed for the .38 on his lap when he heard someone had entered the room. He lowered it when he saw Quinn.

"What's the sad puss for? If you think this is bad, you should've been with us up in Canada back in '15. Me and Frank looked like Swiss cheese." He swallowed hard and asked, "How many did we lose?"

Quinn grabbed an overcoat from the coat rack by the door and threw it around Doyle's shoulders. "Five total. Evans and McCluskey on the roof and three more out front."

Doyle winced. The lines in his face got even deeper. "What about the bastards?"

"All of them but one and we got him alive."

Doyle's face brightened. "Good boy. We'll break him."

"You're not breaking anybody." He grabbed Doyle

around the waist and hauled him to his feet. "I'm getting you to a doctor and right now."

Doyle was wobbly, but Quinn had a good grip on him. He led him out the front toward the Duesenberg.

"Where the hell did everyone go?" Doyle asked.

Quinn opened the back door of his car and eased Doyle in. He knew what would happen if Doyle knew about the threat to the Lounge, so he lied. "I didn't want everyone standing around here when the cops showed up."

He tried to close the car door. Doyle kicked it open. Even with a bullet in him, he had plenty of strength. "I told you that you never could lie worth a shit, kid. What's the real reason?"

"Nothing's wrong, Archie," Quinn forced the door closed. "It's just a precaution, is all."

Doyle reached through the open window and grabbed Quinn's blackened shirt. "Goddamn you, where is everyone?"

He knew Doyle wouldn't let him go until he told him the truth. "An- other crew might be hitting the Lounge. I sent the others over there to see what was going on while I take you to the doctor."

Doyle let go of Quinn's shirt and sank back in the seat. In fifteen minutes, he'd aged twenty years.

Quinn ran around the front of the car and climbed into the driver's seat. He started up the car and leaned on the horn for Baker to hurry up. "Those dirty bastards," Doyle whispered from the back seat. "Going after my club? Why would anyone wanna do something like that?" Quinn leaned on the horn again. "I don't know, but I swear to Christ, they'll bleed for it."

Baker ran out of the headquarters and jumped

into the passenger's seat. "I let it ring a bunch of times, but there's no answer."

Quinn slipped the engine into first gear and pulled away from the curb.

As he sped across Twelfth Street, he kept an eye out for anyone who might be aiming at the car. It was possible that the other crew might be a back up to the first, waiting to finish off anyone left alive from the headquarters.

Then Doyle said: "Take me to the Lounge."

Quinn knew that was coming. He ignored it.

Doyle pulled himself forward with his one good arm and shouted:

"Goddamn it, did you hear what I said? Take me to the Lounge."

Baker tried to ease Doyle back in the seat. "Boss, I really don't think it's a good idea..."

Doyle slapped his hand away and focused all his attention on Quinn.

"Do like I told ya, Terry. Do it now."

"That tourniquet won't keep you from bleeding to death if we waste time by going to the Lounge. If the club's been hit, we can't do much about it now. If it hasn't been hit yet, we've got enough guys heading over there to put up a fight. Either way, you need to get to a doctor and fast."

From the rear-view mirror, Quinn saw Doyle's face go scarlet. "You son of a bitch. I can't believe this is Terry Quinn talking to me now. What about Tommy and Deveraux? What if the band stopped by early to get something to eat before setting up? What if some poor bastard with a wife and kids is in there delivering food when the place gets hit?"

Quinn kept driving. "They're not my problem. You are and you're going to the doctor now."

"But those people are my priority," Doyle yelled. "That place is my priority. It's the only thing I've ever done in my life that meant something to me and you want me to let some low life sons of bitches take it all away from me just because I have a little bit of lead in my shoulder?"

Quinn kept his attention on the street around them.

"Or maybe you don't want to go over there because you've had enough blood for one day? I never thought I'd live to see the day Terry Quinn turned into a shitless fuckin' coward."

Quinn slammed on the brakes. The car screeched to a crooked halt into the middle of the street.

Quinn spun around. Doyle's face was right there, just as blackened as his own. The contemptible sneer had been replaced by a satisfied grin.

"Yeah," he hissed. "I knew that'd get your attention."

Quinn's eyes narrowed. "You really like to push buttons, don't you?"

"These bastards've already shot my best friend and destroyed my clubhouse. I'd rather die defending my own than on a doctor's table."

Quinn turned back around. He drove his fist into the seat in frustration.

Then he yanked the car into gear and brought the big Duesenberg back around toward the club.

Doyle's old smile returned, and he sat back in the seat contented. "Atta boy, Terry! I knew ya had it in ya." He reached down and pulled out one of the two

Thompsons he always kept in a compartment under the back seat. He handed one up to Baker and kept the other for himself. He laid the stock on his lap and balanced the barrel out the open window with his good hand.

Quinn caught another glimpse of him in the rearview mirror. The old man was gone. Other than the hole in his shoulder, Doyle looked twenty years younger. Back in the hunt. Heading toward danger.

"Buck up, me boys!" Doyle roared as he slapped the clip of the Thompson home. "It's time for the Doyle mob to get back some of its own!"

Chapter 14

QUINN STOPPED the Duesenberg short in front of the Longford Lounge. Quinn and Baker spilled out of the car. Doyle covered the street with his Thompson from the back seat.

Jimmy Cain ran out of the Lounge and met them in the middle of the street. "I've got ten guys spread out along the block and fanned out two blocks in every direction. A mouse couldn't fart without one of our boys hearing it."

Quinn was relieved and angry. "Why the hell didn't anyone answer the goddamned phone?"

"I don't know, boss," Cain said. "Everyone's fine. No one saw nothing unusual all day."

Quinn saw the men Cain had spread out on the block were all regular boys. They knew how to handle themselves if things got thick.

Quinn noticed Archie had slumped over in the back seat, the Thompson still across his lap.

Quinn panicked. He reached in through the open window and stabbed two fingers to his neck for a pulse.

The heartbeat was there but weak. The red spot on his shoulder bandage had grown larger. His breathing was getting very shallow.

Archie Doyle was dying.

Quinn was about to jump into the car to drive him to the doctor when he heard the distinct wail of police sirens echo in the distance. The bulls were on their way. They were probably making a beeline for the Lounge after they heard what had happened down at party headquarters.

They'd be looking to question Doyle about the shootout. But if they couldn't get Doyle, they'd settle for Quinn. Quinn knew they'd tear the city apart until they found one of them. Someone would have to answer for the shootout at the warehouse. Doherty couldn't just sweep this one under the rug. The answer was simple:

Quinn gives himself up. Doyle gets to a doctor.

Cain had to handle things on the street while Quinn was being questioned. So Quinn grabbed Baker and pushed him into the driver's seat. "I'll stall them while you get Archie over to Doc Brownell's. I'll call when they let me out."

"But what about you?"

"Who cares?" Quinn snapped. "Worry about Archie instead. His life's in your hands; now get moving."

Cain and Quinn watched Baker drive away. Then Quinn turned to face the approaching police cars. They were coming on fast. They wouldn't be happy when they got there.

"Did your boys run that blind bastard over to the safe house like I told you?" Quinn asked.

"They should be there by now," Cain said. "But I

don't like the idea of giving you up to the cops, Terry. They'll be looking to pin what happened today on someone. I'd hate it to be you."

Quinn waved it off. Archie was all that mattered. "Have your boys make themselves scarce so the bulls don't get them. Then have them drift back around in an hour or so after the cops clear out. You'd better lay low yourself, Jimmy. I'll need you running things while Doherty and Halloran work me over."

Cain reluctantly went to pass the word along to his men.

Quinn stood alone in the middle of the street. Blackened. Sore. His lungs hurt. He'd killed four men and lost five of his own. He didn't dare mourn them. He knew Archie might die. Quinn would've prayed if he thought God wouldn't fall out of Heaven laughing.

The wail of sirens grew closer.

He patted his pockets for a cigarette and a light. He remembered both were in his suit jacket back at the club house. Damned shame. He really liked that jacket.

He felt himself start to weave. His arms felt heavy. A dull ache settled in his right side. He felt at it with a heavy hand. Damp. Probably water from the roll he took in the warehouse. But he didn't remember the warehouse floor being wet. He looked at his hand, but it seemed small and further away than normal. It was sticky and red. Blood? It matched the growing stain on the side of his blackened shirt. Must've been some of Archie's blood that got on him.

The ground began to pitch and wobble beneath his feet. Like he was standing on a ship. Police cars screeched around him. Maybe in front and to the sides of him. He wasn't sure. He didn't care. He saw a skinny man with a pointy hat who looked a lot like Charlie Doherty in a funhouse mirror running toward him. He was screaming something that echoed in the chambers of his mind.

"You stupid son of a bitch," he yelled. "What did I tell you about starting a fucking war?"

Quinn wanted to say something, but his tongue wouldn't work. He showed Doherty his red hand and offered a feeble smile.

He collapsed forward into the detective's shirt. Darkness was coming. God, let Archie live.

The darkness took him.

SOMEWHERE IN THAT DARKNESS, the past returned. Quinn was on that stool again. Madison Square Garden. His dressing room. Surrounded by cops. Kowalski was supposed to win that night. The Boys had ordered Quinn to lose. Bad things would happen if he didn't.

Quinn didn't remember how it happened. They told him he'd hit Kowalski too hard. They told him he sent Kowalski's jaw into his brain. Kowalski died in the ring fifteen minutes before.

Augie, his trainer/manager, wiped the blood from Quinn's chest and face. Augie hugged him and cried. "I'm sorry. I let this happen. I never should've let you fight. I should've thrown in the towel. It's all my fault. I'm so, so sorry."

Someone stuck their head in, and the cops cleared the room, scattered like roaches. Augie and Quinn alone. Augie's hands shook while he cut the wrap off Quinn's hands.

The dressing room door opened and in strode a
dapper Irishman in a smart blue pinstriped suit, a
matching fedora and overcoat. He stood in the middle
of the room. He didn't speak. He just puffed away on
his black Cuban cigar. His jaw cocked up and away at
a sharp angle.

His hands were in his pockets.

Augie started shaking worse. Quinn figured this
was the guy they'd sent to kill him. Quinn didn't care.

The man with the cigar finally spoke. "You put on
one helluva show out there tonight, kid. Never saw a
guy take a beating like that and I've seen a few in my
day." He took the cigar from his mouth. "You know
who I am?"

"You're Archie Doyle," Quinn answered. "The
rum runner."

Doyle laughed. "Sure, I've run rum and just about
everything else at one time or another. Booze, beer,
broads, guns, hemp, dirty pictures, phony real estate. If
you can make a buck doing it, I've probably done it
once or twice. Made a good living, too and I'm still
alive to tell the tale."

"Congratulations," Quinn watched Augie finish
unwrapping his fists. He
was shaking worse than ever. "What do you want
with me?"

Doyle's grin dimmed. "You're pretty cocky for guy
with a price on his head. A lot of people want you
dead for what you done tonight. Bad enough you won.
You have to kill him in the bargain?"

"You didn't answer my question. What do you
want?"

Doyle smiled. "You threw away a good pay day in
there tonight. You could've let Kowalski beat you like

they wanted, collect on the payoff, then fight him for the championship for an even bigger payoff next year and win. Why'd you throw all that away?"

"What's it to you?"

Augie hushed him. "Go easy, Terry."

Doyle answered him anyway. "Because I don't think you even know why you did it. I've watched you fight, kid, plenty of times. I like your style both in and outside the ring. You've got character, real character and brains to boot."

"You ought to put that on my headstone."

Doyle laughed. "And cool under pressure, too. I like that. What you don't know about me is that I'm going places, see? And I'm gonna need good men to help me get there. Men like you." He put the cigar back in his mouth. "I want you to join up with me. Tonight."

Quinn's hands ached. The taste of blood was in his mouth. Blood that wasn't his own. "I'm a fighter, not a gangster."

"You ain't a fighter anymore, kid. That ended the second you killed a man. The commission would've forgiven you most times, but The Boys are sore over all the money you cost them by not diving like you was supposed to. They'll want their pound of flesh. Hell, they've probably got a bunch of goons waiting outside to finish you off the second you leave here. You're tough, but nobody's tougher than a bullet, kid."

Quinn spat and wiped his mouth off with the back of his hand. "You paint a pretty bleak picture, mister."

"I'm honest," Doyle continued. "Or as honest as a louse like me can be. But, if you join up with me, I'll put you square with The Boys. All your problems disappear," he snapped his thick fingers, "just like that."

"Archie!" Quinn heard himself yell.

Pain brought Quinn back. His eyes sprang open, and he quickly closed them. He didn't want to let the pain in. But in that split second, he knew he was sitting upright on a hospital stretcher. Feet dangling over the side. A nurse finished wrapping bandages around his ribs. He lolled his head around to get some feeling back in it. He kept his eyes closed. He knew that the light would start his head hurting.

"How ya feelin', champ?" he heard Halloran say.

Quinn's tongue felt dry and swollen. His head was starting to ache even though he'd kept his eyes closed. "What the hell happened to me?"

"You've been shot," the nurse said. "The bullet went clean through your right side. It didn't hit anything vital, but you have bruised ribs and you smacked your head off the pavement when you collapsed. The doctor believes you have a concussion."

He heard Halloran speak close to his ear. "Probably happened while you was playing cowboys and injuns in the warehouse."

Quinn didn't remember feeling the impact of a bullet in the warehouse.

That bastard in the catwalk must've clipped him after all. But that wasn't important.

"Where's Archie?" Then he remembered telling Baker to take him to Doc Brownell's. He hoped he hadn't babbled anything to Halloran and Doherty while he was out.

"That's what we'd like to know."

That meant they hadn't grabbed him yet. He hoped Baker had gotten Archie to Doc Brownell's in time. He hoped the doc was sober enough to stop the bleeding.

Quinn jumped when the nurse pulled his bandages tighter. "Looks like you're going to live, big fella," she smiled. "But go straight home and go to bed after you leave here. You've lost a lot of blood and I wouldn't want you to pass out again if you were..."

"Yeah, yeah, yeah," Halloran's voice cut her off. "He's got the idea, sister. Quit the yapping and shove off so my partner and me can get down to cases?"

"Drop dead," the nurse cursed, and Quinn heard the door open and close. His closed eyes trick was working, but barely. He wondered if he could keep this up, maybe he could make Halloran disappear.

Then he caught the strong smell of garlic mixed with cheap rum. No such luck. "You can open your eyes, princess. It's just us girls now."

Quinn slowly cracked open his eyes. Halloran's big florid mug was there to greet him. Bloodshot eyes. Flat nose. Lantern jaw.

"Welcome back," Halloran greeted. "We've got a lot to talk about and time's wasting."

Doherty was leaning against the wall, toothpick dangling from the corner of his mouth. He looked even more tired than normal, which was saying something. "We were plenty worried about you for a while, champ, seeing you hit the deck like that."

Quinn's throat was dry from the smoke he'd inhaled, but he'd be damned if he'd ask either of these bastards for water. "What did you find out when you tailed Wallace last night?"

Halloran shook his large head. "You first, smart guy. What happened on Twelfth Street today?"

"People died. Or haven't you figured that part out yet?"

Halloran gave him an open-handed slap across the temple that echoed in the small room.

Quinn lunged at him off the stretcher. The pain from the hole in his side roared and he collapsed to his knees.

Doherty pushed himself from the wall and helped Quinn back up on the stretcher. "See what happens when you buck the system? The more you help us, the more we help you."

Quinn bit off the pain coursing through his body and the humiliation burning in his gut.

"Somebody tried to blow up Archie's clubhouse," Quinn relented through clenched teeth, "and a bunch of my men got killed. A bunch of the shooters, too. Christ, even Halloran could figure that out."

The big detective stepped in for another shot at Quinn, but Doherty pushed him back. "Who stormed the warehouse? How many were there?" Quinn's instinct cut through the pain. All the cops had was a burnt-out building and a lot of dead shooters from Kansas City. Quinn wouldn't give them any more than that. Not until he had time to figure all of this out for himself.

"I didn't see anything, and I didn't get a chance to find out what had happened because you people came along and scared everyone off."

Halloran took off his jacket and rolled up his sleeves. "Oh, boy, I'm gonna enjoy prying the truth out of this one. I've waited a long time to get a piece of you, smart boy, and tonight I'm gonna get it."

"The only thing you're gonna get is dick 'cause that's all I know." Halloran went for him, but Doherty dove between them again. When Doherty had his partner back against the door, he turned back to Quinn. "I can't hold him off forever, Terry, so for Christ's sake be reasonable. We found five Thompsons, but only four shooters. We found some blood on the roof and we need to know if someone got away or if any of them talked before they died."

Doherty left Halloran against the door and came closer to Quinn.

"We're on your side, remember? This thing is all over the news and that gimp bastard in Albany is going to use this as an excuse to tear Walker apart. None of us wants that, do we? Just tell us what happened, and we can help."

Quinn might figure out who was behind this or why. But he needed to know more about Wallace first. "You can help by telling me where Wallace flopped last night."

Doherty shook his head. "You first. We've got witnesses who saw Howard Rothman come by for a sit-down with Archie, then leave before the shooting started. Chief Carmichael thinks Rothman's behind the whole thing, and he wants us to pick him up. That way, Mayor Walker gets the credit and Roosevelt backs off." Doherty put a hand on Quinn's shoulder. "Neither you nor Archie can do much right now anyway. Tell us what you know and let us handle it from here."

Quinn was feeling dizzy again, so he kept it simple. "If you want to know if Rothman's behind this, go ask him."

Halloran laughed from the doorway. "Gee, Charlie. Why didn't we think of that?"

Quinn looked at him. "Because you're a fucking dimwit."

"Rothman's disappeared," Doherty announced. "Crawled into a hole somewhere and no one knows where he is. Looks like you're the last person to see him."

Quinn saw the dilemma, but Doherty spelled it out for him. "A lot of people in Albany think you've grabbed Rothman. Or worse, that you already killed him on account of what happened at the clubhouse. So, where'd you stash him, Terry?"

"I didn't have time to grab him even if I wanted to," Quinn replied. "Rothman probably heard about what happened to Archie and took a powder."

Halloran took a step closer and crouched down, putting his hands on his knees. "You wouldn't be dumb enough to lie to us, would you?" Quinn found the smile he reserved just for Halloran. "Would you be smart enough to know the difference?"

Halloran drew back left hand to smack Quinn again. Quinn grabbed Halloran's wrist and belted him with a hard right cross to the jaw. Halloran tumbled backwards, knocking over steel medicine trays off the counter.

Pain spiked in Quinn's side again. Deeper pain unlike anything he'd ever known. He fell back on the stretcher, bent him in half. He couldn't even find enough wind to scream.

The door of the examining room burst open. The nurse who'd patched him up rushed in. A doctor and Alice Mulgrew were right behind her. Alice pushed her way past the two cops to Quinn. She began kissing him and stroking his head.

"What the hell is going on in here?" the doctor yelled at Doherty and Halloran. "This is a hospital, not one of your goddamned rubber hose rooms in the precinct house. Get the hell out of here before I call your captain and tell him what you've been up to."

Doherty grabbed Halloran's coat from the back of the door and helped his woozy partner out into the hallway. "We'll talk later, champ. You can count on that."

But Quinn was too busy biting off his screams to answer.

Chapter 15

THE MORPHINE PUSHED the pain way, way back.

Quinn's brain started working again. He knew Alice and Jimmy Cain had walked him to a car. He knew his head was on Alice's lap in the backseat. She was stroking his head, telling him he'd be okay. He felt his shoulder holster and the .45 hanging under it. It gave him comfort.

He remembered Doyle.

"Where's Archie?" he heard himself ask.

Alice was looking down at him. She was smiling, but her eyes were red. Her cheeks were wet from tears.

"Where's Archie?"

"He's fine," Jimmy Cain called back from the passenger's seat. "You're in worse shape than he is. You just rest and don't worry about him none." Alice kept stroking his head. "But I'm here, baby, and I'm not going anywhere," she caressed him. The tears started up again. She kissed him. "You just rest easy and let mama take care of everything."

If Cain said Archie was okay, it must be true. The

morphine made him feel calm and hollow.. "How long was I out?"

"The doctor said he gave you enough morphine to put you out for about five or six hours," Alice answered. "That was twenty minutes ago and you're still awake. You're one stubborn bastard."

He tried to sit up, but the car felt like it was spinning. He let his head slip back to Alice's lap where it was soft and warm. "Where are we headed?"

"Back to Lounge, just like you wanted," Cain said. "We got a lead car in front and one in back, full of guys ready to go to work if they need to. Archie ordered you particularly well taken care of."

Quinn perked up. "He's talking already?"

"Jesus Christ," Alice spat, wiping tears away with the back of her hand. "You almost got killed and all you care about is Archie Doyle?"

Her voice made Quinn's head spin. "How is he?"

"Doc said it'll be a while before he can use the arm again," Cain said, "But he'll pull through just fine."

Quinn was getting weak again. He needed to know more before he passed out. "Where's he now? Who's with him?"

"He was too sick to move, so we kept him at Brownell's place. Baker's keeping an eye on him and I've got the place staked out with ten of my best boys." Quinn was about to ask how he'd placed them. Cain beat him to it. "Five in the house, and the other five spread out around the street in doorways all along the street."

Quinn's first instinct was to have Cain drive him over there. But he knew he was in no shape to protect himself, much less Archie. "Good job, Jimmy. And tell Baker he did fine, too. I've been hard on him lately."

Cain reached back and squeezed his arm. "We had a good teacher. Now put your head back down on the pretty lady's lap and relax. We'll have you back home in no time."

A few minutes later, Cain had the car pull into the back alley of the Lounge. He and the driver helped him out of the back seat while five other guys covered the street. They offered to help him upstairs, but Quinn pulled back. He fought a pain spasm and stood strong on his own two feet. He wouldn't look weak in front of his men.

He lightly put his arm around Alice and said, "I'm fine, boys. Get these cars parked and send word over to Archie that I'm okay. Tell him I'll be by to see him in the morning."

"Like hell you will," Alice declared.

Quinn was too weak to argue. He just wanted to go to bed. Cain and his men looked on as Alice guided him up the back stairs, one step at a time. She fished the keys out of his pants and opened the door. Quinn waved down at Cain and his men before they went inside.

Quinn shut the door behind him and collapsed against the wall in relief. He was exhausted and sweating. The medicine and the warm darkness of the room washed over him. He heard Alice fumble for the light switch.

"Thank Christ that's over," he gasped.

A male voice in the darkness said: "It's not over yet."

Quinn grabbed Alice and pulled her behind him as his gun cleared his shoulder holster. He aimed at the place in the dark where he thought the voice came from, ignoring the dull trickle of pain beginning in his side.

A lamp flicked on.

Howard Rothman was sitting comfortably in Quinn's leather lounge chair. Long legs crossed. Gloved hands folded into a gray triangle in front of his nose. He was flanked by two of his goons behind him. Quinn saw that neither man had reached for his gun.

Quinn fought the morphine to keep his pistol level. "What're you doing here?"

Rothman sucked his teeth. "You're always so quick with violence. You really should see somebody about these tendencies. Perhaps get some pills to calm you down."

"People keep telling me that." Quinn thumbed back the hammer. "I know one thing that'd help me feel a lot better right now."

Rothman threw his head back and laughed. His goons laughed, too. "You disappoint me, son. I already know you were taken to the Polyclinic for a gunshot wound to the right side. I even know how many stitches they used to patch you up. I know that Detectives Doherty and Halloran leaned on you about what happened at the clubhouse. And we both know Doherty would never let you leave the hospital with a loaded weapon."

Quinn thought the pistol felt lighter when he'd pulled it. Charlie must've emptied it while he was passed out. "I reloaded in the car ride over here," Quinn lied. The pain started to grow in his side.

Rothman shrugged his narrow shoulders. "Fine. Keep pointing the damned thing if it makes you feel better. I came here to make sure you knew that I had nothing to do with what happened at that clubhouse today."

"Bullshit. I grabbed one of the shooters, Rothman. He said they were ordered not to open up until you drove away."

"If I wanted war," Rothman asked, "would I be here now? If I'd wanted you dead, I could've hit you anywhere between here and the hospital, but I didn't."

Quinn's pain was starting to spike. He tried keeping the gun level, but the morphine was winning.

Rothman went on. "Was I sore at Archie for not pinning your ears back? Sure, but that's no reason to start a war. Wars are bad for business, son, and nothing's more important to men like Archie and me as business."

"What about Bixby?"

"So, I used Bixby to tweak Archie's nose by breaking his Golden Rule or whatever the hell he calls it. So what?"

Quinn felt his legs going, but the gun stayed level. "Are you using Wallace to tweak Doyle's nose too?"

"He's a shit-kicker with more money than brains."

"You're cooking up something with him," Quinn slurred. "I know it."

"With him?" Rothman laughed. "You can't be serious. He dresses like an ice cream salesman, for Christ sake. Things are slow for him in Georgia so I'm helping him buy his way into a couple of places up here. Upstate, mostly. Why do you think I'm working with him?"

Quinn saw three Rothmans now. "Because Ceretti and Johnny the Kid both said Wallace set up Fatty to take a bullet."

Rothman looked back at his two goons, then back

at Quinn. "The Kid told you that? Before you killed him?"

"I didn't kill him, but that's what he told me."

"But Ira's got no cause to be talking to Simon," Rothman said more to himself than anyone else. "I didn't even think they knew each other." He drummed the arm rest with nervous fingers. "I need to talk to Archie about this. Where can I find him?"

Now there were four Rothmans. "Yeah. I just might be that stupid, too."

"Then you talk to him. Tell him I'm not gunning for him, but someone's gunning for both of us. Tell him I'm gonna find out who it is and make sure they don't get another chance."

Quinn felt himself weave back against Alice. "Archie Doyle cleans up his own messes."

Rothman looked him up and down. "Fatty's in the hospital. Doyle's shot up and you're about to pass out. I'll lean on Ira – hard – then square things with Doherty and Halloran. The last thing I need is those two Irish mopes on my back."

Quinn watched the bookie stand up. He thought he still had the gun level but wasn't sure. "Have your lovely lady here stay by the phone, kid. I'll contact you in two hours whether or not I find anything. I've got my own interest in seeing who shot Archie and why. I've made a life out of avoiding trouble and I don't intend to start courting it now."

Quinn watched the room get smaller and started to dim. He shifted his weight to stay on his feet. Words came slow like syrup. "I don't trust you, you yid bastard."

Rothman winked at Alice as he touched a gloved hand to the brim of his bowler. "Pleasure was all mine, toots. Be sure to take care of your boyfriend, here. He doesn't look so good. And when he wakes up, tell him a secret for me. Tell him it's actually Rothmann, with two 'n's. I'm Lutheran, not Jewish, and to keep the 'yid' cracks to himself next time."

The sound of his gun hitting the floor was the last thing Quinn heard before he fell forward into the darkness.

———

QUINN WOKE with a start to the bell. What round was it? It wasn't like a ring bell, but higher pitched like a telephone ringing. He was drenched in sweat. His side ached. He was in bed, naked beneath the sheets except for the tight bandage around his ribs.

The ringing wouldn't quit. He tried to get out of bed. The pain felt like a hot poker wrenching his insides. He fell over sideways on the bed and screamed into the mattress.

A light went on, but the telephone kept ringing. He heard Alice answer it. She rubbed his head and tried to ease him back into bed. "I'm sorry, honey. I'm so, so sorry. I fell asleep and the phone rang before I could get to it."

Quinn rolled slowly onto his back and gasped for breath. The wave of pain started to ebb quicker than before. "Who is it?"

"It's Archie. He wants to talk to you, but I told him..."

Quinn tried to push himself out of bed to get to the phone. Alice put all her weight on him to keep him back down. "Don't get up, honey," she pleaded. "You hit your head again when you passed out, so you're going to be a little dizzy for a while. I'll bring the phone over to you."

Quinn was too weak to do anything else but lay there. He'd known pain before. Broken hands, dislocated shoulders, cracked ribs. Concussions.

Nothing like this. It hurt no matter what he did.

Alice rushed back with the phone. He snatched the candlestick phone out of her hand. She handed him the earpiece and helped him prop the phone on his chest.

"You there, kid?" Archie's voice came over the line strong and clear. "I said are you there?"

"Yeah, barely," Quinn managed. "I'm sorry that I..."

"Knock it off," Doyle yelled at him. "You saved lives today, kid. Mine was one of them. You just do whatever Alice tells you and don't worry about me."

Quinn didn't care about any of that. "What about you? You being taken care of?"

"Sure, sure. Baker, Cain, even Doc Brownell did a halfway decent job. For a drunk, he makes a pretty good doctor. Wanted to let you know that Rothman got word to me. Said he ain't behind all this and that he's looking into things his own way, too. I'm leaning towards believing him."

Quinn tried but couldn't focus that hard. "Archie, get up to the farmhouse until everything blows over. We can't let you..."

"Relax, kid," Doyle said. "Tomorrow's the big wake for the five boys we lost. After I swing by to pay my respects, I'll head up to Millbrook. I promise."

"Just go up to the farm," Quinn slurred. "There's still a five-guy chopper squad out there. The city's not safe for you now."

Doyle laughed his harsh, hoarse laugh. "For someone who's supposed to be a tough guy, you've sure got a soft spot in your heart for me."

Quinn's mouth felt like cotton. He swallowed dry. "I just don't want to see you winding up dead is all."

"Ah, this is nothing. You shoulda been with me back in aught-nine when I had nine bullets go through me and Frankie Sanders in a dance hall on Broadway. I always come out as good as new. This'll all blow over in a couple of weeks, you mark my words. In the meantime, you get your rest and I'll swing by tomorrow to see you before my trip north."

Despite the morphine, Quinn knew Doyle should already be in Millbrook instead of still here in the city. Doyle had to be protected. Quinn couldn't do that from bed. He had to get over to Doc Brownell's place. Take charge. He tried to get out of bed again. The pain in his side spiked big and deep. He crumpled back to the mattress, flat.

Doyle called out to him from somewhere in the darkness. Quinn couldn't answer.

Chapter 16

AT ONE O'CLOCK THE next afternoon, Terry Quinn turned up the collar of his black overcoat and pulled his fedora low on his head. The bitter November wind bit into him as he waited for Doyle in front of McNabb's Funeral Home. A light rain had begun to fall ten minutes before.

His right hand held the .45 in his pocket. He'd almost passed out from the pain when he tried putting on his shoulder holster.

Quinn knew he should've been in bed. But he needed to be here more. He'd been there for two hours, eyeballing the street. The windows and rooftops and everyone who went in and out of the wake house to pay their respects to the families.

They all looked harmless enough. Mostly poor working-class Micks in their Sunday best. Red-eyed and puffy from crying over the tragic loss of youth. Some cried because they knew the boys. Others cried because it could've been their sons in a box. All five men who had died at headquarters had been in their twenties. All came from big families in the Kitchen. Quinn didn't look at the mothers as they passed by. Crying women always got to him. Crying mothers worst of all.

He'd handled his own crying woman earlier that morning.

Quinn had woken up groggy and sore. Too sick to eat. Barely able to stand. Too stubborn to stay in bed where he belonged. Archie needed protecting.

"Please stay in bed, Terry," Alice had begged him between the tears. "Archie knows you're hurt. Even he told you to stay put. He's got enough people to keep him safe. What if them stitches come loose? What if you start bleeding again? Who'll dive in front of a bullet to save you? Let somebody else take care of him for once."

"I owe him," Quinn remembered saying. "I owe him everything."

"Any debt you owed him was paid in full long ago," she wailed. "I can take the danger, Terry. I can take the late nights and the bullets and the blood and the cops and the hospital rooms and the jail cells." She shook her head. The tears came bigger now. "But I can't take the wake house. I can't watch them lower you into the ground. I won't become a widow for you, Terry, and I can't watch you kill yourself for someone like Archie Doyle. I won't do that. I can't. I love you too much."

Quinn had heard this from other women many times before. This time it was different. This time, it hurt.

He answered her the only way he knew how. "If you love me, you'll understand why I have to go to him. And I hope you'll still be here when I get back."

She had looked like she would cry if there were any tears left. "Why should I?"

Quinn did his best to manage a smile before stepping into the shower. "Because I guess I love you too."

The shower had put a dent in the morphine haze. He felt like he had enough energy to get dressed and walk out of the house. He saw Alice had laid out his clothes on the bed for him. She'd even dusted off an old black fedora he'd had in the back of his closet.

But she was gone, save for a small note tucked in his hatband. Just five words:

Because I love you too much.

Now, as he stood alone in front of McNabb's, he told himself it was the cold wind that made his eyes water.

The hole in his side still ached bad. His head was sore. His ribs hurt. He felt like he had a bad fever. He was very weak, but stronger than he'd been yesterday. He focused on the good things.

They were all he had left.

Quinn spotted a gray Cadillac Coupe slow in front of the funeral home. He didn't recognize the car. He inched the .45 out of his pocket. He was in no shape for a gunfight as he was. But as he was, he wouldn't run from one.

He was glad to see Jimmy Cain and a couple of his men climb out in advance of Doyle.

"What the hell are you doing out of bed?" Cain asked him. "You look like shit."

"Stow the compliments," Quinn said. "Archie on his way?"

"Yeah, I ran ahead to look things over, but I'll bet you've already done that."

Quinn kept eyeing the street. "Just the usual weepers. I didn't check inside yet. Take your men inside. I'll walk Archie in."

Cain brought his men inside the funeral home to check things out. A line of mourners was starting to form in the lobby. Soon it would run out the door and into the street. He'd witnessed this kind of scene often since joining up with Archie.

Archie's silver Duesenberg pulled up in front with Baker at the wheel. Quinn went and opened the door for his boss. Doyle stepped out of the back seat, bright and ruddy as ever. A black coat around his shoulders. A black silk sling that cradled his arm beneath the coat.

Doyle glared up at Quinn for a long moment in the rain. He broke into a broad smile. "You stubborn son of a bitch. You oughtta be home in bed with that pretty young singer of yours instead of freezing your ass off for a sorry old man like me."

"And you should be in Millbrook, with a lot of wide-open farmland and your horses."

Doyle laughed and squeezed Quinn's arm. "I'm glad you're here, kid. Hurt much?"

"Only when I breathe. Any word from Rothman?"

"No. But I've got faith he'll pull through."

Jimmy Cain came out of the wake house and met them at the curb. "Inside's fine. Lots of sad faces, but they all look peaceable enough."

Doyle shrugged out of his overcoat to reveal a simple black suit beneath. He let Quinn take his coat and hat. "Now, I don't want you or the boys babying me while I'm in there, understand? Don't crowd me while I'm with the families. This ain't about me today. It's about the five poor boys who died keeping me alive yesterday."

Quinn had seen his boss work the room at a variety of functions over the years. But it was the wakes where the old man really shined. The grief of others brought something out in him, something deep and natural and comforting.

Quinn and Cain stayed back while Doyle walked into the first room where young Liam Sullivan was laid out. Archie quietly waited his turn at the end of the line like everyone else. Eventually, word spread that Archie Doyle himself had come to pay his respects. Sullivan's sister came out to pull him off the line and escort him up to greet Liam's mother. After all, Archie Doyle himself was too important a man to be left waiting in line.

As Doyle walked into the room with her, everyone looked around and gasped. Nurses, deliverymen, truck drivers, day laborers, bus drivers, cops and bartenders all stood out of respect. It was as if a judge had just walked into his courtroom. The irony was not lost on Quinn. They ought to stand, he thought. Most of them only had jobs because Archie Doyle had gotten them for them. Doyle put coals in their furnaces and clothes on their backs. He put money in their pockets.

And sometimes he put their sons in early graves. But such was the price these people were willing to pay for living in the new world.

Quinn watched Doyle take a knee before the seated Mrs. Sullivan. He watched Archie hold the old woman's hand and speak to her softly. Quinn had heard it before, how tragic it was that Liam had been taken from them so young by godless heathens. How he prayed that God would watch over Liam and his family for all their days.

Quinn then watched Doyle give Mr. Sullivan a

firm handshake and tell him he raised a fine young man, and it was an honor to have known him and asked him to please call him if he could be of any service.

Quinn knew this would be a day long remembered by the Sullivan clan and the four other families mourning in McNabb's Funeral Home that day. This was the day that Archie Doyle himself came by to pay his respects. This was the day they shook the grand man's hand.

The four other wakes in various parts of the funeral home played out the same way. The last one, the one for the O'Connor boy, was the rawest. Upon seeing Doyle, O'Connor's mother slapped his face, and pounded his chest as she screamed, "You did this! You got my boy killed! You and your rackets and your booze and your lousy money!"

Doyle motioned for Quinn and Cain to stay back. Doyle let Mrs. O'Connor pounded his chest and his wounded shoulder until she could pound no more. She collapsed against him, sobbing uncontrollably. Doyle held her with his one good arm while she quietly wept. A tear ran down his cheek as he whispered how sorry he was, how tragic it was that her son had been taken from her so young by godless heathens, how he prayed that God would watch over young O'Connor's family for all their days.

Doyle shook hands with other people on his way out. Quinn and Cain met him when he got back out into the hallway.

Doyle wiped the remnants of the tear from his cheek. "Christ, I hate wakes, but I think I hate the wet ones the most." To Cain, he said, "Have Baker bring the car around. I'll be out in a minute." He looked up at Quinn.

"Come with me for a moment, Terry."

Quinn followed his boss down a hall, past the bathrooms to the manager's office. Doyle pushed the door open without knocking.

John McNabb greeted him with open arms. "Mr. Doyle, how wonderful to see you again," McNabb said. He was a bespectacled, quiet looking man Quinn judged to be in his mid-fifties. He bore a permanent look of calmness and understanding, and sympathy most funeral directors acquire. "I'm sorry it couldn't be under better circumstances."

Doyle shook his hand. "It's been many moons, hasn't it Jackie Boy? You don't mind if me and Terry here use your office for a couple of minutes." It was a statement, not a question.

McNabb looked around the office nervously. "I'm sorry, Mr. Doyle. If I'd known you'd require meeting facilities, I would've cleaned up for you."

"Don't worry about a thing," Doyle took a seat behind McNabb's desk.

"We'll manage just fine. We'll only be a few minutes."

McNabb scurried out of the room and shut the door behind him. Doyle struck a match with his good arm off McNabb's desk and lit his cigar. "Degenerate bastard. Son of a bitch takes every dime he gets from this place and puts it on a nag's nose instead of taking care of his wife and kids. He's into me for three large and I'll just bet the dopey hump was just itching to ask me about who's paying for these wakes. He's lucky I don't take this joint away from him."

Quinn took a seat. The pain from the wound spiked. He was getting used to it.

"Please tell me you're still heading up to Millbrook after this."

"I am, and I'm putting you in charge of things while I'm gone."

Quinn heard the words but knew he must've heard them wrong. "Sure, boss. In charge of what?"

"Everything. The gang, the rackets, the money, the boys, the booze. The Lounge too, but you're already in charge of that so I guess that don't count but..."

Quinn felt himself go numb again and he knew it wasn't from the morphine. "You want me in charge? Of everything?"

"Why not?" Doyle let out a long plume of black smoke. "There's nobody else I'd rather have in charge right now and truth is I don't have anybody else. Fatty's too sick to take over and even if he wasn't, he doesn't have the heart for this kind of thing."

Quinn's mind scrambled to find someone else. What did he know about running things? He was just the hired muscle. He did what he was told and kept his mouth shut. There had to be someone else. Then it came to him:

"What about Frank Sanders? You had him run things that time you were in Canada for a while."

"Things change, kid. I love Frankie like a brother, but him and me ain't exactly been seeing things eye to eye lately. Take that talk we had with Walker a couple of nights back. I know he don't think much of my idea about running Al for president again. That's his opinion. But he spouted off in front of people against me before." Doyle waved the whole thing off.

"He's been cloistered up in the Heights too long,

anyway. Besides, Walker likes you better and we need Walker happy, especially now. The happier he is, the more persuasive he'll be with Al."

Quinn's mouth went dry. Doyle was seriously handing him the keys. "But I've never run anything, Archie. I can't do Fatty's job and your job and figure out who shot Fatty. I can't do one of them things by myself, much less all of them at once."

Doyle swung his feet off the desk and leaned forward to face Quinn.

"You're wrong, champ. I've been watching you for a long time now, and believe me, you're ready. And you won't be doing it alone. Jimmy Cain will be right here to help you."

"No," Quinn argued. "Cain's going with you. I want him around if that other chopper squad comes gunning for you."

"I've already got Baker and three good boys heading up there with me. And I ain't exactly helpless myself. I'll be fine. And so will you."

Quinn got dizzy thinking about all the plates Doyle kept spinning. The rackets, the joy houses, the betting parlors, the warehouses, the cops, and the speakeasies. The people that owed Doyle money. The people Doyle paid off. Quinn had never wanted this. None of it seemed right.

"If it's any consolation," Doyle added, "I ran it by Fatty this morning. He's all for it."

Quinn perked up. "Fatty's awake?"

"Sure is and doing better by the hour, the fat bastard." Doyle smiled.

"He said you've done a great job running the Lounge. Running a gang's no different. Just a bit bigger, that's all. You need any advice, Fatty'll help.

Believe me I've only gotten this far because his head's been on my shoulders."

Quinn knew Archie had made his decision and that's all there was to it.

Terry Quinn was running the largest criminal empire on the east coast. "Did you tell Sanders yet?"

"Yeah," Doyle winced. "He wasn't what I'd call 'overjoyed', but he didn't speak against you neither, kid. I'm sure he'll be there for you if you need him, as a favor to me if for no other reason."

Doyle slapped his chair happily as he got to his feet. He came around the desk and Quinn draped the overcoat over Doyle's shoulders. "Quit worrying, will ya? Just keep the money coming in and going out where it should. I'll concentrate on getting Jimmy and Al on board. You'll do fine."

Quinn didn't think so. "Well, since I'm the boss now, I'm ordering Jimmy Cain to go upstate with you."

Doyle laughed and patted Quinn on the cheek. "You're the boss of the gang, sweetheart, not me. Cain stays here. I'll see you in a couple of weeks."

Quinn's mind was flooded with questions about what to do first. Who to talk to. It was all jumbled together in such a knot; all he could think to say was: "Call me when you get to Millbrook."

Archie Doyle smiled. "Yes, mother," then closed the door behind him. He'd just left New York's world of organized crime at his feet.

Terry Quinn now ran New York City.

Jimmy Cain opened the door a few minutes later. The look on his face said it all. "Congratulations, boss."

Quinn had Cain drive him to Fatty's safe house on Twenty-third and Tenth. The brownstone was in the middle of the block and looked no different than the rest of the houses on the street. There were no armed gunmen in front of the building, just a couple of boys with Thompsons in sedans parked at various spots on the street.

Inside, Cain pointed to the first door at the top of the stairs. "We're keepin' your playmate in there," he told Quinn. "The doctor said the concrete scarred his eyes pretty good, but he'll get his sight back eventually. I don't mind tellin' you that it's been a chore keepin' some of the boys away from him, boss. A lot of them really liked the guys he killed."

Quinn had always hated complainers. Now that he was running things, he hated them even more. "Tell them to quit if they don't like taking orders. There's plenty of guys on the street looking for work who won't ask questions."

Cain played it down. "They ain't bein' mutinous or nothin', boss. They're just a little worked up, what with Fatty, Archie and now you bein' hit. They just want to know when we're going to start hittin' back is all. It don't look good, us not doin' nothin'."

"I know. We'll hit back when we know who to hit and not a moment before." He pointed down the hall. "Is that Fatty's room?"

Cain nodded. "The doctor said he's still too weak to be operated on formal, but it looks like he'll be able to live with one kidney after all." Quinn walked down the hall to Fatty's room. He rapped his knuckles lightly on the door before opening it.

Fatty Corcoran was lying on his stomach on an old Queen-sized bed.

The mattress bowed under his weight. His three hundred-plus-pound bulk filled a good portion of it. He had a large bandage wrapped around his considerable girth and extra padding on the small of his back where he'd been shot. His curly red hair was matted to his head by sweat. The bed clothes were soaked through with perspiration.

Quinn knew Fatty's wounds could still get infected. His already overused heart could give out from too much pain at any moment. But he was alive for now and that's all that mattered.

Fatty was dozing. Quinn pulled up a chair next to his bed. He remembered the scene in Zito's apartment two days before. He'd wake Fatty with a little more compassion.

Quinn nudged the fat man with a gentle shake of the shoulder. Fatty looked up from the pillow-scape dazed and confused. He focused on Quinn, blinking his eyes clear. A vague smile appeared on his big face, like a baby waking up. The two of them had always liked each other.

"Hi ya, Terry," Fatty smiled wider. "You're a sight for sore eyes."

Quinn felt himself smiling, too. "Keeping out of trouble, big man?"

"I guess I should call you 'boss' now. He reached for Quinn's hand and squeezed it. "Congratulations, kid."

Quinn played it down. "I'm just filling in until you and Archie are ready to come back."

But Fatty's smile went away. He sank his head back to the pillow. "Archie and I have already had our fair share of come backs, Terry. I can read the writing on the wall. Archie can, too. It says me and

Archie better get out of this business in big, red letters."

"Don't talk like that."

Corcoran's massive bulk raised with a heavy sigh. "I'm not complaining. Archie and me made plenty of dough while the going was good for damned near fifteen years by my count. But the money's drying up and people are willing to take dumb chances for a buck. I don't have the stomach for this kind of life anymore." He smiled again. "And I've got a stomach for quite a bit."

Quinn respected Fatty too much to hear this kind of talk now. Self-pity never solved anything. And despite everything that had happened to him that morning alone, Quinn still needed answers on what happened in Ames that night. "Who do you think shot you, Fatty?"

"I can't think of a soul. Everything's been going fine, except for Archie's fool idea about getting Al Smith to run for president again." Quinn didn't want to get lost in all of that. "What about other parts of the gang? You've always been closer to the day-to-day stuff than Archie. Is there anyone else having problems that might've caused this?"

"Not that I can think of. Frank Sanders had some run-ins with some number runners up in Inwood who were trying to cash in on him being away a lot lately. But he handled that himself."

That caught Quinn's attention. "Frank's been traveling? Where to?"

"Started a couple of months back," Corcoran said, "when he asked for Archie's say-so to expand outside of the city. He'd already gotten as big as he could up in Inwood and the Heights and the only other place he" could go is Harlem. But Archie didn't want a war with the darkies now that he's pushing Al to run."

Again, Quinn skipped all that. "Where'd Frank travel to?"

"Archie told him he should expand up along the Hudson River, Albany, Poughkeepsie. There's money to be made in the boonies for a guy with Frank's talents. But Frank didn't want that. He said he had a line on something in Kansas City that was about to take off, so he's been going there to set things up."

Fatty kept talking, but Quinn didn't hear a thing he said. The hole in his side began to throb but he focused on staying calm. He was running things now. He had to control his temper. All at once, everything started to make sense.

Frank Sanders went to Kansas City. The chopper squad from the warehouse was from Kansas City. The chopper squad hit blind and almost started a mob war between Doyle and Rothman. With Archie on the lam and Fatty laid up, who should benefit from a mob war? The men who stood behind Archie Doyle and Howard Rothman: Frank Sanders and Ira Shapiro.

Quinn remembered Shapiro mumbling something about Doyle's days being over after Quinn shot him. He remembered Sanders disagreeing more and more with Doyle lately.

It all made sense. But where did Wallace fit in? Was he Shapiro and Sanders' go-between? What about Rothman?

His mind was swimming with questions and possibilities Jimmy Cain burst into the room. "Jesus Christ, boss. Turn on the radio quick!"

Quinn flicked on the radio by Corcoran's bedside. A newsman's voice came on in mid-report.

"...have no suspects in custody at this time. Once again, gangland intrigue rocks New York City as Howard Rothman, the infamous lawyer, gambler, and financier, was gunned down in broad daylight. Witnesses report five men in a touring car opened fire on Rothman and two accomplices as they entered Lindy's Delicatessen on 52nd and Broadway. Police officials suspect this is in retaliation for the attempted murder on crime boss Archibald 'Archie' Doyle yesterday afternoon."

Quinn felt himself get dizzy.

Howard Rothman was dead. And whoever did it made it look like the Doyle mob was behind it. The cops would be looking for him and Archie now. They'd need to parade them around in handcuffs to show Albany they were doing something to stop the violence.

They'd raid the Lounge.

They'd raid the speakeasies and the warehouses and the gambling joints.

They'd hit the Doyle organization hard.

Bye bye White House. Hello Sing Sing.

Fatty looked up at him from bed. "You didn't order that, did you?"

"No." But he knew someone who might know more.

Quinn and Cain headed for the blinded gunman's room down the hall.

Quinn threw open the door and found the man lying on the bed with a large white bandage wrapped around his eyes. He flinched when he heard the door splinter. He threw his arms in front of his face to protect himself.

"Who's there?" he yelled into the darkness.

Quinn yanked him out of bed by the night shirt and slammed him against a wall. The hole in his side screamed. "Who hired you to kill Archie Doyle?"

"I told you we didn't know it was Archie's joint," the gunman screamed. "We wouldn't have hit the place if we knew who it was, no matter how much Lenny paid us to do it."

Quinn squeezed. "Yesterday you said Lenny took on a new partner. Who?"

The blind man started crying. "How the hell should I know? Lenny gives orders. He don't ask for advice."

Quinn pulled the blind man off the wall and slammed him against it again. His side roared, but he didn't stop. "Did you ever see this new partner? You're one of Boo's regulars. You must've seen something."

"I don't know. I think I did but that's only because some of the other boys thought it was him."

Quinn pushed back the pain from the wound. He broke out into a sweat. "What did the man look like?"

The blind man's mouth trembled. "I didn't get a good look at his face. I remember he didn't look like the money daddy type. Like he could use a few bucks himself. Wrinkled brown suit, an old shirt and this old brown hat looked like he sat on it, walked with a limp..."

The blind man kept talking, but Quinn had heard all he needed. He let the blind man slide down the wall. He'd just described Frank Sanders.

Son of a bitch.

Jimmy Cain slumped in the doorway. "Jesus Christ, Terry. He don't mean Frank, does he?"

Quinn was drenched in sweat. Pain webbed through his body from the hole in his side. But he had one last question for the blind man. "You said the other group of shooters were supposed to hit the Longford Lounge but they didn't. Why?"

The blind man crawled back up to his bed. "I don't know, mister. Both hits were supposed to happen at the same time. Maybe they got scared off by something."

Or called off, Quinn thought. By someone. But who?

Then the floor felt like it dropped out from under him. He leaned against the wall to keep from falling over.

That's why Tommy the Bartender and Deavers never heard the phone ring at the Lounge.

Baker never called the Lounge. Baker called off the other hit squad instead because they'd lost the element of surprise.

And Baker was driving Doyle up to Millbrook.

Quinn ran downstairs to the car. Jimmy Cain followed. Millbrook was a long way away.

Chapter 17

CAIN DROVE, speeding along back country roads to Doyle's farm in Dutchess County. The trip usually took two hours. It felt like two years to Quinn.

He'd been hoping he was wrong about Baker. He'd called Doyle's house from the gas station. No answer. He feared the worst. He knew Baker didn't have the stomach to hurt Archie but the crew who hit Rothman did.

If Baker was in on it, Quinn bet he'd delivered Archie to them by now. Doyle's farm in Millbrook was the best place to start. It was secluded and easy to defend. Not many people knew about it, not even in Doyle's organization.

Not many people other than Quinn.

The wound in his side ached. Every pothole and divot in the dirt road made Quinn wince. He didn't have morphine to dull the pain. He pulled on a pint of Cain's whiskey instead.

Quinn had never bothered with big questions like "why" before. Archie told him what to do and he did

207

it. But in the two hours between Manhattan and Mill-brook, he found himself asking that question a lot. Why did Sanders turn on Archie after a lifetime of friendship? Why did Shapiro turn on Rothman? Money? Fame? Pride? Where did Simon Wallace fit into all of this?

The more questions Quinn asked, the more frustrated he got. Frustration made him angry, and anger made him scared. Scared about what they'd do to Archie. Scared that he might get Archie killed. The pain in his side ached. He pulled on the pint. The pain dulled but the questions restarted.

It went on like that for two slow hours.

Cain slowed the car to a crawl when they reached the dirt road to Doyle's estate. Gravel crunched beneath the tires.

It was almost four o'clock and the sun was dying fast. A deep purple sky framed Doyle's seven-bedroom colonial mansion on top of a hill overlooking the rolling hills of Millbrook. A black horse fence enveloped the property, following the land as it rose and fell as far as the eye could see.

The house was a quarter of a mile off the main road atop a long, winding driveway. Doyle always posted a car as a guard at the foot of the driveway whenever he was there. But there was no car today. A bad sign.

Quinn had Cain park behind a clump of bushes just off the road. Cain opened the trunk, revealing a standard Doyle mob setup. One shotgun. Two Thompsons. Two .45s. Shells and ammo for all of it.

Quinn took a couple of extra clips for his .45. Cain took the sawed-off shot gun and a box of shells. No need for the Thompsons. If things got thick, it'd be up close and personal.

Quinn knew sound carried in the cold November air. He closed the trunk with a quiet click. He and Cain moved into the tree line along the driveway for extra cover and trudged uphill a quarter mile to Doyle's farmhouse. The cold from the frozen ground seeped up through the thin soles of Quinn's shoes.

The hike and the cold caused the hole in his side to throb even worse. They moved low and quiet in the overgrowth, stopping at every sound that might be the cocking of a hammer or a footfall in the woods. They waited.

They listened. They heard nothing. They moved on.

The features of the house came into view as they got closer. The wrap around porch. The dark blue shutters on the windows. The porch furniture. Quinn remembered quiet summer days he'd spent on that porch, enjoying a scotch and a cigar while Doyle enjoyed the company of lady friends upstairs. The furniture looked odd now that it was Fall.

Quinn spotted Doyle's Duesenberg in the garage. He also saw an unfamiliar green Packard parked off the driveway by the kitchen door. None of Doyle's people drove Packards. That must've been the other crew the blind gunman told him about. Five guns, plus Baker. Three to one odds.

Quinn had faced worse odds.

No guard at the front of the house. No one around back. Everyone was bottled up inside.

The shades were drawn, but he could still see the lights of the first floor were on.

There was no way of knowing what was going on in there from the outside.

They'd have to go in.

Cain crouched behind a tree next to Quinn. "How do you want to handle this, boss?"

Quinn spoke in a whisper. "I'll sneak into the house while you get closer to that kitchen door. It doesn't have a lock on it, so you won't have any trouble getting in. Wait for my signal, then come in blasting. I don't know where Archie and I will be, but I'll make sure we're out of your way."

"What's the signal?"

Quinn held his .45 low as he headed toward the house. "You'll know it when you hear it."

———

QUINN CIRCLED AROUND THE BACK. The quiet of the house unnerved him. He moved fast, but quiet, staying low in the overgrowth until he got around to the side where Doyle's bedroom was. He knew the layout of the farmhouse like the back of his hand. He knew Doyle never slept upstairs. Doyle never wanted to be trapped in a fire or in an attempt on his life. He always slept downstairs in a converted library that had its own bathroom and a large walk-in closet.

The closet had plenty of room for all of Doyle's country clothes. It also had room for a trap door that led to the crawlspace beneath the house. Doyle thought it would come in handy if the house was ever attacked or raided. Doyle and Quinn were the only two who knew about it. Quinn had put it in himself. It had been meant for Doyle's escape. Tonight, it would be used for Doyle's rescue.

The shades on the windows on the back of the house had also been drawn. No one could look in, but no one could look out, either. Quinn holstered his .45 and dove under the house.

He crawled across the frozen ground toward the trap door. Quinn's size made it a tight fit. The cold that had gone through the soles of his shoes now filled his body. The cold and the crawling made the pain from his wound even worse. He couldn't stop.

The ground was littered with dead snake skins and rodent carcasses ripped apart by cats. Discolored cobwebs draped in between the floor beams. He heard rustlings somewhere around him but knew they couldn't be human sounds. He kept going.

Quinn fought the pain by trying to remember the layout of the house. He concentrated on the footfalls on the floorboards just above his head. He knew he was under the living room now, having just crawled past the kitchen.

The sounds from above bounced wildly around him. He heard muffled voices, rapid footfalls, and other things in the darkness. The cold wind whipped beneath the house, numbing not only the pain, but the rest of him, too. He was losing feeling in his feet and legs. He refused to pass out.

Then Quinn heard two sets of footsteps on the floorboards just above him. The voices weren't clear, but he could tell they were yelling at each other. One voice trailed off behind him back toward the kitchen. He hoped Jimmy Cain had kept out of sight.

Quinn reached the trapdoor in Doyle's bedroom closet. He listened and heard a third set of footsteps overhead. They weren't long strides like he'd heard in the living room, but short bursts across the floorboards.

Like someone was in a hurry. They moved in and out of Archie's bedroom several times.

It didn't sound like good news for Archie.

Quinn braced himself for the coming pain as he slowly drew himself up to a crouch and eased the trap-door open. The door was only a thin sheet of wood, but the effort caused sparks of pain to flash before his eyes. He started to sweat again.

He pulled himself up through the hole in the floor, into the closet. His side roared. Stars exploded. He stifled a scream. He distributed his weight evenly on the trapdoor frame, careful not to creak the closet's floorboards. One creak of a floorboard could tip off the gunmen, leaving him trapped in a confined space. He got his balance and eased the trap door shut.

He was inside.

When the pain in his side died down, Quinn felt the wound for dampness. Other than the wetness from crawling along the ground, no blood. He listened at the closet door. Still only one set of quick little noises from Doyle's bedroom. He bent to peek through the keyhole in the door.

The bedroom door was closed. Baker was crouched over Doyle's bed, but he couldn't see Doyle. Quinn clenched when he saw a large slick of blood that trailed beneath the closed bedroom door and out of the room.

Was it Doyle's? Then Baker swore and ran out of the room again. He yelled something to someone deeper in the house.

Not worrying about creaking floorboards now, Quinn shifted to get a better view through the keyhole. He saw Doyle lying in bed; his eyes were closed, muttering to himself. There was fresh blood on his pillow and sheets. Lots of it.

Quinn fought the urge to rush out to help him. That would get them both killed. He waited, but with Doyle's condition, he couldn't wait much longer.

Doyle picked up his head and laughed a soft, wet laugh. He was still laughing when Baker rushed back into the room carrying bandages and fresh towels. Baker threw his bundle on the bed and began tending to Archie's wounds.

Quinn heard a gruff male voice from the living room. "Don't bother, Sean. We're just gonna plug him after we get the money, anyway."

Baker kicked the bedroom door closed and went back to tearing towels into bandages. "Fucking idiots don't listen to me. Nobody ever listens to me. They ignore me and I end up cleaning up the shit."

Doyle was rocking his head back and forth in the pillows, laughing and muttering.

Baker threw down the makeshift bandages and screamed into Doyle's face. "What the fuck are you laughing at? I'm trying to save your life, goddamn it!"

Doyle snapped out of it and grabbed his hands.

Quinn pushed the closet door open and was on Baker in two strides, pinning him against the wall by his throat. The traitor's eyes bulged as Quinn slipped the .45's barrel into his mouth.

Baker gurgled but didn't move.

Quinn was surprised to see Archie had tossed aside his bed clothes and was looking over his own wounds.

"I thought you were out of it," Quinn whispered.

"I heard you in the closet and started acting up to distract him," Doyle said. He grabbed one of the bandages and tied it around a hole in his thigh.

"The little bastard drugged me after the wake and drove me up here. I'm pretty sure his friends outside already killed the three boys who drove up here with us."

Quinn squeezed Baker's throat. "This is how you repay him for everything he's done for you, you miserable son of a bitch?"

Baker squirmed and gagged. His eyes wild and imploring as he struggled to breathe. Quinn warned, "I'm going to take the gun out of your mouth so you can tell me what we're up against. If you scream, I'll gut shoot you and leave you in the woods. Understand?"

Baker nodded. Quinn pulled the barrel out of his mouth and let Baker slide back to the floor. "I swear that it wasn't supposed to happen like this," Baker gasped. "It was supposed to be a simple snatch job is all. Just like Frank and Ira said. I was supposed to play along and babysit Archie while five guys came up and phoned in a ransom demand to you or Fatty. Next thing I know these clowns barge in with the rough stuff. They killed Archie's three bodyguards at the foot of the driveway and headed up here to the house. They were still all hot over killing Rothman. One of them blows past me and heads straight in here to Archie's room. I start screaming, 'This ain't part of the deal!' but he don't listen."

"My hero," Doyle said from bed. "Numb nuts here forgot to take my back up piece from the nightstand. I heard the gun shots at the end of the driveway and was hiding behind the bed when they kicked the door in." He nodded toward the large red mess on the wall next to the door. "The best of him is still there. Got the fucker right between the eyes." He looked down at his right thigh. "The other one caught me in the leg, though."

Baker started weeping again. "I swear, Terry, I didn't want this. I just needed the money and the respect..."

Quinn grabbed his throat again to shut him up. "Did you get a doctor?"

Baker nodded quickly, then pointed up at the ceiling. "All I could get was the vet that works on Archie's horses sometimes. He's the closest, just across the road. I tried to get him to work on Archie, but the other two made him work on their buddy first. He was dead before he hit the ground, but his brother's the leader and he made the doc to keep working on him. Said he'd shoot him if he came downstairs and told him his brother was dead."

Quinn did the math. One shot and two alive. That made three. "I thought it was a five-man squad."

Baker looked surprised. "I don't know anything about that. All I know is that three showed up here."

Two on two. Quinn liked those odds even better. "Where are the last two?"

"The leader's making a ransom call now. I think the other one's in the kitchen. They're both mean and wild and you won't be able to get them both at once by yourself." Baker managed a smile. "I can help you, see? Maybe give you a signal when it's all right to hit them. I mean I already tried keeping Archie alive, see? I already tried to make up for it. I want to help anyway I can."

Quinn grabbed Baker's face and slammed him back against the wall. "Thanks, pal."

He fired two shots into Baker's belly and let the

traitor sink slowly to the floor. A bloody slick trailed on the wallpaper as he sank to the floor.

Quinn went to Archie. He heard the kitchen door crash open. A shotgun blast. No return gunfire. Cain got the one in the kitchen.

One more to go.

He heard someone running down the hall from the living room. A single pistol shot. Another shotgun blast. One more shot. The roar of the shotgun. A thud against the wall, then the floor. Familiar footsteps came from the kitchen, marching up the hallway. Then a light rap on the bedroom door. "Everything okay, boss?" It was Jimmy Cain.

Quinn was already working on Doyle's wounds. "There's a doctor upstairs tending to a dead man," Quinn called out. "Get him down here. But be careful. There might be one more with him."

Quinn ignored Baker's sobs as he tried to put pressure on Doyle's thigh wound. The blood only came faster. He tore one of the bandages lengthwise and pulled it as tight as he could.

Doyle bellowed. Quinn wrapped it around the leg and repeated it before tying it into a knot. The blood flow barely slowed. Quinn concentrated on the original shoulder wound. The hole had opened again, too.

"Ah, this is nothing," Doyle said, with a weak smile. "Don't fuss with that, kid. It's too late now anyway. I'm done for."

"Bullshit," Quinn kept working. "You've lost a lot of blood, but the doc can..."

Doyle was groggy for real this time. "You never did know when to give up, did you? Even in the ring, you never could see the whole play. You could've fought for the title if you'd just been smart enough to take that dive like you was supposed to. But you couldn't take a handout. No, you had to take it on your own. You had to kill the fuckin' guy."

Quinn kept working. "Save your strength, boss."

But Doyle kept trying to slap Quinn's hands away. "They're just gonna keep coming at me, anyway. They'll never stop now until I'm dead and you know it. Just...let...me...go."

Doyle's eyes rolled up into the back of his head. His tongue bulged and he began to gurgle.

Archie was dying.

For the first time since childhood, Quinn felt true terror.

He slapped Archie's face twice to bring him out of it. Nothing. He could feel Doyle slipping away, drifting into eternity. Quinn wasn't ready to let him go. Not yet.

Quinn reared back and slammed his fist over Doyle's heart. Archie's eyes sprang back open, wide, and alive.

The doctor ran into the room with his medical bag. "Don't do that, you damned fool!" He was a skinny little man, but he had enough strength to push Quinn out of the way. "You'll break his chest and puncture a lung. Get the hell out of here before you kill him."

Quinn heard Baker's whimpering from the floor. He pulled his pistol and aimed at Baker's head. Cain did the same. "His whimpering going to keep you from working on Archie, Doc?"

The vet was examining the shoulder wound. "Not really."

"Good." Quinn and Cain put their guns away. "Just concentrate on the man in the bed. We'll worry about him later."

217

Quinn closed the bedroom door behind them. He and Cain stepped over the body of one of Doyle's attackers to get into the living room. He'd been a short, stocky man, but looked to have a solid build. Cain's shotgun blast had caught him in the upper chest and head. Most of his face was gone. What was left wasn't pretty.

Jimmy Cain laid the shotgun against the wall and dropped on the couch. "Baker tell you what happened to them three boys I sent up here with Archie?"

Quinn nodded in a way that told the story.

Cain swore to himself. "Jesus, boss. What are we gonna do now?" Quinn was already thinking about that. Nothing he came up with looked good. Doyle had two big holes in him and was bleeding bad. He might die. He was sure Sanders had sent a goon squad to wipe Archie out and take control of the mob.

Quinn knew he could send some boys to pick up Sanders. But Sanders had plenty of men who liked him. Attacking Sanders could split the Doyle mob in half.

Besides, Quinn was running things now. He had to think like a boss. He had to try to save Archie's empire. For Archie's sake, not his.

But Quinn knew that even if Archie lived, he'd be a marked man for the rest of his life. If Sanders or Shapiro or Wallace didn't get him, some other mob would. And if they didn't, the government would. All this violence had stirred up a lot of resentment against Archie. People saw he wasn't invincible, and they'd keep at him until he was gone.

The old days were over. Quinn wondered if Archie might not be better off dead after all.

That's when it hit him: Archie had to die.

At least for a little while.

Quinn picked up the candlestick phone and jiggled the cradle until the operator came on the line. He gave her Fatty's number and she connected them.

He'd spent the past five years doing his best to keep Archie Doyle alive. He hoped Doyle would forgive him for what he was about to do.

"What're you doin', boss?" Cain asked from the couch.

The call went through, and Fatty picked up. "Aw, Jesus, Terry. Thank Christ it's you. We just got a phone call from some bastards who said they grabbed Archie. They're calling back later with a goddamned ransom demand."

Quinn didn't know who else might be listening in, so he said, "Archie's gone, Fatty. They killed him just before we got here."

Fatty began to sob.

Cain's jaw dropped open and Quinn muffled the mouthpiece against his chest. "Not one fucking word out of you." He went back to Corcoran. "They got him in the leg, but his shoulder opened up again. We killed the two bastards who got him, but Archie bled out before we could save him." Quinn didn't have to act for this part. "That little shit Baker sold him out. Set the whole thing up. He was working with Frank Sanders and Ira Shapiro. I think they hired this Wallace guy to help them sell out Doyle and Rothman to make a grab for the two gangs."

"And neither of them will live long enough to enjoy it." The fat man's voice quivered. "I'll send the boys to round up Sanders and pay the hymie a visit. They'll both be dead within the hour."

"No, you won't," Quinn said. "With Rothman

dead, the cops'll be waiting for us to pull something like that. Just sit tight and keep things running until I get back. I'll send Cain back with Archie's body in a day or two. We're both gonna need some time up here to get things squared away the way Archie would've wanted."

Quinn let Fatty ramble about how dark a day this was before putting the earpiece back in the cradle. He spotted a pack of cigarettes on the coffee table and helped himself. He figured they belonged to the dead faceless man on the floor. He figured the owner wouldn't mind.

Cain's mouth was still wide open. Quinn said, "Keeping your mouth open like that will draw flies, Jimmy."

"What the hell do you think you're doin'?"

"What I'm paid to do, keeping Archie alive."

THE DOCTOR HAD BEEN WORKING on Archie for over two hours. Quinn and Cain waited quietly at the kitchen table. Cain nursed a Highball. Quinn was halfway through a glass of milk. He hated milk, but he didn't feel like drinking, and he wanted something cold.

They ignored the dead man slumped next to the ice box. Corpses had ceased to bother either of them long ago.

Neither man had spoken since the phone call. Not even when they'd dragged Baker into the woods over an hour before. He'd been still begging for mercy when they left him beneath a tree. It didn't matter whether the animals or the blood loss got him first. Dead was dead and Baker had it coming.

The last of the morphine had left Quinn's system long ago. The hole in his side had settled into a dull ache. He was amazed the stitches hadn't opened. He thought of calling Alice to tell her he was okay, but he was afraid she wouldn't answer the phone.

Quinn realized that day was the end of a lot of things in his life. The end of him and Alice. The end of Archie Doyle's reign as Duke of New York, too. He thought of all they'd been through and all they'd done. Quinn had killed thirty-seven people in the five years he'd worked for Archie. Most of them men, but a few women, but not a civilian in the bunch.

Every one of them had been in the Life. Grifters, bookies, gamblers, low-lifes, drunks, junkies, blackmailers, thieves. Remembering that took the sting out of it, helped him sleep nights. He'd done it all for Archie because Archie had gotten The Boys to lay off him five years before. He did it because Archie had been the only consistent force in his life.

Quinn knew the world Archie had shown him was rotten. It preyed on people's weaknesses. It made money from their faults. But it was the only life Quinn had ever known. And it beat what had been waiting for him in the hallway outside his locker room that warm September night five years before.

Quinn vowed to fight to keep Archie's legacy alive. It was important to him because it was important to Archie. But first he'd kill Shapiro. And Sanders. And Wallace.

He flinched when he heard the bedroom door open. Quinn and Cain ran to see him.

The vet stood in the hallway, looking older and

thinner than he had an hour ago. He stepped over the faceless dead man into the living room and dropped himself on the couch. His face and hands were streaked with dried blood.

"How is he doc?" Quinn asked. "Give it to me straight?"

The vet looked up at Quinn with pale blue eyes. "Have you seen that man's body? It's a roadmap of pain. Old fractures, scar tissue, bullet wounds. It's unlike anything I've seen in my entire life." He looked at Cain. "I counted eleven old bullet holes in him, not including the two he got today."

Quinn fought the urge to smack the doc out of it. "Is he going to pull through?"

"I'd imagine so. Judging by the amount of blood he's lost over the last few days; he should have died hours ago. But he is as strong as an ox." The vet gave a weary smile. "And if there's one thing an old vet like me knows, its oxen."

"So, he's gonna make it?" Cain echoed.

"There's always the risk of infection," the vet said, "but seeing what he's lived through before, I'd say Mr. Doyle keeps on living out of sheer habit." It was the best news Quinn had heard in a long time, maybe ever. Everything in him wanted to go in and talk to Archie right then and there.

But Quinn knew that wouldn't accomplish much in the long run. There were more important things here than sentiment. "Do you understand what happened here today, Doc?"

"No and I don't care to. All I know is that Mr. Doyle's been good to me and my family. I'll do what I can to keep him alive."

"I'll get a doctor up here as soon as I can, but it

might take a day or so. Can you hold out until then?"

"Certainly. But you must remember that Mr. Doyle's in grave condition. Even if he was in the finest hospital in the world under the best of care, the slightest infection could kill him." He looked at the dead, faceless man on the floor. "I don't want to be held responsible if he dies."

"Then let's hope he doesn't."

He saw that Cain was still steamed about him telling Fatty that Archie was dead. Quinn clued him in. "And the best way I knew to keep Archie alive was to tell Fatty he was dead. If word got out he was alive, this place might be crawling with people who want to finish the job. Understand?"

"Sure, boss," Cain said, "but what are we gonna use for a body? We've gotta have something to plant in the graveyard."

Quinn looked down at the bloodied, faceless corpse on the floor. "We'll give him the part. He's about Archie's size. With his face gone, so no one will know the difference."

He watched Cain look the corpse over and realize it wasn't a bad idea.

Quinn continued, "I'll clue Fatty in on the plan when I get back to New York. Face-to-face to make sure no one's listening. He'll make all the arrangements."

Cain seemed very confused. "You're going back to New York?"

"Right now. I've got a couple of loose ends to tie up before Archie's resurrection."

Twenty minutes later, Quinn bought some gas at a filling station. And made a phone call to the Chauncey Arms.

Chapter 18

FRIDAY NIGHT WAS Fight Night at Madison Square Garden.

Quinn knew Frank Sanders never missed the fights when he was in town. He doubted Sanders would even let the supposed death of his best friend break his ritual. Especially since he had a hand in it.

Quinn knew the news about Archie's death would spread fast throughout the city. Everyone would assume Sanders was in charge now and would treat him accordingly. And, since his coup worked, there was no need to hide out. Frank Sanders and Ira Shapiro were running things now.

Neither had a care in the world.

Quinn took his time walking through the crowded narrow aisles of the Garden. It was the first time he'd been in the building since the night they took away his license five long years before. One career had ended that night. Tonight, so would another.

The place never changed. The haze from cigar smoke still hovered overhead. The murmur of the crowd and the sound of leather hitting flesh. The creaking of the ring beneath the middleweights as they circled each other.

Quinn spotted Sanders down front, just to the right side of center ring on the aisle. His normal spot.

He spotted two goons he didn't recognize guarding the entrance to Sanders' section. He figured they must be the last two shooters from the Kansas City squad. Sanders must've held them back in case some of Doyle's boys blamed him for Archie's death. The goons eyeballed everyone who passed by and had their backs to the ring. Quinn bet they were looking for him.

Quinn ducked down two sections before Sanders', then cut across through the row. Everyone recognized him and gladly moved for Terry Quinn. Sanders' goons kept facing the wrong way and never saw a thing.

He saw Sanders holding court with several lowlifes, the kind who were always looking to hitch their wagons to the next big thing. Sanders was the biggest thing going and the creeps were all over him, laughing too loud at Sanders' mumbled punch lines.

Quinn stood in the aisle a couple of rows behind Sanders' seat. He kept his hands in his overcoat pockets. He was wide enough to almost fill the aisle and blocked the view of people behind him. But no one heckled him to sit down.

Because you didn't heckle Terry Quinn. "Evening, Frank."

The flunkies craned their necks back to see Quinn. Their phony smiles faded. Their laughter choked off.

Sanders kept his eyes on the ring and took a drag. "Hello, Terry. You missed a good undercard."

Quinn looked down at the five flunkies. "Beat it."

They scurried out of their seats and fled up the stairs. Quinn lowered himself into a seat in the row just behind Sanders. "Nice crew you had there, Frank. Real stand-up boys, just like you."

The two Kansas City goons ran down and flanked Quinn. "Want us to take care of this, Frank?"

Sanders kept watching the fight and waved them back. "Nothing to worry about, boys. I'll call for you if I need you."

They went back up to their spots. This time they'd be facing Quinn and the ring.

That's just what Quinn wanted.

Sanders said, "You've got a lot of balls coming here tonight, Terry."

"Balls got nothing to do with it. I'm paying proper respect to the new boss of the Doyle mob."

"I know you won't believe it, but I didn't mean for it to happen this way."

"Of course not. Because Archie's the type to roll over and let you take over."

"Nothing to joke about, Terry. The way he's been lately? All that nonsense about going legit in a few years? Putting Al Smith in the White House? I half think he wanted this to happen but was too thick to stand down. Too thick or too proud."

"And now he's dead, and you're not."

"Go ahead. Sneer if you want to." Sanders flicked his ash into the aisle. "You've been around for five fuckin' years. I've known the guy for over forty. I loved Archie like a brother. I knew everything there was to know about the man. His balls got us where we are, but his ego was starting to cost us."

"Bullshit."

"Keep saying that, kid. You just might start

believing it. Everything's going to hell. Speakeasies going belly up, the law's cracking down and the politicians are biting the hand what feeds them. And what does Archie do? He pushes Al for another shot at the White House. It was time for him to go and you know it. All he needed was a little shove is all."

"You shove hard, Frankie."

Sanders pointed a crooked finger at him. "None of this had to happen. Fatty getting shot was just supposed to be a warning. That's why Zito only used a .22. Archie was supposed to head upstate and leave me in charge. Then Ira and I move on Rothman and Ira's in charge over there. We box Archie out and that's that. No bloodshed. No one dies. But when Archie wouldn't leave, the whole thing went sideways."

"You've got big dreams, Frank. Growing here and in Kansas City. Your friends out there tell you to hire Zito."

Sanders laughed a nasty laugh. "Fatty told you about that, eh? They gave me ideas, but they didn't know what I was planning. Wallace picked Zito and made the initial cash drop. I paid him the rest out of what I had on hand in the cab stand."

Sanders stopped laughing. "You know, Fatty better watch his step, too or he'll catch one in the head next time. And not from Zito. From that choice Kansas City beef I got watching me up there."

"Hell, I've been killing them all week. Archie nailed one just before he died."

"I'm not surprised. Archie was the toughest bastard I ever knew. If he'd only just been smart enough to let me grow when I asked, this wouldn't have happened."

"One thing's still bugging me. Where does Wallace fit into all of this?"

"What do you care?" Sanders asked. "You're gonna be dead soon anyway."

Quinn smiled. "Everyone dies sometimes, Ace. When's Ira Shapiro's turn?"

For the first time since Quinn sat down, Sanders turned to look up at him. "You know, you never were as dumb as you were supposed to be."

"It's because I'm beautiful. How long does Ira have? It can't be long because you didn't go through all this nonsense to share the spotlight with anyone."

Sanders shrugged. "We're being seen as heroes. The two men who helped avert a war on the streets of the city."

"Make sure they spell your name right on the plaque. So, when's Ira's departure date?"

Sanders went back to watching the fight. "About fifteen minutes from now. I got a dame dressed up as a nurse to inject him with an empty needle. Archie would've been impressed."

"Get him before he gets you and with an arena full of witnesses to say you were here."

"Like I said, Archie would've been impressed."

Quinn let Sanders watch the fight for a bit. It was a bad fight, just a couple of middleweights pawing at each other, afraid to throw. "When do I get mine?"

"I've been thinking about that," Sanders said. "Wallace wants you done quick. But you've been loyal to Archie for years and deserve the chance to get away clean. So, I'm giving you a choice: blow town tonight and never look back. Or you'll be dead before sunrise."

Quinn leaned forward and spoke into Sanders' ear.

"Even if I'm dead by sunrise, I'll still outlive you, fucko."

"And here I was, thinking you was a smart kid." Sanders kept his eyes on the fight and raised his hand to beckon the two goons. "Damned shame."

"If you're not waving for your two friends from Kansas City, you'll be waving a long time. They're dead."

Sanders jerked around in his seat and looked up the aisle, then all over the arena.

Quinn didn't have to look. He knew they were dead.

"The biggest trouble with hiring a guy like Carmine Zito is that it's tough to keep an eye out for a guy when you don't know what he looks like. It's even worse when he's good at not being noticed."

Sanders was on his feet now, his eyes wild. "Bullshit."

Quinn grinned. "Keep saying that, kid, and you might start believing it. Zito doesn't like being used and he thinks you used him to shoot Fatty. You probably didn't think I'd find him, but I did. You probably figured I'd kill him if I found him."

Quinn shook his head. "But I didn't. He doesn't like you very much, Frank. And he's going to kill you. Here. Tonight. And you'll never see it coming because you don't know what he looks like."

Sanders kept looking at the crowd, his head moving like a chicken pecking at birdseed. Thousands of men of various shapes and sizes. Some talking to each other. Some screaming at the fighters in the ring. None of them looked like a hired killer.

The good ones never do.

Quinn loved every moment of it. "All those faces

and any one of them might be Zito. But he'll introduce himself to you soon enough, Frank. When he sticks a knife into your belly."

Sanders scrambled into the aisle and ran up the stairs.

"And here I was thinking, you was a smart kid."

Quinn touched the brim of his hat and yelled after him. "Give my regards to Shapiro and Rothman."

Quinn watched Sanders hobble up the aisle, frantically looking around him for his assassin. He barged through a row of fans cheering the fight and stepped on dozens of feet, knocking men and little kids out of his way.

Quinn lost sight of him when he got to the far side of the section and bolted up some stairs.

Quinn found an untouched bag of popcorn left behind by one of Sanders' stooges. He sat back and began to watch the fight. It was the first thing he'd eaten all day. In a couple of days, actually. He was always amazed at how danger could kill an appetite.

Both fighters flinched when a woman's blood curdling scream pierced the hum of the crowd, followed by calls of 'Murder! Murder!'

The spectators jumped to their feet and looked toward where the screaming was coming from. Some people started to leave, but most stayed where they were.

Quinn stood slowly and walked up the aisle. By the time he got to the top of the hallway, he recognized a cop who was running past him. "Hey, Murphy. What's all the commotion about?"

"Someone just knifed Frank Sanders on his way out of the building, slit his belly wide open," the young officer said. "Two other clowns were just found with their throats cut in the bathroom. I never seen so much blood in my life."

"Anyone see who did it?" Quinn asked.

"Nah, the bastard ran off into the crowd. But we'll find him, I promise you."

Quinn doubted it.

He made his way over to a phone booth and called Wendell Bixby. After a couple of minutes, the newspaper's secretary got him on the line. "Hey, Terry. Howard Rothman and Archie Doyle, both R.I.P. Sorry for your loss. Care to give me the scoop on who's next?"

"You get an address on Simon Wallace?"

Quinn heard Bixby fumbling threw his notepad. "He's a real difficult guy to pin down. I talked to a couple of doormen at some of the places he's gone. Two of them said he's bragged about how he's got a suite at the Plaza when he's drunk a couple of times, but..."

Quinn hung up the phone. Doyle had people at the Plaza. Finding the room number wouldn't be hard.

Rothman was dead. Sanders was dead. Shapiro was probably dead by now, too.

But Simon Wallace was alive.

And Quinn was going to do something about that.

Chapter 19

THE DOORMAN at the Plaza was into Fatty Corcoran for five bills. Quinn told him the debt was forgiven if he told him where Wallace lived. The doorman kicked loose in record time: Suite 1001 but Wallace always had a guard posted in the hall outside.

Quinn had seen the bodyguard. He wasn't worried.

Still, it paid to be safe. Quinn had the elevator boy take him up to the eleventh floor, then he walked down one flight of stairs to the tenth floor. Quinn drew his .45 and paused at the door on the tenth floor. He listened for voices, footfalls, anything.

Nothing.

Quinn eased the door open slow. He was lucky it didn't creak or make any noise. He took a long, slow look down the hallway.

The same stocky longshoreman Wallace had brought with him to the Lounge. He was sound asleep in front of a pair of white double doors at the end of the hallway. Wallace's suite: 1001. An empty tray of food was on the floor at his feet. An open newspaper at his side.

Quinn liked double doors. They popped right open if you hit them hard enough.

He had an idea.

Quinn stepped into the hallway and let the door close behind him with a quiet click. He kept his gun down as moved toward the sleeping guard. As he got closer, Quinn saw the 'Please, Do Not Disturb' sign dangling from the brass doorknob of the double doors.

Someone was about to be very disappointed.

Quinn dropped the .45 into his overcoat pocket. He backhanded the sleeping man off the chair. Quinn picked him up off the floor and drove his knee into his stomach twice. He grabbed him by the back of the pants and collar and whipped him around, throwing him through the middle of the double doors. They splintered wide open.

Quinn pulled his gun from his pocket as he walked through the shattered doorway. He walked on the unconscious bodyguard and into the entrance hall of the suite.

Simon Wallace was on a bed with red silk sheets and pillows. He had two naked black girls with him. They looked a few years shy of eighteen. They were screaming as they tumbled off the bed onto the floor together, holding each other to hide their nakedness.

Wallace glared out at Quinn from the bed; the red silk sheet barely covered his pale, thin body. His brown hair was mussed. His face was flushed. He looked nothing like the powered, coifed dude who had strode into the Lounge a few days before.

Quinn knew hate when he saw it. He was seeing it now.

Quinn pointed the gun rat him. "Hope I didn't interrupt anything." Wallace didn't say a word. His dark little eyes quivered beneath his brow.

Then he threw his head back and laughed a long, deep belly laugh not unlike the laugh Rothman had given in Doyle's office. But this laugh was deep and genuine.

At least it made the black girls on the floor stop screaming.

Wallace laughed until he collapsed back into the sea of red pillows. He clapped his hands like a fat kid at a birthday party. Except Wallace was neither fat nor a kid.

"Bravo, Terry Quinn, bravo." Wallace wiped the tears from his eyes. "You really have exceeded all of my expectations." He motioned down at the two naked black women on the floor. "This doesn't involve them, does it?"

The girls looked up at Quinn hopefully.

Quinn said, "Get going."

The girls grabbed up whatever clothes they could find on the floor and pressed it to themselves as they ran from the room. Quinn didn't watch them go. He kept his gun and his eyes on Wallace instead.

"You're sense of timing is really extraordinary," Wallace sighed. "You barged in here just as things were beginning to get interesting."

Quinn didn't care about his love life. "Why did you help Sanders kill Archie Doyle and Howard Rothman?"

Wallace laughed again. "Enough of the small talk, eh? Ah, poor, poor boy. A guard dog that's lost its master is the saddest canine of all. You know, if you weren't pointing that gun at my head, I might be inclined to pity you."

"Stick pity up your ass. Why did you help Sanders and Shapiro kill Doyle and Rothman?"

"I haven't helped anyone kill anyone. They did it all themselves. All I did was push them in the right direction. I was their muse if you will."

He slowly stretched for a large gold cigarette box on his nightstand. Quinn fired. The box disintegrated, sending cigarettes everywhere.

Wallace yanked back his hand and pinned himself back against the headboard. "For Christ's sake! I was just getting a cigarette!"

Cigarettes from the box had scattered all over the floor and the sheets. "Answer my question or you catch the next one in the belly."

"Of course," Wallace threw up his hands. "You're cross. And why shouldn't you be? After all, Archie Doyle is dead and that's put you in a bad mood."

"I'm getting really tired of asking this. Why did..."

Wallace surprised him by actually interrupting him. "This is your biggest failing, Terry. Your inflexibility. It's what drove poor Sean Baker away you know. He never thought anything he did was good enough for you or Archie. He looked up to you, you know. Much the way I believe Johnny looked up to Ira. Both so young and eager to please, but slow to think. And so easy to turn."

Quinn fired a round into the headboard about an inch away from Wallace's skull.

Wallace flinched, but not like before. "I wouldn't do that again if I were you. I might panic and do something stupid, like lunge at your gun." He folded his arms across his pale, bare chest. "You'd kill me, of course, but then you'd never get an answer to that one precious question that's been gnawing at you: my involvement in this tawdry melodrama of yours."

Quinn didn't know how to handle Wallace. Most guys he went up against either fought back or cowered. Wallace did neither. He just threw words at him.

"So?" Quinn said. "Start talking."

"And miss witnessing such a rare occurrence of your powers of deductive reasoning being brought to bear?" Wallace shook his head. "I've rather enjoyed your transformation from button man to detective. I'd like to see how far you got. You go first."

"You're in no position to bargain."

"And neither are you," Wallace laced his fingers behind his head. "Now, give me your idea of what happened, or I keep my mouth shut."

Quinn didn't like following Wallace's lead. But the little bastard was right. He had to know where Wallace fit into all of this. He had to know how far the rot went so he could cut it out.

"Sanders and Shapiro wanted to take over, so they hired you to help them do it. You arranged Fatty getting shot by Zito and helped them hire those Kansas City chopper squads to hit Archie and Rothman. Ira was closer to Rothman every day than Sanders was to Archie, so you flipped Baker to turn traitor. Sanders and Shapiro take over and everyone lives happily ever after."

Wallace shook his head in admiration. "You pieced together more than I thought you would. Sanders underestimated you and so did Shapiro. I made the mistake of listening to them." He smiled. "I probably should've killed you first."

"I wish you'd tried."

"There's only one thing wrong with your hypothesis. You believe that I worked for Shapiro and Sanders. Not so. They worked for me."

Quinn's eyes narrowed. That didn't make sense. "What?"

"Of course. I have lots of people who work for me in New York City. Shapiro, Sanders, Baker. Even Detective James Halloran of the New York Police Department. Or Big Jim as you call him. He's one of my best employees." He looked over Quinn's right shoulder. "Isn't that right, Jim?"

Quinn felt the cold gun metal press into the back of his neck.

"You always liked to run your mouth too much," Halloran said. "Now toss the heater on the bed. Do it nice and slow."

Quinn did what he was told. The steel moved away from his neck, and he turned enough to get a look at Halloran. Unfortunately, he looked reasonably sober. Sober enough to level a .38 at Quinn's stomach and smart enough to back far enough away so Quinn couldn't make a play for the gun.

Quinn offered the smirk he reserved only for him. "You've got your hands in a lot of pockets, Halloran. I didn't think you were that smart."

"Me and Mr. Wallace have known each other a couple of years now," the big cop said. "I damned near busted a gut when Doherty had me trail him when he left the Lounge. Follow him? Hell, I drove him home."

"Detective Halloran has been a great help to my organization," Wallace said as he slipped out of bed and into a silk smoking jacket. "But given what I've learned about you tonight, Terry, I'd like to give you a chance to join my organization. Of course, I'd like to discuss that with Mr. Shapiro and Mr. Sanders first."

"I'd like you to discuss it with them, too. They're both dead."

Wallace stopped tying the belt of his smoking jacket in mid-motion.

"You're lying."

"Nope. Sanders said he had Ira snuffed in the hospital about an hour ago. And I had Zito take care of Sanders in the Garden just before I came here. Carved that bastard open like a Christmas goose."

Wallace looked at Halloran, then back at Quinn before laughter bent him in half. Halloran laughed, too.

Wallace sat back on the edge of the bed and caught his breath. "Good God, man. It's like something out of a horrible opera. A farce, for God's sake. Why, had we known you were this thorough, my people would have given you the job instead of Sanders. You've set our plans ahead by months, years, my boy!"

"We?" Quinn kept his hands up. "Who's we?"

Wallace finished tying the belt of his smoking jacket around his narrow waist. "I'm not foolish enough to get into specifics with you, but I'll let you in on an open secret. Men like Rothman, Doyle, and others like them all over the country have held sway over most illegal activity for over a decade now. Gambling, liquor, prostitution, and narcotics have been regionally controlled by a relatively small number of men for far too long. There are forces coming to power who want the criminal element to organize itself in a more efficient, national manner."

"Bullshit. Doyle already has his hooks into mobs all over the country."

"Yes, but power held by one man can lead to greater problems," Wallace reminded. "Look at what happened in Chicago under Capone. Then look at how quickly things quieted down once Capone was removed. With disbursed organization comes less chaos, which leads to less public outcry, which leads to less government interference which ultimately leads to greater profits. Doyle had become too complacent, and Rothman had overextended his power, especially with the legislature in Albany. We knew neither Doyle nor Rothman would go quietly, and a nasty street war would ensue. As we sought to avoid that at all costs, we used Shapiro and Sanders to move them out for us. Change is often painful, Terry, but necessary. I'm sure you understand."

None of this made much sense to Quinn. "Who's this 'we' you keep talking about? Who do you work for?"

"A consortium of interests who have grown tired of the Rothman/Doyle monopoly and who've grown fearful of Doyle's plans to influence national politics."

"Like Archie getting Al Smith to run for president."

"It's a ridiculous notion, but it served as the spark that lit Sanders' treasonous fire weeks ago. I just fanned the flames to my own advantage. And now that Doyle, Rothman, Shapiro, and Sanders are all dead, my allies can assume control much quicker than they planned." Wallace saluted Quinn. "I have your meddling to thank for that."

"I'm not going to ask you again. Who do you work for?"

"What difference does it make? As you'll be dead soon, telling you would be harmless enough, but I'm afraid Detective Halloran isn't as discreet as you."

"You better hope he's as good as you think he is. If he's not, I'm coming back here and kill you."

"He's good enough."

Wallace went to the nightstand, took a large envelope out of the drawer and tossed it over to a chair near Halloran. "There's your payment in advance. I suppose just killing him here would be awkward?"

The cop shrugged. "It'd be a hell of a lot easier to shoot him and leave him here after you clear out if you don't care about him being found."

Wallace sighed. "Unfortunately, I do care about him being found. If he's dead too, it'll all look too neat. Too planned. People may ask questions and there'll be enough of that as it is. Where do you usually dispose of problems like this?"

"I got a couple of places," Halloran answered.

"I'm sure you do. On your way then and make sure it's painless if you can," Wallace cautioned him. "I'm sure you and Mr. Quinn have had your differences in the past, but I think he deserves a little professional courtesy – from one mercenary soul to another."

"Sure. Let's go, Quinn, and keep them arms up. No funny business."

Halloran trailed a good distance behind Quinn with the gun still aimed at his midsection. Quinn stepped over the bodyguard who was still lying among the splinters of what used to be the door. Wallace walked them out, "I'm sorry things didn't turn out better for us, Terry. Perhaps we'll meet again in another life."

Quinn kept moving. "That might be sooner than you think."

The little man saluted him and disappeared back into the suite. Halloran jerked the gun toward him. "Let's go, hooch punk. And forget the elevator. You might get too frisky in a small space and do something stupid. We'll take the stairs all the way down, nice and easy. Then we're going to do a little sightseeing."

Quinn walked down the stairs to his destiny with a gun at his back.

Chapter 20

HALLORAN MADE QUINN DRIVE.

Quinn couldn't see Halloran in the rearview mirror. The bastard was smart. He sat in the back seat right behind Quinn. He'd have to find another way to read the big cop.

"Give her some gas and head downtown on Fifth," Halloran directed. "Nice and slow."

Quinn pulled away from the Plaza's curb and headed downtown. He heard Halloran unscrew the cap off a steel flask. "And don't try no funny stuff, neither. I've got this cannon aimed square at your back. One dumb move and you'll catch one but good." He took a belt from the flask. "Just drive like I tell you and you'll be better off."

It was after eleven o'clock at night and traffic was light. As the blocks passed by, Quinn ignored the growing pain in his side. Whipping the bodyguard through the door hurt more than he realized. He may have even opened his stitches but didn't dare take his

242

hand off the wheel to check. Halloran might get nervous, and he was plenty nervous already.

Quinn took stock of his options. It was a damned short list. His gun was on Wallace's bed ten floors up. He didn't have a backup piece, and no one knew where he was. No would be looking for him, either. He had a gun aimed at his back by a crooked cop who'd been looking for a reason to kill him for years.

Then it hit him.

Maybe he could use that to his advantage.

Halloran hated his guts because deep down, Halloran was afraid of him. And he was taking healthy pulls on that flask for courage. If Quinn could get him to lose his temper, it might create an opening. But he'd have to do it slow because if Halloran caught on to what he was trying to do, it could backfire. At this point, all Quinn had to lose was his life. And he was going to lose it anyway if he followed Halloran's orders. A traffic light turned red. Quinn stopped short and Halloran jerked forward.

Quinn spotted a cop car with two patrolmen parked on the Doyle side of Fifth Avenue. Chances were, they were on Doyle's payroll.

"Don't get any ideas, smart guy," Halloran warned from the back seat.

"Remember I'm a detective and they'll believe anything I say."

Quinn laughed. "The shield in your pocket might make you a cop. But you're not much of a detective."

"I'm enough of a detective to be on this side of the gun."

Quinn heard him take another pull on his flask. "Getting up some courage?"

"Quit talking and drive," Halloran wiped his mouth with the back of his hand.

The light turned green. Quinn took his time giving it some gas but moved along slow.

"Mind telling me where we're going or are we just gonna tool around like a couple of swishes on a joyride. Maybe take a little late-night stroll through Central Park and grab some cotton candy?" Quinn winked back at him. "I bet you'd like that, wouldn't you, sweetheart?"

"Sure. But I'm gonna like putting a bullet in that smart mouth of yours even better. Take Fifth Avenue until you hit Broadway at Twenty-Third Street, then take Broadway all the way down."

"Keep heading downtown?"

"There ain't nowhere to go on Broadway but down. Especially for you tonight."

Quinn figured that meant they were heading out east. Brooklyn or Queens or Long Island some place. Weeds, swamps, lots of woods. Several dozen places to dump a body. Quinn had made similar trips dozens of times. But he wanted to pull it out of Halloran, to get on his nerves and stay there. "Don't tell me. We're going to Brooklyn?"

"You ask a lot of questions for a dead man."

"That's the right of the damned. A dying man's supposed to be granted his last request, or something like that."

"The only thing I'm gonna grant you is a bullet in the gut. Now shut up."

Quinn knew he was getting to him. "I know you're scared. But icing a guy is never supposed to be easy. I still get a little nervous and I've planted plenty of guys."

"Scared? Killing you is one of the highpoints of my life. And I never bought that bullshit about all the guys you supposedly killed anyway. I figure you mostly had it done. You ain't half as tough as people say you are."

"At least I never turned traitor."

"Traitor? You rum peddling scum make me laugh. Traitor. Betrayal. You bastards run booze and whores and crooked crap games and kill people and act like you're honorable men. Loyalty?" Halloran took another pull from the flask. "The only real loyalty I got is to the dead presidents in my billfold."

"Money's all that matters, heh?"

"That's right."

"Just like a whore."

"Whatever you say, croaker. Boy, I'm really going to enjoy shutting that smart mouth of yours once and for all."

They were getting closer to the Brooklyn Bridge. Quinn knew he didn't have much time. He had to keep working on him until he could make his move, whatever that move was going to be.

"Funny thing about killing people in our line of work. Don't kill enough and you lose your edge. Kill too much and it becomes a habit. If you're not careful, you get sloppy and sloppy gets you caught."

"I told you to shut up."

"Level with me about something. How long do you think Wallace is going to let you live after tonight? With me dead, you're the only guy who knows what he's done. Killing you would tie up a lot of loose ends."

He heard Halloran starting to breathe heavier. "At

the end of Broadway, take the Brooklyn Bridge and head east."

Quinn kept driving. "I don't blame you for dodging the question. I wouldn't want to think about it either. You can't trust guys like Wallace to live up to their end of the bargain. A smart cop would steer clear of Wallace types. Take Doherty for instance. Now that's my idea of a smart cop."

"You would think that. Taking scraps from Doyle don't make Doherty smart."

Quinn kept it up. "Scraps from Archie's better than taking shit from some swish in a white suit."

"Wallace ain't a fruit and Doherty's no angel, believe me." Quinn heard him pull on the flask again. "Oh, Charlie comes across as a straight shooter, but he's a no-good drunk with a wife and kids in the Bronx and a mistress up in the Heights."

"But he's his own man, unlike you." Quinn turned left off Broadway and on to the Brooklyn Bridge. "That's why you're here and he's not. Wallace is gonna whack you the second you're through with me."

"I ain't gonna stick around and give him the chance. See that satchel on the floor next to you?" Quinn looked at the passenger seat and saw a leather satchel on the floor. "With what he paid me tonight, plus what I already got squirreled away in that bag," Halloran went on, "I'll blow this town with wind in my sails and money to burn. Probably head to some place nice and warm where a bunch of native girls in grass skirts will serve me drinks on the beach. But don't worry, Quinn. I'll come back to piss on your grave someday."

They were on the bridge now and Quinn gave the

engine just a little more gas. "I don't think you'll live that long."

"Just shut up and drive," Halloran slurred. Quinn could hear the liquor taking effect. "I don't need no advice from a punk with a gun to his back."

"I'm just trying to give you a little friendly advice is all." Quinn slowly fed the car more gas as they crossed into the Brooklyn half of the bridge.

"Where I'm going, it could be the difference between the up elevator and the freight to the basement."

"Wherever you wind up, save a seat for me."

"Are you kidding? The way things are going, I won't have time. You'll be right behind me."

"Keep driving. Take Adams Street when we get off the bridge and head south."

Adams Street. That meant Halloran was taking him to the Gowanus Canal. One of Quinn's favorite dumping spots. Close to Manhattan. A ton of old warehouses. The few people who lived there weren't the curious type. You could plug a guy on the shoreline and let the body fall into the murky water of the canal never to be seen again. No holes to dig. No blood to clean up. If the bullet didn't kill him, the shit in the water would.

"Adams Street only heads south, dimwit." He only had about ten minutes left to break Halloran. Quinn worked him harder.

"I know that, goddamn it," Halloran's words were thicker now. "I'm just making sure you know it."

"I know a lot," Quinn turned right onto Adams Street. "Just like I know Wallace has plans for you." He made a show of checking the sideview mirror, then the rearview again. "Rothman, Doyle, Shapiro, Sanders.

All dead. Let's say you run. Let's say you even get out of town. How far until Wallace and whoever's paying him decide to hunt you down. You're a loose end, pal."

"Shut up!" Halloran yelled. Quinn still couldn't see him in the mirror. "You've got your own problems. Take a left on Atlantic, then a right on Hoyt."

Quinn gave the car even more gas as they entered the warehouse district. By now, they'd built up good speed. The streets were deserted and dark. The only light came from the car's headlights. Quinn knew he didn't have much time left.

"So, you're just gonna march me out to the canal, shoot me, dump me and walk away?"

"That's what Wallace paid for and that's what he's going to get."

Quinn knew he was running out of time fast. He made a bigger show of checking the mirrors again. "You really are a stupid bastard, you know that? You think it's gonna be that easy?"

Quinn heard the cop's jaw clench tight. Halloran's pride had taken a beating the whole ride out. It was swollen and sore by now. "I've had just about all the kicking I'm gonna take from you, punk. Fuck what Wallace said. I'm gonna give it to you in the gut and watch you bleed out slow. Then I'll drop you in the canal and watch you drown, you son of a bitch."

Quinn knew it was now or never. He pointed at the rear-view mirror. "I've got a feeling you'll be right in after me. Because the two guys who've been following us since 23rd Street might have other plans."

He heard Halloran jerk around to look out the rear window. Quinn gunned the engine and aimed the car for the side wall of a warehouse. He flicked off the headlights and slammed on the brakes as he yanked the wheel hard to the right.

The car went into a wild skid in total darkness and slammed hard into the brick wall of a warehouse.

Quinn had been ready for the impact, but he was still a bit dazed. He shook the cobwebs loose and tried to get out of the car fast.

Halloran snatched Quinn by the throat, squeezing his thick fingers around Quinn's windpipe slow and tight. Quinn tried to wrench the hands from his neck when he realized: Halloran was using both hands. Halloran didn't have the gun.

But Quinn couldn't breathe.

Quinn tried digging his fingers into Halloran's hands and the big man's grip began to weaken. Quinn twisted around slowly in the front seat, ignoring the pain burning in the wound in his side. He got his balance and fired a straight right into Halloran's face. He heard the cop's nose break.

His grip was broken. Halloran fell back screaming.

Quinn dove into the back seat after him. He couldn't let Halloran get that gun.

The big cop's nose was broken, but he kicked and punched wildly.

Quinn pummeled him as hard as he could in the cramped confines of the back seat. One of his blows felt like it hit a kidney and Halloran cried out.

Halloran's arms flailed. The passenger door swung open.

Quinn found Halloran's throat and it was his turn to squeeze. Now with the door open, Quinn had room to pitch forward and put all his weight on Halloran's windpipe. But all those awkward punches had killed his hands. The pain made him squeeze that much harder.

Halloran's thumping became weaker, and he started to gurgle. But just as Quinn realized he was leaning halfway out of the car, Halloran's hand shot out, grabbed the door handle, and pulled it shut. The glass window shattered on Quinn's head.

Quinn tumbled back into the car, reeling from the blood and the pain from the glass.

Halloran recovered and began stomping at Quinn's wounded side, his aim incredibly accurate. Pain exploded in Quinn's side. The roar of his own blood rushing in his head drowned out his screams.

Quinn refused to let himself black out. He reached back and fumbled with the door latch. It opened and he spilled out onto the ground.

The freezing night air hurt his lungs, but it kept him from passing out.

Halloran launched himself out of the car with a primordial scream; his face was a broken red mask of blood. Quinn brought up his knees into Halloran's stomach and flipped the big man over him. The sudden added weight of Halloran's bulk was like a spear going through his side. He cried out again and rolled on his side to dull the pain.

Despite the agony, Quinn knew he had to get to his feet. He was weaker than he thought and fell to one knee. The blood from the new cuts from the glass trickled into his eyes, blinding him.

Halloran connected with a roundhouse uppercut beneath the chin, sending Quinn back against the car. Quinn swung blindly at where he thought the cop should be but hit nothing but air.

He heard Halloran laughing. Quinn swung at the place where the sound came from but missed again.

Halloran belted him with a left cross to the jaw.

"Got something in your eye, Precious?" He followed up with a right deep to the gut that brought Quinn to his knees.

"I've gotta admit I was wrong, though," Halloran chuckled. "I thought putting a bullet in your brain was going to feel good. But this? This is even better."

Quinn knew the bastard would beat him to death if he didn't do something. He heard the dirt in front of him shift and he wondered if Halloran had just stepped closer.

Quinn fired a straight jab that caught Halloran square in the balls.

Halloran wheezed as he doubled over and staggered back. Quinn followed it up a blind uppercut that connected with Halloran's nose or jaw. Quinn couldn't see where it landed but heard that crunch of bone meeting bone.

Quinn fell back against the car and slid to the ground. He didn't know if he'd knocked Halloran out, but he knew he'd hurt him. And if the big bastard came back after him, so be it. Quinn didn't have enough left in the tank to fight him off.

He hurt in too many places to care anymore. He welcomed the darkness that slowly enveloped him, taking away his pain.

——

QUINN DIDN'T KNOW how long he'd been out.

He tried opening his eyes, but the blood from his head had caked over the eyelids. He could see just enough to know he wasn't blind. He didn't know if he'd been out for five seconds or five hours, but he knew it wasn't dawn yet.

He was still leaning against the car where he'd fallen. He used it to help him get to his feet. He felt along the car until he found the rear door. He went in the back seat and fumbled along the floor until he found Halloran's flask. He opened it and poured the rest of the rum over his head. It stung like hell but would kill off infection.

He rubbed some of the rum over his eyelids and flaked off the blood. They still stung, but at least he could see.

The first thing he saw was Big Jim Halloran's dead eyes gazing up at him. His head lolled over to the side.

From the looks of it, Quinn had hit him hard enough to send his nose up into his brain.

Lucky shot for Quinn. Not so lucky for Halloran.

Quinn rummaged through the dead cop's pockets. He found Halloran's cigarettes and lit one. He took the smoke deep into his lungs. The tobacco dulled Quinn's many pains.

Quinn knew he was worse off now than he'd been in the car ride out there.

He flexed his stiffening hands. His knuckles scarred and bloodied. He didn't think anything was broken, but they'd be sore as hell for at least a week. The hole in his side hurt like hell, but it hadn't bled as much as Quinn had feared. The cuts on his head weren't deep, but he'd probably need stitches. That meant a doctor. Even doctors on the payroll asked questions and he was in no position to give answers. Now he not only had Wallace still on the loose. He had a dead cop on his hands. A cop he'd killed.

Quinn had done all of this to try to save Doyle's empire. Now he realized that empire was beyond saving. Yes, Rothman and Sanders and Shapiro were dead but that didn't help Archie. He was still alive and Wallace's employers – whoever they were – would still want him gone. Younger, hungrier gangs – probably Sally Lucania and the other Italians – would rise to take Archie's place. Pretty soon, they'd probably want their own mayor running things.

No matter how Quinn cut it, The Doyle Era was over.

Quinn thought about going back and wiping out Wallace but figured the little shit had probably cleared out of his hotel room five minutes after Quinn and Halloran left.

And Quinn had a dead cop at his feet. A crooked cop, sure, but still a cop.

Quinn took a deep drag on his cigarette and looked down at Halloran's corpse. The son of a bitch was just as much trouble dead as he'd been alive. Quinn knew Doherty might've been crooked, but he was at heart a decent man. He wouldn't stop looking for his partner's killer until he found him.

Quinn flicked his cigarette into the Gowanus Canal. He was beginning to think he would've been better off letting Halloran put a bullet in his brain and dumping him in the canal. In many ways, Halloran was better off than he was.

And that's when it hit him.

What if Halloran had killed him after all?

Quinn remembered Halloran talking about the satchel in the car and having enough money to blow town with. Quinn went back to the car and opened it, finding about ten grand in cash and the five hundred dollars in the white envelope Wallace had thrown him.

Quinn hated to admit it, but Halloran was right. It was enough for a new start.

Quinn went back to Halloran's body and emptied the pockets on the ground. He found Halloran's badge, police identification card, driver's license, and house keys. He flicked on the headlights of the car and picked up the police identification card. Halloran's ugly mug stared back at him.

Thin lips. Lantern jaw. Ugly bastard.

Just like Quinn.

Sure, Quinn was thirty pounds lighter and a bit taller than Halloran, but the resemblance was close enough.

Quinn put his own wallet and license in Halloran's jacket pocket.

He searched the warehouse yard and found a length of thick rope and an old hunk of metal that looked like it had been part of an anchor at one time.

Quinn smiled. His luck was starting to change.

He tied one end of the rope around the piece of anchor. He tied the other end around Halloran's ankle. He pushed the anchor over the side and watched it pull Halloran's body down with it.

The Gowanus Canal had been a cesspool since the 1880s and had almost fifty years of sewage, garbage and debris floating through it. It was a safe bet no one would come out to check up on Halloran's work. Even if they did, the muck in the water went to work on a body almost immediately.

All anyone would find would be Quinn's identification in the pockets of a rotting corpse.

Quinn pocketed Halloran's badge and ID. He found his black fedora on the floor of the front seat and put it on.

The day before, Terry Quinn had been made the

boss of New York. Today, he became James Halloran. Detective, New York Police Department.

What a difference a day makes.

Quinn knew Wallace might want to tie up loose ends by killing Halloran. The key word there was might. Wallace and every cop in the NYPD would be out to get Terry Quinn. Becoming Halloran wasn't perfect, but nothing in Quinn's life ever was.

Quinn knew if he was going to survive, he'd have to get out of town.

Fast.

He tossed the satchel on the passenger seat next to him and started up the car. With Halloran's stash, plus the money he'd stashed in his safe and everything else he'd saved up over the years, he'd be blowing town with a good chunk of change. More than most people made in a couple of years.

Not bad for a fugitive ex-boxer with no brains to speak of. A man could live a long time on a bankroll like that if he was careful. And Quinn had always thought of himself as a careful man.

Quinn started the engine and put the car in gear.

He thought about swinging by Alice's place and asking her to come along. She'd blamed Doyle for all their problems. Now that he was on his own, maybe they could have a chance. She'd sure make life on the run a lot easier to take.

But he knew a girl like her would slow him down and make it harder for him to blend in. He'd have a tough enough time doing that on his own without her tagging along.

He wouldn't admit he loved her too much to put her in that much danger. He didn't dare.

Maybe in a year or so he'd send for her. She might even come.

As Quinn drove over the Brooklyn Bridge, he caught an eyeful of lower Manhattan. The tall buildings looked regal against the brightening darkness of the late night, early morning sky. It was twilight time again.

Magic time.

His time.

Quinn gunned the engine and sped across the deserted bridge, into the unknown.

Take a Look at the third novel:
SLOW BURN

FROM BEST-SELLING AUTHOR TERRENCE MCCAULEY COMES A RIVETING, GRITTY AND AUTHENTIC CRIME THRILLER OF 1930'S MANHATTAN.

New York City - August 1932

Caught between the Great Depression and a massive heatwave, New York is a city on the edge. Businesses close up shop, breadlines grow longer, and riots are almost a daily occurrence.

When corrupt NYPD Detective Charlie Doherty is assigned to investigate a dead body in a flophouse, he knows there's more here than meets the eye. He quickly discovers that the girl's death is tied to one of the most powerful families in New York, and a kidnapping case that could tear the city apart.

In a chase that takes Doherty from the mansions of Fifth Avenue, to the slums of the Lower East Side, all the way to City Hall itself, Doherty is in a race against time to find the people responsible for putting his city on a slow burn.

COMING NOVEMBER 2021

About the Author

Terrence McCauley is an award-winning writer of Thrillers, Crime Fiction and Westerns. A proud native of The Bronx, NY, he currently lives in Dutchess County, NY where he is writing his next work of fiction.